Also by Jennie Marts

COWBOYS OF CREEDENCE
Caught Up in a Cowboy
You Had Me at Cowboy
It Started with a Cowboy
Wish Upon a Cowboy

CREEDENCE HORSE RESCUE
A Cowboy State of Mind
When a Cowboy Loves a Woman
How to Cowboy
Never Enough Cowboy

EVERY BIT A
Cowboy

JENNIE
MARTS

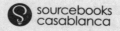

sourcebooks
casablanca

Published by Sourcebooks Casablanca, an imprint of Sourcebooks
P.O. Box 4410, Naperville, Illinois 60567-4410
(630) 961-3900
sourcebooks.com

Printed and bound in Canada.
MBP 10 9 8 7 6 5 4 3 2 1

This book featuring a hairstylist has to be
dedicated to my own hairstylist heroine:

Melissa Chapman
Hair Therapist Extraordinaire

For the last fourteen years, you've cheered on my writing career
while we've spent hours talking plots and character motivation
in between laughing, crying, and sharing life wisdom.
You've cut and curled and colored my hair,
but most of all you've been my friend.
Thank you

CHAPTER 1

IT HAD SEEMED LIKE JUST ANOTHER ORDINARY DAY AT Carley's Cut & Curl for salon owner Carley Chapman—until her stylist's water broke in the middle of doing a highlight. And then a pissed-off customer barged in the front door as the salon's receptionist was helping the pregnant hairdresser out the back, leaving Carley with a half-finished perm, an incomplete color, and a brawling catfight as one angry customer confronted another.

Carley forced her voice to remain calm as she slowly took a step away from the two women, their faces contorted in rage as one held her best pair of shears while the other brandished her flat iron like it was a sword. "Just put the scissors down, Amber," she said to the one closest to her. "I'm sure we can work this out."

Amber Wilcox and Brandi Simms were two of her best customers, so she didn't want it to seem like she was taking sides. They each could be counted on for a regular cut and color appointment every other month, although Brandi *was* the bigger tipper. But she didn't want to lose either one of them due to anger or a hair-care-tool–related injury caused by an argument over a man. Especially the man in question. Buster Jenkins was no prize, and certainly not worth losing a finger for.

It had happened so fast. Carley was still reeling over Erica, her stylist, going into labor—she wasn't due for another week—when Amber had charged into the salon. The bell over the door was still jingling as Amber grabbed the shears off the tray, her eyes wild and flashing with anger. The pink ends of the cape flapped as Brandi shot out of the chair and grabbed the flat iron from the next station.

"There's nothing to work out," Amber said, waving the shears recklessly through the air. "Except the end of our so-called friendship. I heard about the way you were flirting with Buster down at the Creed last night," she practically spat as she referred to the *Creedence Tavern*, one of the town's most popular restaurant and pubs. "I ran into Monica Morris in the grocery just now, and she couldn't wait to tell me how you belted back three raspberry margaritas and then tried to turn Taco Tuesday into *Topless* Tuesday by claiming the strap of your cheap-ass dress just *happened* to break."

A gasp came from the direction of the hair dryers where two more of Carley's regular customers sat. Lyda Hightower, who was married to the mayor of their small mountain town of Creedence, Colorado, loved to drop in for a blowout before her numerous charity events, and Evelyn Chapman, who was not just a customer but also Carley's former grandmother-in-law.

The downtown building where her salon was housed and the adorable eighty-year-old woman were the only things of value Carley had gotten out of her failed three-year marriage to Paul Chapman, and Evelyn had a regular Wednesday afternoon appointment for a weekly wash-and-style and a quarterly perm.

Evelyn, the one getting the permanent that day, sat waiting in the chair next to Lyda, a magazine in her lap and her head covered in neat rows of purple rods. She reached over to turn off the other woman's hair dryer, presumably to be able to hear better, just as Lyda was speaking, and her voice carried loudly through the salon. "I wouldn't believe a thing that comes out of that woman's mouth. Monica loves gossip more than sugar, and I've seen that woman positively inhale the better part of a chocolate cake."

Brandi ignored the comment as she held her ground, the layers of foil covering her head flapping as she yelled back. "For your information, I only had *one* margarita, the strap of my dress really *did* break, and Buster was the one flirting with *me*."

"How dare you," Amber shrieked, flames practically shooting from her narrowed eyes. "My Buster would never flirt with the likes of you."

"Her Buster would flirt with the likes of anything in a skirt," Lyda whispered to Evelyn, although everyone in the shop heard.

Before Amber had stormed in, it had been a fairly normal Wednesday afternoon at the salon. A haircut, a blowout, and a perm or highlight and cut was an average day for Carley, who had been running the salon mostly on her own for the last several years. Erica, already a mother of two, took clients by appointment only and usually came in a few days a week. Their receptionist, Danielle, worked the desk a few afternoons after school and did an occasional shampoo, but that was more as a favor to Dani's mom, who secretly paid the bulk of the girl's salary. But otherwise, Carley ran the shop herself.

She swept the floors and put the stations back together each night, so everything was in place and ready when she opened the door the next morning. She loved walking into the shop and seeing the black-and-white-checked floors and bubble-gum pink walls with Paris-themed decorations, the air still carrying the scent of the lemongrass and eucalyptus candles she burned daily to mask the smell of some of the stronger hair-care products.

It was her happy place—where she created beauty and made others feel good about themselves. Not just through her skills as a stylist, but also the way she listened and tried to offer helpful advice when customers shared their problems with her. She loved that her shop was a haven for sharing and friendship. It meant everything to her—which is why she'd literally sold her soul to keep it.

She had seen a lot of things in her days as a hairstylist, weeping hysterics over a color job gone wrong, more Bridezillas than she could shake a piece of wedding cake at, and had even had a request to do a cut and curl on a beloved Afghan hound, but this was the first time she'd seen two women screaming and threatening each other with her hair tools.

She shifted from one foot to the other, weighing what to do. She could maybe toss a spare cape over Amber's head and try to wrestle the scissors from her. Or an easier, and less dangerous, option might be to offer them each a free blowout.

Before she had time to decide, the bell of the shop door jangled, and Deputy Knox Garrison eased in, the worn soles of his cowboy boots silently sliding across the polished tile floor.

Conversation stopped as every woman turned her attention to the handsome lawman. Well over six feet tall, he wore jeans and a neatly pressed light-gray uniform shirt with a shiny gold star pinned above his chest pocket, his muscled biceps stretching the fabric of the sleeves. His chiseled jaw was clean-shaven, and his thick, dark hair curled a little at the nape of his neck, just visible below the rim of his gray felt Stetson.

Knox tipped his hat, his shoulders loose as he drawled out an easy greeting. "Afternoon, ladies." His gaze was sharp as he took in the scene, but he stayed calm and relaxed as he eased closer to the women. "I hear there's a bit of a dustup going on in here."

Carley swallowed at the dustup happening inside her—as if three dozen monarch butterflies had just taken off and were flying around her stomach like they were trying to get out.

She'd met the tall deputy last month at the Heaven Can Wait Horse Rescue Ranch where her sister, Jillian, and her ten-year-old nephew, Milo, volunteered. Then she'd seen him again a few weeks ago, also at the horse rescue ranch, when her sister married the newly appointed Sheriff Ethan Rayburn, who she guessed was now Knox's boss. Or he would be, after the happy couple returned from their honeymoon.

No time to think about the dance they'd shared at the wedding or the harmless flirting or the deep brown color of his eyes that made a girl want to melt into them. *Nope, no time for that.* Not when she had a beauty shop brawl she was trying to contain.

Amber snorted. "There's no dustup. Nothing for you to worry about anyway. This is between me and the floozy who's been hitting on my man."

Brandi waved the flat iron like she was conducting an orchestra. "I was *not* hitting on anyone. I'd ordered the *Nacho Average Nachos* platter—you know the one where they pile the chips and cheese as tall as your head—and I was reaching across the bar in front of Buster to grab the hot sauce when my strap broke."

Knox nodded. "Those nachos are amazing. And in no way average. Now, I can see how a situation like this could be misunderstood and certainly upsetting, but I'm still gonna need you each to set down your weapons and take a step back."

"And be careful with those scissors, Amber," Carley said. "Those are my best shears, and I just got them sharpened last week."

"They are good shears," Lyda agreed, nodding toward Evelyn. "She gave me the wispiest bangs with them last week."

Carley glanced at Knox. "I'm serious—those things are razor sharp. They could probably be classified as a deadly weapon."

"I'll keep that in mind," he said to Carley before addressing the women again, this time in a slightly more authoritative voice. "Did you hear that, ladies? You are wielding deadly weapons. Nobody really wants to *kill* anyone here, do they?"

Amber's face paled as she looked down at the scissors. "No, of course not."

Whispers of foil sounded as Brandi shook her head. She gingerly set the flat iron back down on the tray. "I never wanted to hurt anyone."

"Me neither." Amber shoved the scissors onto the stylist station next to her. They hit a wooden box of hair clips and sent it flying off the station.

Carley reached for it—the box had been a gift from her grandmother—but she was too late. She winced as it crashed to the floor and the hair clips scattered across the linoleum.

"Oh, no," Amber said, drawing her hands to her mouth. "Sorry about that."

Not as sorry as I am. Carley swallowed as she peered down at the box. The top had broken off in the fall, and several small pieces of wood had fallen out of the inlaid design on the lid and had slid across the floor. She pressed her hands to her legs to keep from dropping onto the floor and collecting the precious pieces. "I'm just glad no one got hurt," she forced herself to say. Although she *was* glad neither of the women had resorted to using their weapons of choice.

"Are you going to let this go?" Knox asked Amber. "Or do we need to go down to the station to discuss this some more?"

"*The station?*" the two women asked in unison.

He dipped his chin, his expression stern. "This is a pretty

serious situation. It sounds like threats were made and accusations were thrown." He tilted his head toward Brandi. "Are you thinking about pressing charges?"

Brandi shook her head so hard one of the foils almost broke free. "Heck no."

"*No?* You sure? Even though she came at you with a *deadly weapon*?"

"'Course I'm sure. Amber's my cousin. Our moms would be so mad if one of us got the other thrown in jail."

Amber nodded vigorously. "Yeah, they would."

"Listen, Amber, I'm sorry about all this. That *was* a cheap-ass dress. I bought it at the church garage sale for two dollars, and I *swear* the strap just broke last night. Thanks to my cravings for those stupid nachos, the dress was too dang tight, so it's not like it fell off or anything—it didn't even move. And there was no way in heck I was coming on to Buster. Besides him being your guy, you know I've been in love with Jimmy for just about as long as I can breathe. There will never be any other guy for me."

Amber's shoulders slumped, and she let out a heavy sigh. "Yeah, all right. Sorry about that. See you at Aunt Suzy's on Sunday?"

"You know it. Kickoff starts at two, and we haven't missed a Broncos game in years. Even though we all know they haven't been the same since we lost Peyton Manning."

A murmur of agreement rippled through the salon.

Amber acted as if she wasn't sure what to do with her hands, then finally settled on crossing them over her chest. "You bringin' your spinach dip?"

"Always do."

"Okay, see you there." She turned to leave then gazed back at Knox. "Okay if I just slink out of here with my tail between my legs?"

Knox nodded. "Stay out of trouble, though." He raised his hand for a fist bump. "Go Broncos." Amber offered him a sheepish grin as she bumped his fist, then slipped out. He ran his glance over the rest of the salon as if assessing the situation. "Everybody else, okay? Anybody get hurt?"

"Only my heart," Carley muttered as she glanced forlornly at the shattered box.

"Don't worry," Knox said, bending down to scoop up the pieces. "I can fix that." He gingerly placed the broken pieces of wood inside the box and carefully set the lid on top.

"No, you don't have to."

"It's no problem. I've got woodworking tools in my shop, and I like to fix stuff."

"He does," Lyda Hightower said. "He fixed my back gate just last week. That last windstorm nearly tore it off its hinges. Which reminds me, I've got a box of Twinkies sitting in the front seat of my car just in case I ran into you."

Carley raised an eyebrow in his direction. "Twinkies?"

Knox shrugged and offered her a sheepish grin. "I noticed her gate was broken on one of my patrols and told her I'd fix it for a box of Twinkies. I don't know what it is about the silly things, but I can't help it, I love them."

"My car is unlocked," Lyda told him. "Just grab them on your way by."

"Will do." He took another step closer and lowered his

voice as he reached into his chest pocket, pulled out a business card, and passed it to Carley. "My personal cell is written on the back. Call me if you need anything. Or just text me if you want to talk. Or whatever." A slow grin tugged at the corner of his lips. "Although I have to say this is a pretty elaborate way to get my number."

He was close enough now that she could smell the woodsy scent of his aftershave mixed with the starch of his immaculately pressed uniform shirt, and the combination was causing a stir in places that hadn't been stirred in a very long time. "Who says I was trying to get your number?"

He shrugged. "Maybe I was just hoping you did. I've been out to the horse rescue ranch several times the last few weeks and kept hoping I'd run into you so I could ask for yours."

He'd been purposely trying to run into her? That thought both terrified and excited her. Her ex had done such a number on her, she'd spent the last several years just trying to reclaim the self-worth he'd stolen from her and focus on building the business she loved. She'd worked so hard to gain back her confidence and self-assurance through creating a place where women felt valued and beautiful, both inside and out. Dating hadn't been much of a consideration, and she wasn't planning to pursue an actual relationship with another man for a very long time, if ever.

But that didn't stop her heart from doing a few extra beats at this very hot cowboy's interest.

"That seems like a lot of trouble to go through…" Carley pointed a finger to the front of the shop, surprised at the coy tone of her voice…but still using it. "When my number is written on the outside of that glass in eight-inch-high hot-pink numbers. You probably drive by it ten times a day. You could've called me anytime."

"Or scheduled a haircut," Lyda threw in helpfully, then returned her gaze to the magazine she was pretending to read.

"Yeah, but that would've been too easy. I was hoping you'd *want* to give it to me." The playful grin that crossed Knox's face caused more stirring, and Carley had to force herself to breathe, and *not* to think about the double entendre of that sentence.

"You won't have any trouble finding her at the horse rescue after this weekend," Evelyn offered, not even trying to act like she was still interested in her magazine. "She's moving out there this Saturday."

Carley shot her a look, but Evelyn ignored it.

"Oh, yeah?" Knox asked. "You need any help? I've got Saturday off, *and* I've got a truck."

"Everyone around here has a truck."

"Yeah, but not everyone offers to use them to help people move." He flashed her another grin, and the butterflies took off on another kamikaze flight through her belly. "Don't you know, you never turn down an offer to help haul your stuff somewhere new?"

"I appreciate that. I really do." And she would definitely appreciate the gun-show his muscles would perform as he moved her things. "But my sister and her husband get back from their honeymoon on Friday, and they're going to help me."

His shoulders fell just the slightest. "You've got my number now, in case you change your mind. Or just want an extra hand. And that's my personal cell on the back."

"Yes. You mentioned that already."

"Did I? Well, feel free to call. Or text me. Anytime."

She looked up at him, not sure what to say next or how to end the conversation. Should she shake his hand or just go with an awkward wave?

Before she had time to do either, the timer on her counter went off, sending a shrill ring through the salon and making her jump. She snatched up the timer and silenced the ring. "You're ready for the sink, Evelyn," she told the older woman.

"What about me?" Brandi said, pointing to her foils. "These things have been on for like twenty minutes now."

Carley's eyes widened as she looked from one woman to the other. "Oh, shoot. I wasn't thinking you'd both be done at the same time. I've got to get your permanent solution rinsed out…" she said, taking a step toward Evelyn, then turning back to Brandi. "But if we don't get that color solution washed out of your hair soon, you'll turn into a bleached blond."

"That wouldn't be so terribly bad," Brandi said, pushing out of the chair. "I *have* heard that blonds have more fun. Although that Gina over at the bowling alley is as blond as they come, and she's always in a bad mood."

"I'd wager that has more to do with having to work in the bowling alley or being married to that weasel Darryl than the color of her hair," Evelyn murmured to Lyda.

Carley hurried to one of the sinks and turned on the tap. "I'll just have to try to wash you both at the same time."

"I can help," Knox said, setting the wooden box on the counter and unbuttoning his cuffs.

"You?" Carley asked. "I don't think shampoo and rinse are listed in your deputy duties."

"Maybe not, but emergencies certainly are. This one might not fall in the realm of cataclysmic, but it's at least pushing an urgent predicament," he said, grinning as he rolled up his sleeves.

"Oh, he can do me," Evelyn said, shooting up out of her chair. Realizing what she'd said, she tucked her chin demurely toward her chest. "I mean mine. I mean he can rinse my hair."

"See?" he said, flashing her a grin as he motioned Evelyn toward the sink. "And I do have a sister, so I'm not totally without knowledge of hair and styling skills."

"I don't want you to get permanent solution on your shirt though," Evelyn told him. "Just to be safe, you should probably take it off."

CHAPTER 2

"Evelyn," Carley hissed. Heat rushed to her cheeks as she shook her head at Knox, who was already working on undoing his buttons. "You should definitely *not* take your shirt off."

His lips curved into a slow grin that had her insides doing a loop-da-loop and chanting, "Take it off" like they were at a male revue. "It's okay, darlin'. I'm wearing a T-shirt underneath." He pulled the sides of his shirt open like he was a superhero revealing his suit underneath, and a disappointed sigh at the white cotton underneath instead of muscled abs could be heard from at least one of the women in the shop.

"Well, that's disappointing," Evelyn muttered, voicing what they were all thinking.

"Would you behave?" Carley scolded as she playfully swatted at Evelyn's knee.

"Where's the fun in that?" she asked, her bottom lip going out in a pout. "Don't you know well-behaved women rarely make history?"

"*History?* You're eighty years old. What history are you still trying to make?"

Evelyn huffed out an indignant breath. "I'm only seventy-nine and a half."

Carley arched an eyebrow. "Really?"

"Well, I was at one point," she said, settling herself into the chair in front of the sink.

"The water should be warm enough now," Carley told Knox as he folded his uniform shirt and set it on the counter. "Just start running it all over her head and rinsing that solution out." She motioned for Brandi to take a seat and started pulling foils from her hair and dropping them into the sink.

"Got it," Knox said, checking the water with his hand before spraying it over Evelyn's head. He reached for one of the rods. "Should I start taking these curler things out?"

"No!" she and Evelyn said at the same time.

"Don't do anything except run water over her hair and wash the solution out. It takes like five minutes to get all of it rinsed away," Carley told him.

"I can do that." He held his hand over Evelyn's eyebrows to shield her face from the water. "It's really not that different from when I give my dog a bath."

"Watch it, buster," Evelyn said, whacking a hand toward his knee.

"I'm just kidding, Miss Evelyn," he said, with a chuckle. "But I do think I'm getting the hang of this."

Carley had tossed the used foils and was rinsing Brandi's hair, but she looked over to watch him move the nozzle in a circular motion, efficiently spraying water over Evelyn's curler-covered head.

The older woman reached over her shoulder and patted his hand. "You're doing great, honey."

He offered her a pleased smile. "Thanks, Miss Evelyn."

He really is, Carley thought as she rinsed the last of the color from Brandi's hair, then worked through a glob of shampoo. But she didn't trust him to do the finishing solution or the next steps—not that the finishing solution and curlers were complicated, but she'd still feel better if she did them herself. "Okay, switch," she told him.

"Switch?"

"Yes, I don't have time to start Brandi's haircut, so you come over and give her a deep moisturizing treatment while I finish Evelyn's hair." She peered down at Brandi. "Is that okay with you? The treatment is on the house."

Brandi's cheeks colored pink. "Yes, of course... I mean sure, it's okay with me...if he wants to..." She shook her head, then closed her mouth and her eyes and sank further down into the chair.

Knox moved to the other side of the sink, and Carley was all too aware of his broad chest and bare muscular arms as he slid around her to trade places. She nodded to a blue bottle behind the sink. "Squirt three pumps of that into your hand, then work it through her hair from the roots to the ends."

"Got it." He followed her instructions, and Brandi let out a groan of pleasure as his fingers worked over her scalp.

Her eyes popped open, and her hand flew to her mouth. "Oh, my gosh. Did I make that sound out loud?"

Knox lifted one shoulder in a small shrug.

"Yeah, ya did," Lyda offered from her chair. She'd given up on the hair dryer and was leaning forward to be part of the conversation.

"I'm so sorry. Pretend you didn't hear that," Brandi told

EVERY BIT A COWBOY

him, closing her eyes again. "That head massage just feels amazing."

"I understand," Knox said, tilting his head toward Carley. "I've been told that I have magic fingers."

Carley swallowed and lowered her gaze back to the rods she was releasing.

But Evelyn's head was twisted toward Knox. "Hey," she said. "I want a deep moisturizing treatment with an amazing head massage too."

"Me too," Lyda said, checking the diamond-encrusted watch on her wrist. "I don't have to be at my event for four more hours. I've got plenty of time."

"Me first," Evelyn said. "I can barely remember what magic fingers feel like."

Carley nudged Knox in the side as she playfully scolded him. "See what you've started?"

He chuckled as he helped Brandi to sit up and was wrapping a towel around her head when the phone rang. After a quick glance at Carley, who was only halfway through removing Evelyn's permanent rods, he held up his hand. "Don't worry. I got this." He strode across the room, his long legs easily eating up the floor, and picked up the phone on the third ring. He winked at Carley as he spoke into the receiver. "Carley's Cut & Curl. Deputy Knox Garrison speaking. How can I help you?"

Carley grinned down at Evelyn. "I'll bet whoever's calling is shocked to hear his voice."

"They might try to schedule something more than a haircut," Evelyn replied, wiggling her eyebrows.

"You are killing me today. When did you get such a dirty mind?"

"Oh, I've always had it," Evelyn said. "We just don't normally have handsome cowboys with magic fingers around to inspire me."

Their conversation was interrupted as Knox's voice deepened and took on a more authoritative tone.

"What kind of an emergency?" he asked. "Are you hurt? Is anyone bleeding? Can you get somewhere safe?" He listened a second then replied, "Ma'am, I can't understand you when you're yelling like that. Do you need to hang up and call 911?"

He held the phone away from his ear, and the caller's voice could be heard screeching through the receiver. "Yes, I *am* the police. And no, nothing bad is happening at the salon. Carley's here, she's just busy so I'm helping her out. But you said this was an emergency, so I'm trying to ascertain if I should send a squad car or an ambulance."

More screaming came from the phone, then Knox's brow furrowed in concern. "A skunk, you say? Sounds like you don't need an ambulance, you need to call animal control." He winced as the volume of the caller's voice rose an octave. "Now, ma'am, there's no need to use that kind of language. I need you to take a breath and calmly tell me your name and what in blue blazes is going on."

Carley's hands moved by rote as she circled the sprayer over and around Evelyn's head. None of them spoke as they were all riveted by Knox's call.

He nodded a few times as he listened intently and slipped in a couple of murmured, "Gotcha's," and an "I understand."

"Okay, hold on," he finally said. "I'll ask her." He covered the mouthpiece with his hand. "Margie Ruggle is on the phone, and best I can make out, she tried to bleach her own hair with some," he paused, "four letter word that rhymes with plucking, gosh-awful box solution she got down at the drugstore, and now she's washed it out and it's still half gray, and half black, and she looks like a skunk."

"Oh, dear," Lyda said. "That does sound like an emergency."

Amber nodded in agreement.

Knox turned his head toward Lyda and raised his eyebrows. "Certainly not the kind of emergency I'm used to dealing with. The way she was carrying on, I couldn't tell if she had a skunk in her house or if she'd just been stabbed and was bleeding out."

"Well, it definitely sounds like a *hair emergency*," Carley said. "Tell her not to do anything else to it. Like seriously, *don't even touch it*. Just come down here to the shop and let me take a look at it."

He peered around the salon at the already waiting customers. "You sure? It seems like you've got your hands full."

She nodded. "Yes, I'm sure. It'll be fine. This is what I do."

"So, you're kind of like a hairdresser superhero, fighting color emergencies one hair crisis at a time."

"Something like that," she said with a laugh. She liked that he thought of her as a superhero. She'd certainly never considered herself as anything so important.

Knox relayed the message to the caller, then hung up the phone. "She said she'd be here in half an hour." He rubbed his hands together as he crossed back to Carley. "What else can I do?"

Carley shook her head. As much as she and the other women in the salon were enjoying the attention of the cute cowboy, her current hair crisis was handled. "Nothing else. I'm good now. I appreciate the help, but you'd better get out of here or I'm gonna have to add you to the payroll."

He laughed, a deep rich chuckle, and the sound of it did funny things to Carley's spine. "All right, if you're sure." He grabbed his shirt from the counter, then gingerly picked up the broken wooden box before tipping his hat as he headed toward the door. "Have a good afternoon, ladies."

"Thanks for coming by," Carley said. "And for all your help."

"Stop by anytime," Lyda offered, as if she were inviting him back for tea. "And don't forget to grab those Twinkies."

"I won't," he said, giving Carley one last glance before he headed out the door.

"That man is positively swoony," Lyda said, fanning herself with her magazine. "I'm tempted to break something else at my house just to have him come back over so I can watch him fix it."

"I think you have too vivid of a fantasy life." Carley teased her as she guided Evelyn toward an empty stylist chair.

"I don't think yours is vivid enough," Evelyn told her as she planted her fanny in the seat and spread the pink cape she wore over her lap. "That deputy is clearly interested in you."

"Oh, no," Carley said, brushing off her comments as she

dabbed at Evelyn's hair with a towel. "I think he was just being nice."

"He didn't offer his number to anyone else in the salon. Or mention that it was his personal cell. *Twice*. I think you should call him. He seems like a great guy. And so cute."

Carley picked up a comb that had teeth on one end and long silver tines on the other and used it to pick out the curls springing up around Evelyn's head. "I appreciate the thought, but it doesn't matter how great…or how cute…he is, I'm not getting involved with another man." She lowered her voice as she leaned closer. "You *know* why."

The older woman's expression pinched in anguish. "I know. But that deputy is nothing like my grandson. Knox Garrison is a *good* man."

Carley let out a sigh as she locked eyes with the other woman in the mirror. "I thought your grandson was too."

CHAPTER 3

"WHERE ARE YOU?" CARLEY MUTTERED THE FOLLOWING Saturday morning as she checked her phone again. No messages, no missed calls from her sister. It was ten after nine, and Jillian was never late. She hadn't spoken to her sister in days. Between her staying busy packing and the spotty reception in the mountains where Jillian was camping, they'd barely even been able to text.

They'd had a few weeks before Jillian's new hubby, Ethan, officially took office, so he and Jillian had decided to rent a camper and spend their honeymoon exploring Montana. Thankfully, it was a big camper, because they also took Jillian's son, Milo, *and* their pets, which included two dogs and a mini-horse named Applejack, who saw herself as more of a dog than a horse anyway. Before they left, they'd ended up inviting Ethan's grandpa, Amos, to join them as well.

With that crew, Carley could imagine they'd had quite a few adventures, and she couldn't wait to hear about every single one. Up until a month ago, the two sisters and Milo had been sharing her small apartment, and she missed her sister and nephew.

Head librarian and super-mom Jillian was one of the most organized women Carley knew, so she hadn't been worried that her sister wouldn't show up. But she was start-ing to worry now. Especially since her calls over the last few hours had gone straight to voicemail.

She tried the number again, praying as she listened to the rings. One. Two.

Click. "Hey, Sis."

Oh thank goodness. Carley slumped against the stack of boxes next to her in the kitchen. "Jillian, hi. Are you okay?"

"Yeah, we're great. We just saw a buffalo. Sorry if I lose you, the reception is awful here."

A buffalo? "Where are you?"

"Yellowstone."

"As in Wyoming?"

She heard Jillian's easy laugh, and it only made her miss her sister more. "Yeah, that's where the park is. Although some of it's in Montana, so we could be in either state. I'm not sure, but I *can* tell you it's just gorgeous here."

"I'm sure it is. But you're supposed to be here, in Colorado, helping me move out to the ranch."

"No, that's next weekend."

"No. It's *this* weekend."

"I don't think so. It's on my calendar."

Carley groaned as she looked around her apartment at the mountains of boxes. "Well, I took this weekend off, and I've already packed everything, even my toothbrush." She peered into her empty kitchen. "And I don't even know which box the coffeemaker is in. There's no way I can wait another week."

"I'm sorry, Sis. You know we'd help if we were there. Why

don't you call Bryn? I'm sure she and Zane can help, and she'll probably bake you a casserole too."

"Yeah, okay." She hated asking anyone for help. Her car was small, but maybe if she tied her dresser to the top and took several trips—like twenty, then she could do it herself. She hung up with her sister, promising to call her again that night, then dialed Bryn.

"Yeah, of course, we're planning to help," Bryn said, when Carley asked her if she remembered she was moving out to her ranch that day. "But I thought it was next weekend."

"That's what Jillian said too." She scrubbed her hand across her forehead. "I must have screwed up the date."

"No worries," her friend, and new landlord, said. "It's fine if you move out today. The bunkhouse is ready. The door's unlocked, and the key is hanging on one of the hooks in the kitchen. But Zane and I are in Denver, so we just won't be able to help." She let out a disappointed groan. "Shoot. I was planning to make you a baked ziti to welcome you out for your first night at the ranch. You can probably find something in my freezer if you want to look."

Carley's stomach growled at the thought. She'd been working so hard that morning, she hadn't had a chance to eat anything. "I'll be fine. I'll see you when you get back."

She hung up and paced the tiny parts of the floor that weren't covered in boxes. There *was* someone she could call. But she really shouldn't.

She prided herself on doing things on her own. Her ex had spent the majority of their marriage telling her what she couldn't do and how she was going to fail at everything she tried. Proving to *herself* that she wasn't a failure and proving *him* wrong were two of the driving forces behind why she was so determined to make her shop a success. But this wasn't business. This was her home. It was much more personal.

And it wasn't just her pride. She hated that she couldn't just take care of this move herself, but there was more to it. Calling him felt like she was sending a different kind of message. And she wasn't looking to get involved with anyone. She had enough on her plate trying to manage her business.

But he *had* offered to help. And there was nothing saying that they couldn't be friends. Just not friends with benefits, more like friends with a truck.

She dug his card out of the pocket of her purse and called the number on the back.

He answered on the first ring. "Hey, Carley."

She arched an eyebrow at her phone. "How'd you know it was me?"

He cleared his throat. "Well…I…just…okay, so maybe I have seen your number on the front window of your shop. I'm a deputy sheriff. I get paid to notice and remember things that are important."

Things that are important? Her stomach dipped in a swirl of nerves. No, not nerves. She was just hungry. Or maybe just nervous about asking him for help.

Say something. Anything.

"How's the moving going?" he asked, filling the awkward silence.

"Well, that's the thing. Apparently, there was a mix-up in the dates, and I don't actually have anyone to help me."

"I can fix that."

"I hate to ask—" she said, but he cut her off before she could finish her sentence.

"You're not asking. I'm offering."

Carley jumped as a knock sounded at the door. "Hold on, there's someone here." She crossed the room to pull open the door and couldn't be more surprised to see Knox standing there, wearing a gorgeous grin and holding a tray of coffees and a bag of fast food.

He had on jeans, square-toed cowboy boots, and a faded blue T-shirt that stretched around his sizeable biceps. "Hey," he said, tipping the brim of his hat. "Any chance you're hungry?"

Oh my. Down girl. He's talking about the food.

"I'm starving," she said, opening the door as she clicked off her phone and shoved it into the side pocket of her leggings. She lifted one of the coffees out of the tray as he set it and the food on the kitchen counter. "And coffee," she said, inhaling the rich scent. "You have no idea how much I needed this. I could seriously kiss you right now."

He arched an eyebrow then grinned again as he swept his arm around her waist and pulled her against his chest. "Dang, if I had known all it would take was a cup of coffee to earn a kiss, I would have brought you some sooner."

For a second, she couldn't speak. Her mouth had gone dry, and she was sure he must be able to feel the thump of her heart as it pounded hard and fast against their pressed chests. "Uh…um…I didn't actually mean…it was just a figure of speech…"

He tilted his head as his gorgeous, brown-eyed gaze dropped to her lips...and her heart dropped into her stomach. "You sure? It's pretty good coffee."

Tearing her gaze from his, she glanced down at the cup smooshed between them. "It's from a fast-food place."

The corners of his lips tugged up. "But it's still hot."

Gulp. *It sure as heck is.*

She wasn't sure what to do, so she lifted the cup, took a sip, then grimaced. "It needs sugar."

His grin widened, and a sexy glint lit his eyes. "Got it." His voice dropped to a low, slow drawl. "Next time I'll bring more kiss-worthy coffee that's sweeter and has more heat."

She swallowed again. *Holy hot cowboy.* She hadn't felt a hard-muscled chest pressed against hers in months, maybe a year. She couldn't even remember the last time she'd gone on a date. And it had been even longer since she'd entertained the notion of kissing someone. But her brain was sure entertaining the idea now, and her body was egging it on.

Before she had a chance to decide either way, Knox let her go and reached for the brown paper bag next to the tray. "I wasn't sure if you preferred bacon or sausage or biscuits or muffins, so I just got a selection of them all."

"I'd arm wrestle you for any one of them," she said, pressing a hand to her stomach and hoping he hadn't just heard it growl at the mention of bacon and sausage. "I haven't eaten anything." She peered into the bag. "There's like six sandwiches in here."

He shrugged. "I told you I couldn't decide. Plus, I thought Ethan and Jillian would be here."

"That explains the four coffees," she said, digging out a sausage and egg biscuit and inhaling as she peeled back the paper. "I haven't had one of these in years, but it smells like heaven. And don't worry, I'll drink theirs. My coffee maker is packed, and I've already been feeling the effects of caffeine withdrawal." Which might explain why she was considering locking lips with the hunky deputy a few minutes earlier.

Yeah, right. Blame it on the caffeine.

She shushed her inner critic by shoving the biscuit into her mouth and sinking her teeth into the buttery goodness of the flaky crust. A groan escaped her lips as she chewed. "So good," she muttered before taking another bite.

He pulled a second sandwich from the bag and leaned against the counter as he unwrapped it. Keeping his gaze on her, his lips curved in an easy grin.

"What?" She covered her mouth as she realized she was wolfing down the biscuit like she was starving and it was the first meal she'd seen in days.

He shook his head. "Nothing. I was just enjoying watching you eat. And wishing I would have brought you another sausage biscuit."

"No way. I'm already going to have to hold myself back from eating a second one. And I can't resist those hash browns. Which is why I never let myself get these. I haven't had one in forever. I usually eat cereal or yogurt for breakfast. And I try to steer clear of too many trans fats."

He took another bite of his sandwich. "Why? Those are the tastiest ones."

A laugh escaped her lips. "Yeah, well, all I have to do is look at them and those tasty fats transfer right to my hips."

His gaze traveled over her body and lingered around her waist. "I can think of worse places to be transferred to."

She shook her head. "Just eat your breakfast."

"Yes, ma'am."

They finished their breakfast quickly, and Carley finished her coffee and cleaned up the wrappers. "How did you know to show up right when I needed you?"

"I didn't. I just took a chance that you might need an extra hand and figured you wouldn't turn me away if I brought coffee and food."

"You figured right."

Knox rubbed his hands together as he looked around the room. "I brought my truck and a trailer, so we should be able to get this all in one trip. Just tell me where to start."

She jerked a thumb at a half-empty box on the kitchen counter, then pointed toward the stacks of boxes filling the room. "I just need to finish packing the last little bit of pantry stuff, but I've dragged most everything else out into the living area here. The bunkhouse is furnished, so I'm mainly just bringing boxes and some of this loose stuff. I've already sold my sofa and extra furniture I'm not taking with me."

He picked up a cardboard box and nodded toward the door. "Sounds good. I'll start taking stuff down while you finish packing up. I'll bet we can knock this out in less than an hour and have you all moved in by lunch."

"I like your optimism," she said, grabbing the remaining

canned goods and cake mixes from the pantry shelves and dumping them into the box. "And lunch is on me."

"Deal."

———————

A warm, late summer breeze blew through her open car window an hour later, and Carley inhaled the scent of hay and freshly mown grass as she turned into the driveway of the Heaven Can Wait Horse Rescue Ranch. Her new home.

She loved the ranch, loved volunteering with Jillian and Milo, and being here always made her feel good. She was hoping the move out to the country might be the thing to finally settle that feeling in her stomach that never quite accepted any place she'd lived as her true home. Part of her kept the hope alive that someday she'd find the elusive place that quieted her soul and gave her that feeling of genuine belonging, but another part of her had given up hope of ever finding it.

The Callahan ranch came pretty dang close though. The farm oozed hominess with its old yellow two-story farmhouse on one side of the drive and a large barn with faded red paint on the other. Two nice-sized corrals flanked either side of the barn, and chickens roamed inside the fence surrounding a small chicken coop.

Touches of Bryn were everywhere, from the cheery blue pillows on the porch swing to the array of colorful pots spilling over with flowers on the steps leading up to the house. A neat fenced-in garden sat next to the house with one sign reading "Love grows here" on the left side of the gate and one reading "Free Weeds...Pull your own" on the right.

She'd been here enough times to recognize the horses she drove by on the other side of the fence. Prince and Beauty had been Bryn's first rescues. Beauty's colt, Mack, and a mini-horse named Shamus had been next, and the two smaller horses trotted along the gate, keeping up with her car as if they wanted to say hello. A few dozen head of cattle filled the corral and the pasture beyond, and one let out a low moo, almost as if welcoming Carley back.

She laughed as she pulled up in front of the bunkhouse and saw a hefty hog and a yellow-and-white cat curled up together on the front porch. Tiny, the pig, wore a bright blue ribbon around her neck, and she opened her eyes and let out a happy snuffle as Carley climbed out of her car. The cat stretched and yawned, then poked her paws into the pig's side and settled back into sleep—which could equate to an exuberant greeting in cat language.

It might not be her forever home, but Carley could be happy here.

Speaking of which, several of her happy parts were dancing around her insides as Knox exited his truck and came up to stand beside her.

"This is such a cool place," he said, gazing toward the bunkhouse.

"I know. I love all the history behind it. Bryn's grandpa built it for his ranch hands, then her cousin, Cade, renovated and updated it into two side-by-side apartments earlier this summer."

It had the look of a log cabin with a long front porch and thick cedar posts. Galvanized steel buckets overflowing with pink trumpet flowers sat on either side of the stairs, and a blue-and-white quilt was folded over the back of a blue-cushioned glider swing. Flower boxes bursting with colorful pansies hung in front of the two wide front windows, and identical red welcome mats sat in front of the matching screened doors that opened to each apartment.

"Bryn might not be here, but it looks like she sent the welcoming committee," he said, reaching down to scratch under Tiny's chin. The pig stretched her neck out to give him more scratching space, then let out a contented sigh before dropping her snout back onto the porch.

"Only in the country," Carley said, grabbing a box from the back seat and carrying it up the porch steps. Skirting around the rather large swine, she pulled open the door to her side of the bunkhouse and stepped inside. Pausing to inhale the subtle scents of vanilla, cinnamon, and cedar, she inhaled a tiny gasp as Knox bumped up against her back.

"Sorry," he said, although not seeming that sorry as he wrapped his arms around her sides to help support the box she was holding. "I was trying not to step on the cat."

The feline in question circled Knox's legs, then Carley's, then leisurely crossed the living room and jumped up to curl into the corner of the sofa.

Her mouth had gone dry, and Carley couldn't seem to move. All it would take was one step forward and she could set the box on the counter, but for just a few seconds, she let herself enjoy the sheltered feeling of her back against his chest and the delicious sensation of being held in the circle of his strong arms. Forcing her feet to move, she stepped forward, clearing her throat as she tried to speak. "It looks like I've already got a roommate."

"I wouldn't feed her, or she'll never leave," he said, walking into the living room area. "Although I wouldn't blame her. This place is great. And you can't beat that view." He turned to gaze out at the panoramic view of the gorgeous, snow-capped mountains perfectly framed in the large picture window.

"I agree." She loved the open concept of the space and the modern farmhouse décor. The floors were the original hardwood and added an extra country touch. The main area had the kitchen on one side, the living room where Knox stood on the other, and a large kitchen island that separated the two. A bouquet of dried-up wildflowers in a glass jar sat in the center of a small dining room table that was pushed up against the window. A bookcase crammed with books was in the corner, a television resting on top of it, and a blue overstuffed sofa surrounded by a mismatched coffee table and end tables were the only other furniture in the room.

Knox sidled a little closer, doing that thing where he dipped his head and lowered his voice before he crooned something flirty. "You know, those mountains aren't the only gorgeous view around here."

His words, and the low timbre of his voice, sent a rush of heat along her spine. Dang. Why did everything that came out of this man's mouth have to sound so sexy? He could probably read her the items on a takeout menu, and she'd get turned on by the way he said "chicken fried steak." She needed to rein this in. Yeah, he was cute...okay...maybe not so much *cute* as *hot as hell*...but she didn't need or want to get involved with another man. She'd learned her lesson with Paul.

She planted a hand on her hip, determined to appear unfazed by the cowboy's flirtations. "Stop trying to butter me up. I already said I'd feed you lunch." Dang. That was supposed to sound casual and cool, but even she heard the coyness in her voice.

Her coolness didn't dissuade him at all. If anything, he seemed to take it as a challenge as his lips curved into seductive grin. "Lunch isn't exactly what I'm hungry for..."

He left the statement open-ended, as if passing the flirty ball back to her side of the court. But as much as her body was responding to his words with surges of heat and crazy stomach flutters, this was one game she wasn't prepared to play.

CHAPTER 4

K<small>NOX KNEW HE'D BE TAKING A CHANCE BY PICKING UP</small> food and just showing up at Carley's apartment that morning, but thankfully, his efforts had been appreciated.

He didn't know what it was about the blond hairdresser, but something about being around Carley set his pulse racing and his heart pounding so hard in his chest, it felt like it was trying to break free.

It was more than just the fact that she was beautiful— although she was gorgeous, and just enough on the tall side that she fit perfectly against him when they'd slow-danced at her sister's wedding. She also made him laugh, and he admired her dedication to family, supporting her sister and doting on her nephew. She was someone he wanted to spend time with, and he hoped she'd give him a chance to get to know her better.

He couldn't remember the last time a woman had taken up so many of his thoughts. And he did think about her— imagining how it would feel to slide his hands along her lush curves and run his fingers through her thick curly mess of hair, the chestnut blond shade reminding him of the color of his favorite horse.

But there was still something more. She had a

vulnerability about her, just a shadow of insecurity that told him someone—probably that bastard ex of hers—had hurt her. That hint of pain had all his protective instincts kicking in and all he wanted to do was shield her from anyone ever hurting her again. Too bad that hurt also came with defensive walls that seemed a hundred feet high and kept shooting up every time he dared to get too close.

"This is the last of it," Carley told him, grabbing the final box from the front seat of her car. She nodded to her back seat. "If you wouldn't mind grabbing the TV, we can finish with this load."

"I've got it," he said, hefting the television into his arms and closing the car doors behind him.

He couldn't help but enjoy the view as he followed her in. She had on sneakers and leggings and a loose pink T-shirt in a wrap style that fit snug over her hips and split open in the back, revealing some kind of black bra contraption that had a thick lacy band and thin straps that crisscrossed over her back and shoulders. He wasn't sure how it worked, but it was sexy as hell with the little straps and the glimpses he kept grabbing of the bare skin of her shoulder blades and lower back. He also shot up a silent prayer of thanks to whoever invented the snug-fitting leggings and convinced women to wear them. Because Carley Chapman wore the hell out of them.

"We did it," she said, setting her box on the floor in the kitchen. It was the last one she'd packed, and she'd had to leave it open because it was so full. Boxes of Pasta Roni and cake mixes perched precariously on top of the pantry items and a six-pack of soda hung off one side.

He swallowed at the dryness in his mouth and tried to shake the vision of him sliding his hands inside the open back section of her shirt and skimming them over the smooth skin of her waist. He tilted his chin down to the television in his arms. "Where do you want this?"

"You can put it in my room," she told him, leading him toward the first bedroom.

"Nice," he said, setting the television on top of the dresser. "We've been here less than an hour and we've already made it into your bedroom."

Oh, geez. What was it with him and the cheesy comments? He never flirted like this—which was probably becoming quite obvious to Carley—since he was so terrible at it.

She planted a hand on her hip. "You are on a roll today. Are you always this shameless a flirt?"

He shook his head, then dipped his chin to his chest. "No, actually I'm never like this. And even though part of me is as embarrassed as heck, there's something about you that brings out this devilish side of me, and I guess I'm hoping that if I keep throwing out outrageous comments, I'm either going to get you to kiss me or earn a good laugh from you. And I'm actually pretty good with either response."

"At least now I know what you're after."

He raised an eyebrow. "So does that mean a kiss is a possibility?"

"More likely a laugh, but I appreciate your commitment to your strategy."

"I'm nothing if not thorough..." He nodded to a taped-up

pile of shelving on the floor. "How about if I shut up now and just help you put that bookshelf back together and get those pictures hung up?"

"That sounds good."

"I'll just grab my tools from the truck."

———————

Seriously? A tool belt? Carley swallowed as she watched Knox hook the belt around his waist, then let it ride low on his hips. What was it about a guy wearing a tool belt that had her lady parts screaming that they needed to be hammered? *Wait, bad choice of words.* She meant that they were broken and needed to be fixed…with his tool…er…tools.

He pulled his hammer from the loop on the side and held it up, almost as if reading her mind. "Do you have something you need me to nail?"

A laugh burst out of her. Whether it was nerves or that his comment was just too cheesy, she couldn't hold back the laughter.

He lifted one shoulder as he offered her a sheepish grin. "That one was probably a little too much."

"But you did get me to laugh."

"One mission down, one to go."

"You still think you're gonna earn that kiss?"

His lips curved into a slow sexy smile. "I'm still gonna try."

"I wouldn't expect anything less," she said, still chuckling as she hoisted a box onto the desk and ripped off the tape.

They worked in companionable silence, except for the

sound of Knox's screw gun as he assembled her bookshelf. She unpacked her clothes into the dresser and closet, continually aware of his presence as they brushed against each other as they moved around the room.

She could smell his aftershave and the clean linen scent of laundry detergent as she turned from the closet and accidentally bumped into his chest. The fabric of his faded T-shirt was so soft, and his shoulders were so broad, she just wanted to cuddle into his chest. Either that or climb him like a tree. The man was seriously sexy. His shirtsleeves hugged the solid muscles of his biceps, and his forearms flexed and corded as he pounded nails into the wall and hung her pictures.

She wasn't normally this affected by a man. Heck, she was around men all the time, but none of them had her heart pounding like a jackhammer in her chest or her libido on DEFCON 1 alert every time she was within a foot of them.

Knox was a great guy. Or he seemed to be in the last month that she'd known him. He was fun to flirt with and she'd be lying if she said she didn't appreciate his attention. But she wasn't looking for a man or a relationship, no matter how strong his arms or how broad his shoulders were. Or how catching a glimpse of his bare stomach when he reached up sent darts of heat coiling through her most sensitive places, places that hadn't felt heat like that in a long time.

Images of them tangling in the covers filled her thoughts as she shook out a fitted sheet and tucked it around the corner of the bed.

Forget the hunky cowboy. Focus on the room. Not the bed.

Yeah, right. There wasn't much she could think of that

would deter her mind from Knox, especially with the way his chest pressed against her back as he leaned around her to reach for a loose corner of the sheet.

"Here, let me help you with that," he said, grabbing a section and pulling it toward the opposite corner. "Nice sheets," he commented, running his hand over the mint green fabric. "Soft."

She nodded, trying to push away the image of his hand running over her body the way he'd just run it along the sheet. Dang. What was wrong with her? Her body felt electric with all the tingles and shivers his stupid, sexy grin was causing. Had there been some kind of aphrodisiac in those breakfast sandwiches? "Thanks. They're flannel. I've had them forever." She passed him a corner of the comforter.

"They look pretty cozy," he said, pulling up the bedspread and folding the top edge down like she'd done. He patted his side of the mattress. "Want to try it out with me?"

"What do you mean...?" she sputtered, heat rushing to her cheeks.

His face broke into a grin. "I just meant to take a nap. Geez, where's your mind?"

Apparently naked and in bed with you. Her imagination was now running wild with images of them naked and under the comforter. She could almost feel the cool cotton of the sheets against her skin.

She glanced up to catch that knowing grin on his face again. "From the pink in your cheeks, I can guess where your mind went. Which is okay with me."

"My mind went to the same place as yours. Of course I

knew you were talking about a nap. We haven't even kissed yet."

He raised an eyebrow and dropped his voice to that easy drawl that made the butterflies take off in her stomach. "There's an easy remedy for that."

It would be easy—the easiest thing in the world to fall into his arms and lose herself in Knox Garrison for an afternoon. But the hard part would come afterward, when she backed away, which she knew she would. She just couldn't let herself trust that any man—no matter how good he seemed—would stick around. And not destroy her again.

An afternoon with Knox might be worth the risk.

The room suddenly seemed to have shrunk in size as Knox came around to her side of the bed. He reached for one of the pillowcases on the nightstand behind her, and she sucked in a quick breath as his arm brushed against her hip. As if it had a mind of its own, her hand raised up and came within an inch of touching his chest. Hovering in the air, it was as if an electric force field were holding it there, so close to touching him, her hand wanting to bridge the distance while her mind kept it at bay.

"Could I get a pillow for this?" Knox asked, peering down at her.

He was so close. She could see the tiny flecks of gold in his deep brown eyes, and she just wanted to sink into their gaze.

"Could I?" he asked, his voice low, as he leaned just a tad closer.

Could he what? Kiss her? Toss her onto the bed and have his way with her?

Before she could answer, she jerked as a sound came from the kitchen. "What was that?"

His lips curved into a sexy smile. "Dang. I know my heart's pounding pretty hard, but I didn't think you could actually hear it."

She cocked an eyebrow. "Really?"

His grin turned sheepish. "Yeah, even I heard how corny that sounded."

A hushed slide followed by a scrape of wood sounded, and she gripped his arm. "See, there it is again," she whispered. "I told you I heard something."

His brow furrowed, and he tilted his head toward the door as if that could help him to hear better.

Another whoosh followed by a thump.

"Sounds like someone's here," Knox said, already moving toward the door. His hand went to his hip as if reaching for his service weapon. But he wasn't in uniform, and she caught the motion of his fingers as they flexed closed then opened again. "You expecting anyone?"

"No."

"Stay here," he said, just as she took his hand and squeezed it in a death grip.

"No way. I'm coming with you. What if it's a serial killer?"

He looked down at their hands, and she swore she caught the ghost of a smile pull at the corners of his lips before another whoosh sounded and his expression turned guarded. He cautiously approached the doorway, then slowly moved his head around the frame, his muscles tense.

The tension left his shoulders, and he let out a chuckle.

Tilting his head toward the door, he said, "You were almost right. It's not quite a serial *killer*, but you could call him a cereal sniper because it looks like he's trying to take off with your Lucky Charms."

"What?" She peered around him and the door frame to see a black and white billy goat in her kitchen, his teeth clamped onto one of the flaps of her open pantry box as he systematically pulled it toward the screen door they'd propped open earlier when they'd been bringing stuff in. The goat would take a few steps back and then pull the box toward him, sliding it over the hardwood and making the whooshing and thumping sounds they'd been hearing.

Carley stepped into the hallway. "Hey, let go of that." She'd met Otis before, the ornery goat trying to abscond with her Lucky Charms. "And don't think I don't see you two as well." She pointed to Shamus, the mini-horse Bryn had rescued earlier that year, standing in the doorway, and Tiny, the pig, on the porch behind him, innocently watching as if she had nothing to do with the moving box heist.

Otis ignored her, and instead doubled his efforts as he tugged the box closer to the door.

"Oh, no, you don't," she said, hurrying down the hall and grabbing the other side of the box. "You wanna give me a hand here, Deputy?" she called back to Knox.

He laughed as he followed her into the kitchen. "I'm not sure what the right move is here. Do I try to help you get the box away from him or do I try to get him to drop the box?"

"I'm not sure, either. You're the one trained for crisis situations."

"I don't think I've ever had a goat crisis before."

"This is Otis. He's always sneaking around trying to steal stuff, especially if it's edible."

"Oh yeah, I've heard the story of how Ethan rescued your half-naked sister from the hay loft after Otis had stolen her skirt."

"That's nothing. My friend Nora was *all the way* naked when she had a tug-of-war with him over her towel after she'd just gotten out of the shower."

"*Half*-naked? *All the way* naked? Dang, now I feel like I'm getting the short end of the stick in this goat battle." He reached for her edge of the box. "I'll spot you if you want to strip down to your undies real quick. We don't want to buck the trend."

"Nice try, buster. But not a chance."

He arched one eyebrow. "Would you consider at least taking your top off?"

She had to laugh. "Would *you*?"

"Heck, yes."

"You goofball," she said, still laughing. "Just help me save this box."

"You sure?" he asked, reaching for the bottom of his shirt. "I'll do it." Before he could pull it off, Otis must have sensed a break in their concentration and given one more massive pull at his side of the box. The cardboard ripped, sending Pasta-roni and cake mixes toppling out and the six-pack of soda that had been precariously perched on the edge of the box sliding off the side. It crashed to the hardwood, and the top of one of the cans burst open and soda shot out, spraying directly at Knox's chest.

The soda spray must have frightened Otis because he let go of the flap and took a step back. Never one to give up a fight, he snatched a box of vanilla cake mix and made a mad dash out the door.

Carley fell back on her bottom, laughing as Knox waved his arms in an attempt to try to fend off the last sprays of the pop.

"Should I go after him?" he asked, as the soda can fizzled out.

Carley shook her head. "Oh, let him have it. It's not like he can actually make the cake."

"Right? You mean because he doesn't have vegetable oil and three eggs?"

She laughed again. "I was thinking because he doesn't have an oven. But you make a valid point too."

"Man, this stuff is sticky." He pulled his wet shirt away from his chest, then offered her another one of his flirty grins. "I think you're gonna get your request because I've gotta take this shirt off."

CHAPTER 5

CARLEY SWALLOWED AS KNOX LIFTED HIS SHIRT OVER HIS head, transfixed by the amazing display of hard muscle and bare skin. Dang, the man looked like he was carved out of marble. If she looked close—and she was *really* looking— she could see a few flaws, a thin line of scar tissue running across his chest, another scar on his shoulder, and one about the size of a quarter on his right pec that looked suspiciously like a bullet wound.

Why did that suddenly make him seem even more sexy? It made more sense that the kind of guy she'd want to date—*if* she wanted to date, that is—would be one who would *avoid* getting shot.

She needed to do something, say something, anything to stop her from continuing to stare at his half-naked body. Or worse, to fling herself at him and beg him to take her against the kitchen counter. "I kind of think you deserve that," she finally said, feeling like the sarcastic teasing route was the best way to go.

He chuckled as he turned on the water and held the shirt under the faucet. "If you knew the thoughts I'd been having about you taking *your* top off, you'd be sure of it."

She grabbed a towel off the kitchen counter and tossed it at him.

He deftly evaded the towel as he wrung out his wet shirt. "Can I stick this in your dryer?"

"Sure." She led him toward the small laundry room tucked behind the bathroom at the end of the hall. An old washer and dryer filled most of the space, leaving just enough room for a hamper and a small utility sink. She knew the room wasn't very big, but it seemed to shrink even more as Knox followed her in. He stood behind her, their bodies almost touching as she tossed his shirt in the dryer, threw in a fabric sheet, and set the timer for thirty minutes.

The rumble of the old dryer started as she turned around and ran smack into a wall of hard muscled chest. Make that hard, *naked* muscled chest.

She peered up at him, knowing she should back away but unable to move. He looked down at her, the soft expression on his face changing to one of desire as his gaze dropped to her mouth.

Her lips parted as if in hopes of a kiss, and she drew in a small shallow breath. Something was happening here, and she seemed powerless to stop it. The air itself seemed charged with…what? Electricity? A current of energy? Yeah, that about summed it up…an electric current of crazy sexual energy.

Geez. What was the matter with her? Knox was just a man. What was so special about this guy that started her tingly bits humming and had her thinking stuff like "crazy sexual energy"?

She didn't know what it was. But it was something. Something that was taking her over, so when he leaned in even closer, her sexually charged body told her cautious brain to "stuff it" and she leaned in too, her body aching to press against his.

He reached up a hand and pressed the back of his fingers to her cheek. His voice was low, barely above a whisper. "I really do like you, Carley."

"I really do like you too," she whispered back.

He leaned down and softly brushed his lips against her neck in that spot right below her ear—the spot that made her hum with anticipation. His voice vibrated against her skin. "All I can think about is how much I want to kiss you."

"Mmm-hmm." Her mouth couldn't seem to form words. All that seemed to come out were little sighs of pleasure.

"I won't kiss you until you say 'yes' though." As he spoke, his lips grazed up her neck and over her cheek. His breath was warm, and his voice husky as he spoke into her ear. "You have to tell me it's okay. Is it okay? Can I kiss you, Carley?"

She might just die if he didn't kiss her soon. Her body was so warm, she feared she was in danger of internal combustion. Her hands gripped his muscular biceps, just the feel of his strong arms exciting her even more, as she breathed out the single word. "*Yes.*"

She felt him still, then his tense shoulders relaxed as he slid his arm around her waist and pulled her close. The hand that had been touching her cheek moved slowly across her face until his thumb grazed her bottom lip.

It seemed as if the tenseness in Knox's muscles had shifted to hers, her whole body was taut with the anticipation of his lips finally meeting hers. So soft, so careful, as if she were something fragile that might break. Then his light, tender kiss deepened, as if he wanted to consume her.

Her fingers ran over his smooth, broad shoulders, then clutched his back as she tried to pull him closer. He lifted her up, setting her on the dryer as she wrapped her legs around his waist. His hands were everywhere, cupping, caressing, skimming over her arms, then holding her cheeks, then digging into her hair as he devoured her. There was no other word for the onslaught of passion and desire as he feasted on her mouth, sampling and sipping, asking, then taking, until she was no longer sure where his breath ended and hers began.

She had no idea where this was coming from, this intense wave of passion, but she was caught in it, unable to escape its clutches. And in the flaming heat of that moment, she didn't want to.

She didn't want anything except this man's hands on her and the press of his body against hers. She let out a small moan as his hands slid inside the slit of her shirt, and she felt his fingers brush over the bare skin of her back, then skim up the sides of her breasts.

She could feel the warmth of the dryer through her leggings and the steady thrum of the machine as he rocked against her, the hard swell of him rubbing against the center of her feminine core.

The vibrations and the heat of the machine combined with the last few hours of suppressed sexual tension and all the fantasizing about him had her so turned on, she couldn't even think. All she could do was feel. Then the emotion and ecstasy completely took her over as he ravished her, touching her skin and wrenching the sleeve of her shirt down to place hot kisses along her neck and shoulder.

He took her mouth again just as his hips ground into her in exactly *that* spot…the thin fabric of her leggings rubbing against the friction of the denim of his jeans…the sensations building…and building…

Oh. Ohh. *Ohhhh.*

The intensity of it caught her off-guard as the spasms ripped through her, swelling then ebbing then flooding her with heat and pleasure. A shuddering moan escaped her as she dug her fingers into his back, clinging to him as she rode the wave of euphoria.

He stopped, holding still, then slowly pulled his head back, his eyes wide as he peered down at her. "Did you just…?"

She let out a shaky breath. "Yeah, I did. I mean, it's been a long time for me…and you were wearing that tool belt… and no shirt…and did I mention that it's been a *really* long time for me?"

"You did mention that."

She lowered her gaze, embarrassment further heating her already warm cheeks. But when she dared to look back up at him, a slow grin was spreading across his lips. A grin of pride tinged with just a hint of self-importance.

She shook her head. "What are you smiling about? I'm sure it was just the vibration of the dryer."

"Too late, darlin'. You already mentioned my tool belt. Come on, now. Forget the dryer or how long it's been, you gotta give me *some* of the credit for that one."

She lifted one shoulder in the smallest shrug. "Okay, maybe you get a little credit."

He ran his hand up the outside of her thigh, drawing goosebumps out along her skin. "Maybe we need to try that again, just so we know for sure to offer where credit is due."

That idea had heat swirling and coiling in her stomach and her sensitive spot humming with expectation. "Or we could just call it a draw."

He dropped his chin to press a warm kiss against the side of her neck—in the same spot that started this whole thing happening. His voice was ridiculously sexy and sent more hums through her as he softly asked, "Now where's the fun in that?"

Her nipples ached at the prospect of another round of "fun," and she pressed her hips against him, the bulge behind his zipper telling her he was just as excited about the idea as she was.

She really should stop this before it went even further. If he kept kissing her like he'd been doing, more clothes than just his shirt were bound to come off. Her brain kept trying to convince her that was a bad idea, but her body was over-ruling its objections as his lips found hers again.

Then she was lost, enraptured by the feel of his arms as he pulled her close and the press of his hungry lips as they slanted against hers.

She froze mid-kiss, pulling away as she heard the distinctive creak of the front door opening followed by an elderly female voice calling down the hallway. "Yoo-hoo. Anybody home?"

Carley's eyes went wide. "It's Evelyn," she whispered, adjusting her shirt as she hopped off the dryer.

"Oh, shit. Do you think she knows I'm here?" he whispered back.

"Yes, your truck's outside," she said quietly before raising her voice. "Be out in a minute."

"It's gonna take me more than a minute to be presentable to Miss Evelyn," he said.

Carley held back a giggle as she slid past him. "I'll distract her while you…get yourself together."

"Good. I'll just take a quick cold shower and try to solve some algebraic equations in my head."

"Algebraic equations? I thought guys always thought about hockey stats or something else equally boring."

"Not me. And hockey stats aren't boring. I love hockey. But I hate algebra. Thinking about cleaning out the moldy food in the refrigerator sometimes helps too."

She made a face. "You're weird. Hot. But still weird…" She peered down at his *dilemma*, which hadn't lessened in the least. "Whatever it takes. Miss Evelyn might not have the best eyesight in the world, but there's no way she'll miss that."

His lips curved into a sexy grin that had her stomach swirling and her lady parts yearning for another ride on the dryer. "Thank you. I'm taking that as a compliment."

"Oh my gosh." She laughed as she playfully swatted his arm. "X equals Y plus nine squared to the root of seven…"

He raised an eyebrow. "Did you even take algebra?"

She laughed. "Yes, and that's exactly how I remember it,

a bunch of letters with random math-sounding words and numbers in between."

"Okay, okay." He laughed with her as he scooted out of her way. "I'll try to do some actual mathematical equations and be out in a sec."

She took a deep breath, then smoothed her hair and exited the laundry room. "Evelyn, hi," she said to the woman standing in her kitchen.

"The door was open, so I let myself in. Hope that's okay." She held a Pyrex casserole dish, and the cat had left the sofa and was weaving around Evelyn's ankles, leaving a trail of yellow and white hair on the woman's pant legs.

"Of course. I'm always happy to see you, but what are you doing here?"

"I knew Bryn was out of town, so I wanted to welcome you to your new home by bringing you a hot dish. But it seems like you already have one of those," she said, nodding toward the hallway where Knox was coming out of the laundry room and pulling his T-shirt over his head.

Warmth flooded Carley's cheeks. "It's not what you think."

"Whatever you say, dear," Evelyn said, gazing at Carley with an impish grin that told her she knew exactly what to think.

"Really, his shirt just got wet, and we threw it in the dryer," she sputtered.

"Of course it did. What other reason would he have for taking his shirt off?"

"Hey, Miss Evelyn. Good to see you," Knox said, peering

at the dish in her hands. "I don't know what you've got in there, but it smells amazing."

"Oh, it's nothing. I just threw together a little lasagna."

He groaned and pressed a hand to his stomach, both the sound and the action reminding Carley of their time in the laundry room. "Lasagna is my favorite."

Evelyn's face broke into a pleased smile, and Carley swore she saw the older woman's cheeks pinken a little. It seemed Knox had that effect on more than just her.

"I'll just put this in the oven and set it on low so you can eat it whenever," Evelyn said, busying herself by putting the dish in the oven and turning it on. "Then I'll scoot and let you two get back to whatever you were doing."

"Laundry," Carley insisted. "We were just doing laundry."

"I'm sure that's right," Evelyn replied, giving her a wink before waving her fingers at Knox. "You take care, Deputy Garrison."

"You too. Thanks again for the lasagna," Knox said.

"My pleasure." She opened the screen door, then let out a little yelp. "Did you know there's a rather large hog sunning herself on your porch?"

Carley chuckled. "Yes. She probably smelled the lasagna. Although I've been told that she prefers not to be referred to as a hog." She heard the pig give a snort in agreement.

"Sorry, dear, didn't mean to offend," Evelyn said, sticking out her hand to give the pig a few affectionate taps on her head as she walked past.

The scent of Evelyn's hot dish had been too tantalizing, so Carley and Knox had filled their plates with slabs of cheesy lasagna and taken them out to the front porch to eat. They chatted easily about people they knew, and Knox had told her about how well Sienna, the new rescue he often came to visit, was doing.

They sat side-by-side on the cushioned glider, the view of the ranch and the mountains spread out in front of them. Carley was surprised by how comfortable she felt with him and how often he made her laugh. Although, as easy as it was to talk to him, she still noticed every time their knees touched, or their shoulders made contact, like they just had as he'd taken their plates and set them on the table in front of them.

It was crazy. She'd just surrendered herself to him on the dryer an hour ago but now her stomach was still getting fluttery every time their knees touched.

He leaned back with a contented sigh. "Well, how does it feel to be in your new home?"

"That's funny," she said, turning to look at him as she scooted her body into the corner of the glider. "I was just thinking about that earlier. But I was thinking about how I've never really found a place that truly felt like home to me."

"Never?"

She shrugged. "My dad left us when we were kids, and my mom moved Jillian and me around a lot. She always had a good reason—always searching for the next best thing—new job, new town, usually a new man. We got to the point where no place really felt like home—or maybe we just never let ourselves get too attached or let ourselves think of any place like that."

"No place?"

She shook her head. "No. Not really."

"What about when you got married?"

She huffed out a bitter laugh. "For sure not with Paul. We moved several times too, and I just never felt settled with him. Even when I did make the effort to try to create something homey for us, nothing I ever did was good enough, so I guess I just quit trying."

"I know I've never met him, but I really hate that guy."

"Don't. He's not worth wasting the emotion on."

"Good point. So back to you, what do you think *would* make some place feel like home?"

"I don't know."

He picked up her feet and held them in his lap. "Close your eyes." She tensed and started to pull her feet back, but he held on, slipping off her shoes then massaging one of her arches with his thumb. "Come on. Trust me. Just close your eyes."

She warily settled back against the cushion and closed her eyes. Mainly because of the magical massage he was giving her feet.

"Now, when you think of the word *home*, what do you see?"

"I told you, I don't know."

He kneaded her sore heels. Dang, the man had great hands. And the sole of her foot easily fit into his palm. "Stop thinking about your feet," he told her. "Just imagine you've gotten off work and you're driving home. You turn off the road and pull up to a house and all the tension of the day leaves your shoulders because you've just arrived home. Now tell me what that house looks like."

She let out a sigh. "There is a place, I guess."

"Tell me about it. What color is the house?"

"Blue."

"Good start. Keep going."

"It's like a two-story farmhouse, kind of Victorian-looking with dormer windows upstairs, but it still has a bit of a log cabin feel to it because the bottom part of the house is stone. It's got a wide wraparound front porch with big pine trees next to it. And it has a red front door."

"A Victorian-looking log cabin farmhouse?"

Knox's question had a funny tone to it, and she opened her eyes. "Yep."

His expression was thoughtful and a bit perplexed. "And you said a red door? You sure about that?"

"Oh yes. It has to have a red door and a white porch swing and two white rocking chairs on the porch next to the door."

"That's a pretty specific-sounding description. Have you seen this house before?"

She searched her memory. It had been a long time since she'd thought about the house, but she could still see it clearly in her mind. "Maybe. I'm not sure. You know, our grandparents lived here in Creedence when Jillian and I were kids and we used to come visit them. We loved it here. That's why I ended up coming back. But I feel like maybe I saw a house like that one time when we were driving home from a day of fishing with my grandpa. It was set back in the trees, like up against the mountains, and I remember thinking that I wished I could live there someday. But I'd been sleeping on that drive back so I'm not sure if I really saw it or just dreamed that I did."

"You've obviously got a pretty clear picture of it in your mind," Knox said.

"Yeah, I guess I do. So, we must have driven by it." She shook her head. "Maybe that's dumb—a house I *may* have seen once as a kid, or possibly dreamed up, is the place I picture when I think of *home*."

"I don't think it's dumb at all. It must have been a good memory."

"It was. And it was a good day. I remember I caught the biggest fish that day, and that hardly ever happened. It had been just Jillian and me with our grandpa, and he had taken us up to a new place, some little mountain stream. My grandma didn't come with us that day, but she packed us a lunch and I can remember us sitting by the creek, with the sun sparkling off the water, and eating cold fried chicken and my grandma's lemon bars. She made the best lemon bars ever. And I remember there was a shallow area in the creek, and my grandpa let us swim around in it. Probably scared off all the fish, and the water was freezing, but we didn't care. When we left, we were wet and exhausted and probably smelled like fish, but it was a perfect day."

"Sounds like it."

"Gosh, I haven't thought about that in years. I'm going to have to call Jillian later and see if she remembers that day."

"I'll bet she does. Stuff like that can stick with you. I was close to my grandparents too, and I have great memories of times we've spent together."

She settled back against the seat again and let herself enjoy the feel of Knox's hands rubbing her feet. "You know, my grandparents meant the world to me. I like that yours were important to you. That might have just added another tally in the 'Knox-box.'"

"The Knox-box, huh?" His lips curved up in a grin. "How many tallies do I have on my side so far?"

"Enough that it's making it harder to remember why going out with you is such a bad idea."

"I'll keep that in mind." He didn't say anything more, but his grin widened as he continued to rub her feet. Which might have added one more tick to the box.

CHAPTER 6

CARLEY HUMMED ALONG WITH THE RADIO AS SHE DROVE into town that Monday morning. She'd been busy the day before, unpacking and organizing and settling into her new place. She'd made time to take a walk at dusk, her favorite time of day, and had enjoyed the company of Tiny and Shamus who strolled along the pasture path with her. Otis had started to come with them but must have turned back once he realized there was no food involved.

She'd been pleasantly surprised to find how much she enjoyed the company of the mini-horse and the pig—both were good listeners, and she swore Tiny smiled at her a couple of times when she was telling them her thoughts about what was going on with Knox. And even though she'd told him she wouldn't, she couldn't help setting out a few scraps and some water for the yellow-and-white cat who'd claimed residence in Carley's lap as she'd sipped a glass of wine on the porch after her walk.

Jillian had called, and they'd had a few minutes to catch up, her sister sharing all the drama and excitement of spending her honeymoon with her son, a mini-horse, two dogs, and an occasionally grumpy old man. But she'd hung on every word when Carley had told her about Knox helping her move in and *their* excitement in the laundry room.

"Wait," her sister had said. "Back up. You're telling me Knox took you to O-town *on the dryer*?"

"Oh yeah. And it was quite a trip."

"But that's crazy. You never get naked on a first date. And you haven't done the deed in forever. This guy *must* be something special."

"I *still* haven't done the deed. And I *wasn't* naked. That's the crazy part of the story. We both had our clothes *on*. Well, Knox was missing his shirt, but I was fully dressed. I'm still not exactly sure how it happened. It had to have been the dryer."

"Wow. Good to know. And just so we're clear, once we get home, Ethan and I will be stopping by the bunkhouse while you're out to 'do some laundry.'"

They'd giggled and cracked a few more dirty puns before hanging up. Talking and laughing with her sister had been just the thing Carley had needed.

But Jillian was right about one thing. Knox did seem to be something special.

As her car rumbled over the original brick-paved main street of Creedence, she tried to take her mind off the handsome deputy by admiring the quaintness of the town. The small mountain town had a population of less than fifteen hundred, but the residents took pride in their city and the downtown area was adorned with mock gas lamps, lots of planters overflowing with colorful flowers, and green awnings that complemented the massive range of mountains the town was nestled against.

A grand stone courthouse occupied the town square with cute shops and businesses surrounding it, then filling several blocks of Main Street. It was the perfect walking town with boutiques and gift shops mixed in with a grocery store, the bank, the drugstore, and a couple of quaint coffee shops within a few blocks of each other. At the far end of town sat the Creedence Country Cafe where Bryn worked, the feed store, and the Mercantile, where you could buy anything from stamps to socks to fishing waders.

It was the perfect town, and Carley did love Creedence. If there ever was a place she could call home, it came the closest. There was something about the mountains—not just their beauty and mystery, but the way it seemed as if the majestic peaks were watching over them, keeping her residents tucked in safe and guarding them from the outside world.

Her building sat between a bookstore and the Ladybug Dress Shoppe. Its redbrick facade had flowerboxes filled with pansies in front of each window and one long green awning spanning over both the entrance to her shop and the yoga studio next door. Autumn Green and her studio had pretty much come with the building. And even though she and Autumn had their occasional differences, the yoga instructor paid her rent on time, kept the property neat, and with her bustling crowd of health enthusiasts, also kept business in the downtown area. After her classes let out, her patrons often grabbed coffees or lunch or just ran errands downtown and they had plenty of crossover customers who partook of Autumn's classes and Carley's hair-care services.

As she pulled into her normal parking space to the right of her building, Carley was surprised to see Knox standing in front of the shop holding two teal takeout cups, the signature color of *Perk Up*, her favorite coffee shop located a few doors down from the salon. So much for getting her mind off him. "Hey, there," she called, climbing out of her car.

"Good morning, beautiful."

Her cheeks warmed at the compliment. She hadn't been called "beautiful" in a long time, at least not by a handsome cowboy. "What are you doing here?"

"I accidentally ordered an extra vanilla latte, then I remembered you telling me this weekend that kind was your favorite, so thought I'd see if you could use a little extra caffeine this morning."

"Accidentally ordered an extra of my *exact favorite* kind of coffee? Well, isn't that a coincidence?"

"And a heckuva one at that," he said with an innocent grin. "And the darndest thing is that it's even iced, just the way you said you liked it. Would you believe it?"

"No. Not really," she said, but she couldn't help smiling back at him as she reached for the cup. "But I'll take the coffee anyway."

"Looks like someone left you a note," he said, gesturing to the sheet of paper taped to her front door.

"It's from my neighbor," Carley said, already recognizing the pink page with the yoga studio letterhead and Autumn's familiar loopy handwriting, as she unlocked the front door. She pulled it from the glass as she walked in, reading the note aloud, "'Dear Carley, This is Autumn, from next door'...she always introduces herself in her notes. Even though they're on letterhead, and I've been her landlord for almost five years now. Well, technically you could say Evelyn is still her landlord. She and I share ownership of the building, but I mostly take care of it. She used to own it with Paul, but he signed his half over to me in the divorce settlement. It was the best thing I got out of our marriage. That and my relationship with Evelyn. She's like a grandmother to me. And I've always treated her better than Paul ever did."

"How could anyone not treat Miss Evelyn well?" Knox asked. "She's the sweetest."

"I know, right?" She turned back to the note and kept reading. "'I heard you had a confrontation in the salon the other day and wanted to mention that I do offer a Conflict Contemplation Class for folks who have disputes or disagreements. I'd be willing to offer your customers 15% off the class, since we're neighbors and all. If they're not interested in a class, I could always whip them up a half-price batch of my "special-secret-ingredient" Rocky Mountain High Brownies—they're great for "mellowing" out arguments. Let me know. Have a good day. *Namaste*.'"

"Wow," Knox said. "That's quite an offer. Have you tried her special-secret-ingredient brownies?"

Carley chuckled as she tossed the note on the counter. "No. Not my thing. Although she did offer them to me a few months ago, along with her Conflict Contemplation Class, when she and I were arguing over if we should spend an extra hundred dollars apiece to get eco-friendly coconut husk welcome mats for our shops when ours wore out."

"A hundred extra dollars for a welcome mat? The place you wipe the dirt off your feet?"

"I know."

"I probably would have sided with you on that one," he said. "Do you all argue a lot?"

She shook her head. "No. We usually get along fine. She's sweet, and her heart's in the right place, but we share the building, and she rented from Evelyn before I took over, so we still have our occasional skirmishes."

"Like the kind I broke up the other day with the scissors and that curling iron thing?"

"That was a flat iron, there's a difference," she corrected. "And no. We haven't resorted to using weapons, hair care or otherwise. At least not yet."

"Good. Let's keep it that way. I don't want our first date to be postponed because you're behind bars for assaulting your neighbor with a hair styling doohickey."

She took a sip of coffee, then offered him a coy smile over the top of her cup. "Who said anything about a first date? Have I agreed to a date yet?"

"Not yet. But I feel like I might be wearing you down." He flashed her one of his roguish grins. "Speaking of *wearing*, I left a few shirts in the washer this morning and wondered if I could bring them over later to throw in your dryer?"

She laughed but was saved from having to come up with a clever answer by the bell above the door as Erica wheeled in a stroller. "Hey, there. Anyone up for a new baby visit?"

"Oh my gosh, yes," Carley squealed as she hurried toward

her stylist, giving her a gentle hug before peering into the stroller. "Oh honey, she's just precious."

"Isn't she though?" She lifted the tiny bundle from the stroller and passed her to Carley's waiting arms. "This is Lily. We named her after my grandmother."

"She is sooo sweet," Carley said, her chest tightening as the baby wrapped her fingers around her pinkie. She'd wanted kids right away when she and Paul had first gotten married, but he'd always had a reason to put it off—not enough money saved, not enough room in their apartment, too much time spent on the road chasing another rodeo. She was glad now that they hadn't had kids and didn't have to drag them through their ugly divorce, but her heart still hurt at the years wasted that she'd thought would have been spent as a mom. She hugged the precious bundle closer to her chest as she turned back to Erica. "You look amazing. And I can't believe you're out and about already."

Erica shrugged. "Oh, shoot yes. She's an easy baby, and she's my third, so no rest for the wicked *or* new moms. She gets me up early, so this morning I've already put supper in the Crock-Pot, dropped my oldest off at soccer practice, my middle at piano lessons, and mopped the kitchen floor. I was just taking a break to grab a latte at the coffee shop and to come show off my new girl."

"After a morning like that, your coffee's on me," Knox said, pulling out his phone and tapping at the screen. "I'm texting Victoria over at Perk Up right now to tell her to put your coffee and a pastry on my tab."

Carley was surprised at the tinge of jealousy she felt at

Knox having the cute coffee-shop owner's number in his cell phone. Before she could think too much about it, the bell rang again as two more customers entered the shop and were immediately drawn to the new baby in her arms.

"Ohhhh, isn't she sweet?" one said as the other held out her arms for her turn to hold her.

Carley passed Lily to her, already missing the sweet bundle. She let out a breath and peered around the shop, searching for something to busy her hands with, and caught Knox looking at her, a soft expression on his face, almost as if he knew holding Erica's baby made her happy and sad at the same time.

It wasn't the first time she'd felt like he just *got her*. It had been so long since she'd felt any kind of connection with a man that it kept tripping her up how many moments like this they'd had. She wasn't used to sharing secret smiles and having that feeling that one of them just knew what the other was thinking. But she had that feeling with Knox, and as much as her heart seemed to be getting all giddy every time it happened, she wasn't sure if the rational part of her was as happy about it.

Another customer stopped in to buy some conditioner and took her turn holding Lily. "She's just the cutest," she said passing the baby back to her mother.

"I should probably get going," Erica said, as she took her daughter. She turned to Knox. "You want to hold her before I go, Deputy?"

"You bet. I love babies," Knox said, taking Lily and cuddling the baby close to his chest. He gently bounced her and murmured sweet nothings as she stared up at him, her tiny lips pursed in a perfect pink bow.

The other women in the beauty shop stared at them, seemingly transfixed by either the sweet infant or the hunky cowboy who'd so deftly swept her into his arms. Was there anything quite as aww-inducing as a tough guy cuddling a newborn?

"Wow, I'm impressed," Erica said. "Most men are scared of babies."

He flashed a sidelong glance at Carley. "I am not *most* men. And it takes a whole lot more than this adorable bundle to scare me."

Lily must have taken his declaration as a challenge, because she took that moment to projectile vomit a spray of milky white liquid onto the front of his shirt.

"Oh, no," Erica said, passing Knox a burp rag as she took back the baby. "Sorry about that. I fed her before we came in, and she does that sometimes after she eats. I can pay to have your shirt cleaned."

"Don't worry about it," Knox told her as he wiped the spit-up from his shirt. "The department has a service, and I can assure you this is not the worst thing this shirt has ever seen." He looked at Carley, his grin conveying another one of those secret messages. "Looks like I've got something on my shirt. You got a place where I can clean this up?"

"Come on," she said, leading him toward the back of the shop and ignoring the swirl of butterflies in her stomach at the memory of the last time he had something on his shirt. "I'll check in with you later. Thanks for bringing Lily in," she called to Erica. "She's adorable."

"And don't forget your coffee *and* a pastry are on me," Knox said. "Maybe get two. You need to keep your strength up with that cutie." He waved before ducking behind the curtain with Carley.

She wet a hand towel at the sink and dabbed at the spot on his shirt.

"I swear every time I'm around you, something is getting spilled on me," Knox told her. "It's like the universe is conspiring to get us naked together."

She tried to laugh off his joke and pretend that her body hadn't just responded to him saying the words "naked together" as she pressed the dry side of the towel against the wet area on his magnificently muscled chest. "*Or* maybe you just happen to get stuff spilled on you a lot."

"I'm not sure you really got the spot well enough. I'd be happy to take my shirt off," Knox said, glancing around the back room. "There's gotta be a dryer around here somewhere. *Please* let there be a dryer here."

"Stop it," she said, playfully nudging his arm. "I do have a dryer, but I've also got a shop full of customers. Who are all probably wildly speculating about what we're doing back here, so we should get back out there."

"We could always give them something to talk about." He wrapped an arm around her waist and pulled her close. Leaning in, he nuzzled her neck, his voice low as he said, "Give me four minutes, and I bet I could find a way to get your cheeks flushed and your hair mussed."

She fought the thrill of heat that ran down her spine and that small voice that was begging her to give him the time.

Instead, and with massive amounts of willpower, she pulled away. "Only four minutes, huh?"

He grinned down at her. "Yeah. But just imagine what I could do if you gave me an hour."

She barked out a bawdy laugh. "I'll keep that in mind," she said as she playfully pushed him out of the back room. Her hand was still on his forearm—how did she keep finding ways to touch him—as they emerged from behind the pink curtain.

The laughter died on her lips as she spotted the brown-haired man standing in the middle of the shop.

She hadn't seen him in almost five years. Not since they'd signed the divorce papers.

Anger, resentment, shock, and that sneaky bastard of an emotion—abandonment—all flooded through her as she opened her mouth to speak, then closed it again when no words came out. After what seemed like hours, she finally managed to sputter his name. "P-paul? What the hell are you doing here?"

CHAPTER 7

CARLEY WAITED FOR AN ANSWER AS SHE STARED AT THE man who had walked out on her all those years ago.

He smiled good-naturedly—yes, actually *smiled* at her—as if his abandonment hadn't really happened and they were just a couple of old friends who hadn't seen each other in a while. "Hey now. Is that any way to greet your husband?"

"*Ex*-husband," she corrected. "And what were you expecting? A homecoming parade in your honor?"

He shrugged. "I do love a good parade."

"I'll tell you where you can stick your parade," she muttered softly, then realized all the women in the shop were watching their interaction. Forcing herself to stay calm, she raised her voice to a normal tone and said, "Well, you can forget that. What are you doing here anyway?"

He lifted his shoulders in an easy shrug. "I was in town. Thought I'd just stop by for a little visit."

"Well, hi, bye, don't care how you're doing. There's your *little* visit. You can leave now."

Paul nodded over her shoulder. "Aren't you going to introduce me to your friend?"

Knox's body tensed behind her. She'd almost forgotten he was standing there. "I'd rather not."

"Deputy Sheriff Knox Garrison," Knox said, sticking his hand out as he introduced himself.

"Good to meet ya. Paul Chapman." Paul's voice took on a territorial tone as he took his hand. "Carley's husband."

"*Ex*-husband," she and Knox said at the same time, and Carley took a little too much satisfaction in seeing Paul's slight wince at the strength of Knox's grip.

Paul took his hand back but continued to study the deputy. "And how do you two know each other?"

"None of your business. That's how," Carley said, planting a fist on her hip.

The mike on Knox's shoulder squawked with a call from dispatch. "Deputy Garrison, we need you back at the station."

Knox leaned his mouth toward the mike and uttered a reply of some kind, words that Carley couldn't hear or comprehend. She was too distracted by the sight of her ex-husband, a man she'd hoped never to see again. And she didn't believe for a second that he'd just come back for a little visit. He *always* had an agenda.

She had no idea what he could have up his sleeve. But she was sure it wasn't good.

"I gotta go," Knox said, slipping an arm around her waist and pulling her to his side. He leaned down and spoke close to her ear, close enough for everyone watching—and every eye in the shop was watching—to assume there was at least some level of intimacy between the two. "I'll call you later."

Carley might normally have bristled at the attention, but it was worth the chance of a rumor starting about her and Knox just to see the pained expression of envy on her ex's face.

Like a tennis match, it seemed every head in the shop in unison turned one way to watch Knox walk out the door, then turned back to see what Paul would do next.

Now that Knox was gone, he seemed to slip back into his easy what-he-thought-of-as charm. She might have also thought so at one time, back when she believed all the insincere promises he made, then so easily broke, but she saw through his snake-oil salesman appeal now. He leaned an elbow casually on the reception desk. "So, sweetie pie... what's new?"

Gag. She wanted to puke at the old endearment. "The door. Feel free to use it."

"Geez. Why are you so touchy? I'm just trying to be friendly." This is what he did—acted all hurt like he was being so sweet, and she was just being bitchy. He wasn't so sweet when he'd told her he didn't love her anymore, *and* didn't think he ever had, right before he walked out *their* front door.

"I've got enough friends," she told him.

He nodded his head toward the door. "Like Deputy Dog?"

"Like none of your business," she repeated.

He let it go and plastered on a smarmy smile as he looked around the salon. "The shop looks good. You've made some nice improvements. And business on Main Street seems to be picking up more from what I remember."

A frisson of panic stole through her gut. Is that what he was here for? Was he coming after the shop?

Knox tapped his fingers on his desk. It had only been a few hours since he'd seen her. Was it too soon to call?

Maybe he should just send a short text. Make it seem casual. Nothing like the "hey, I really like you and wouldn't we make beautiful babies together?" words he had running through his head. And those were the least of them.

He was also thinking sappy ones about how he loved her smile and spent way too much time thinking about how he could coax more of them out of her. And then there were the thoughts about them naked and rolling around in the sheets continuing what they'd started on the dryer. Yeah, none of those words should be typed into a text.

Screw it. He was calling her. That's what a friend would do. She'd had a shock seeing her ex that morning. It was perfectly reasonable to call just to see how she's doing.

He second-guessed his decision the whole time he was digging out his phone, scrolling to her contact info (he'd just barely restrained himself from adding her to his favorites already), and listening to the phone ring, once, twice…he should just hang up…

"Hey, Knox." Carley's voice came through the phone, sending a little wave of nerves running through him. Although she must have him added to her contacts too if she knew it was him calling. That thought made him smile.

Geez. What a chump he was.

"Hey, Carley," he said, wiping his sweaty palm on his thigh. "I was just checking in on you. You know, seeing how you were doing after seeing, you know…" What was wrong with his brain, and why was he finding it so hard to form words?

"He who must not be named?" she said, then softly laughed at her own joke. "I don't know. It's weird. And a little unnerving. And I don't believe for one second that he's here for an innocent visit, so I just keep waiting for the other shoe to drop."

"Sounds stressful. How about I pick you up after work and take you out to dinner?" *Real smooth, Garrison.* "I mean, just so you have one less thing to worry about today. Now you know supper is on me."

He held his breath, waiting for her answer and not sure if he'd saved himself. Way not to push her. He'd only called to check up on her, but now he'd somehow asked her out on a date. He waited another beat, then exhaled as he heard her reply.

"Yeah, sure. Why not? A girl's gotta eat."

Okay, so maybe not the most romantic of answers, but still…he'd take it. She'd agreed to go to dinner with him and that was the most important thing.

"Great. I'll pick you up around five. Will that work?"

"Sure. I've got a blowout scheduled for four, so I'll text you when I've finished."

"You *schedule* your arguments? Who are you fighting with? The yoga instructor?"

"What?" she asked, confusion in her voice. Then she laughed. "No, not *that* kind of blowout. I'm washing then blow-*drying* out someone's hair. They've got an event tonight so I'm doing their hair before they go out."

"That's a relief. Although there is a certain kind of logic to planning an hour in your calendar to have a squabble. Then you either get it all over and done in an hour's time and can move on with your day or, more than likely, you would have forgotten what you were arguing about by the time the appointment reminder came along."

She laughed again. "I like the way you think. But let's try not to have to schedule that appointment. Okay?"

"Agreed."

"I'll see you around five."

"Affirmative. See you then."

"Oh, and Knox," she said softly. "Thanks for checking in with me. It helped."

"That's what friends are for," he said. "See you tonight."

That's what friends are for? He gave himself a mental head slap. Why had he said that? He didn't want to be her *friend*. Well, he did. But that's not *all* he wanted to be. And by throwing the *friend* word in there at the end of the conversation, did he just negate the whole idea of this being a date?

For such a smart guy, he could be a real idiot. Especially when a gorgeous blond hairdresser was involved.

He turned back to his computer and pulled up the latest report he was supposed to be working on, determined to keep his mind *off* Carley and *on* his job for the next few hours. He'd written four sentences when the door to his office flew open, and Paul busted into the room.

"Sorry, Deputy," Janice, his admin said, hot on the intruder's heels. "I tried to get him to wait, but he insisted he needed to see you. He said you two know each other."

Her desk was to the left of Knox's office door, and she didn't usually let people get by her without letting him know first. But most people weren't Paul Chapman.

"It's fine, Janice," he told her. "I've got it."

"Yeah," Paul said, his tone dismissive. "It's fine, Janice. Deputy *Dog* and I go way back."

Wow. Super original, Paul. Like that's the first time I've heard that one.

Janice raised an eyebrow, then her gaze traveled disdainfully up and down him, ending with a slight sniff of her nose. Knox wondered if she knew the history between him and Carley. She'd grown up in this town and not much got past her, so he assumed that she did. "*Fine,*" she said, mocking the same tone of Paul. "But you let me know if you need me, Deputy *Garrison*, and I'd be happy to take this trash out."

Oh yeah, she knew. And it sounded like she was *Team Carley*, all the way.

He held back a smile as he leaned back in his chair and assessed the man Carley had somehow fallen for and agreed to marry. He must have been one hell of a salesman if he'd convinced her to buy what he was selling. How could she not have seen through his blowhard disposition?

He sure did. Everything about this guy just rubbed him the wrong way. And not just because he'd hurt Carley, although Knox was sure that was probably coloring his judgment. But there was more to it. Paul came across like he was always running a con. And he hated how the guy acted all smug like he was better than everyone else.

"What do you want, Paul?"

He tried for a casual shrug. "I just wanted to come in and have a chat."

"About what?"

"About what's going on with you and my wife."

"*Ex*-wife," Knox was quick to remind him. "How about we talk about what you're doing back in town instead."

"Okay. That's easy." Paul's lips curved into a greedy smile. "I came back to get what's mine."

A tiny sliver of dread snaked its way through Knox's chest. Did Paul come home to try to win Carley back? Would she fall for this guy's lame attempts again? *No way.*

"And what is that, exactly?"

"So, what's the deal with you two anyway?" Paul asked, leaning his hip against the side of his desk and ignoring the question.

None of your damn business, was what Knox wanted to answer. But instead, somehow when he opened his mouth, the words that came out were, "We're dating."

Okay, so they hadn't officially gone on a date yet, and putting aside the fact that she just now had barely agreed to go out on *one* date with him, and even that he might have accidentally made it sound like a meal between friends, this seemed like a bit of a stretch.

But things had been going well with them, at least until this doofus had shown up and was trying to throw a wrench in things.

Paul scoffed. "*Dating?* That's crazy. Carley hasn't dated anyone the whole time we've been divorced."

Knox bristled. "How would you know?"

"I've still got plenty of friends in this town." He patted the desk and stood as if he were dismissing the matter *and* Knox. "I was a little concerned it might be serious. But I'm not worried now. I knew she wasn't over me."

It felt like this guy was trying to make him feel like a fool. Not to mention the way he was demeaning Carley, as if her opinions didn't matter. He couldn't let him get away with that.

"You're wrong," Knox told him, standing up and coming around from behind his desk. He had several inches on the other man, but he pushed his shoulders back, so he stood even taller. "It *is* serious. And she's been over you for years."

"Yeah, right," Paul said, although a little of his bluster had diminished. "I don't believe it. I know Carley doesn't go out with *anyone*. And especially not with a guy like you."

What the hell did that mean?

"Like I said, you're wrong. She *does* go out with a guy like me. We've been seeing each other for a while now."

Shut up, man.

What was he doing?

Paul looked him up and down, as if assessing his worthiness, then let out a condescending chuckle. "No way. Maybe you've gone out a couple of times, but I don't believe she'd get serious with you."

"Well, we're actually engaged. Is that serious enough for you?"

What the hell was he doing? He'd really stepped in it now.

"*Engaged?*" Paul narrowed his eyes. "I haven't heard anything about Carley getting engaged. And this town's too small for that to be a secret."

He made an excellent point. Knox scrambled for an explanation. "That's because we haven't officially made an announcement yet. We were waiting for her sister to get back." There. Maybe he could salvage this outlandish declaration he'd made.

"So, then I've still got time," Paul said, giving him an arrogant wink before sauntering out of his office. "See ya around, Deputy."

Time for what?

Knox followed him to the door, hating that he'd had the last word. But the wide-eyed look he saw on the receptionist's face before she dropped her gaze and busied herself with her papers on her desk told him she'd heard their whole conversation.

Or at least the part that mattered.

"Janice..." he started to say before his name was called from across the station.

"Garrison, grab your gear," one of the other deputies hollered as he headed toward the door. "We've got a situation, and we need you on this one."

His conversation with Janice would have to wait, he thought as he reached for his stuff. Hopefully she wouldn't say anything to anyone until he got back. Or until he'd had time to warn Carley about his stupid ego and his dang big mouth.

The salon had been busy all afternoon with more customers than usual stopping in to buy hair products or set an appointment. Word must have gotten around that Paul was back in town and had made an appearance at the shop.

Carley could have done without the visit from her ex, but the uptick in sales that afternoon almost made seeing his smug face worth it.

The bell over the door rang, and two women from her church pushed in together, as if one were trying to beat the other inside.

"Hi, ladies," Carley called out to them. "I'll be with you in a second."

"Oh, no hurry," the shorter one said. "I was just passing by your shop and thought I'd stop in to remind you that my cousin has started doing wedding cakes over at her bakery, and they're just gorgeous. She uses real flowers and everything."

The other woman had scanned the shelves and picked up a five-dollar sample of eucalyptus hand lotion, one of the least expensive items on the shelf. She pulled a five-dollar bill and a business card from her purse and set them on the counter. "I heard this hand cream was wonderful, so I thought I'd stop in and grab a sample. My daughter uses it all the time. You might have heard she just started working at the Little Flower Market, and they do amazing wedding bouquets. I'll leave you one of their cards. And I wrote my girl's name on it, just in case you want to mention her."

"Okay. Thanks for letting me know." Why were they telling her this? She had been doing more bridal parties this summer. Maybe she was earning more of a reputation for her work, and they wanted her to pass on the information to the brides she scheduled. "And I hope you like the lotion. It works great for our dry Colorado hands."

"Oh yeah, I'm sure it will be wonderful. Don't forget about the card."

The other woman pushed her way in front of her. "And don't forget about my cousin."

"Okay, I've got it," Carley said, although she didn't really get it. "Thanks for coming by."

———————————

Later that afternoon, Carley took a twenty-minute break to grab a coffee and pick up a couple things from the grocery. Sipping the iced vanilla latte only made her think of Knox again and how sweet and thoughtful it was that he'd brought her a caffeine boost that morning. Everything seemed to make her think of him lately.

He really was a good guy. And he must be wearing her down if he'd talked her into a date tonight. Although right before he'd clicked off, he'd mentioned something about that's what a friend would do, so maybe this *wasn't* a date. Maybe it was just supper between two friends. Thinking of it that way seemed to ease some of the nervousness that tightened her chest when she even *thought* the word "date."

She'd spent the last several years swearing off men. Despite some casual flirting and an occasional lunch offer, she didn't really go out on dates. And what did it mean that the first time she not only considers dating but agrees to a meal out, her stupid ex happens to show back up in town? Was that a bad omen?

Stop it, she told herself as she grabbed a cart and tossed in the couple of things she needed. She didn't believe in omens. But thinking about Paul had her brain scrambling again trying to figure out what he was doing here. *Ugh*. She hated wasting any brain-time on that jerk.

Trying to push away any thoughts of Paul and his likely nefarious motives, she tossed a Snickers in her cart and headed for the checkout. *What?* It was one chocolate bar. And she could use the sugar.

"Hey, Carley."

She stopped at the sound of someone calling her name and turned to see Susan Johnson, a woman she'd known for a few years now and who was an occasional customer at the salon. She had a photographic memory for all her clients' salon needs, even if they didn't come in often. Susan was blond highlights and a shag cut.

Carley waved as she took her place in line.

Susan slipped into line behind her. She had a goofy grin on her face as if she knew something Carley didn't or maybe like they were in on some kind of secret together. She lowered her voice to a conspiratorial tone. "Just wanted to be one of the first to tell you congratulations."

"Thank you. I guess. Although I'm not exactly sure what you're congratulating me for," she said, thinking Susan must've heard that she'd moved out to the rescue ranch, as she took a sip of her coffee.

"For...you know..." She lowered her voice again and

gave Carley's side a little nudge. "You and that hunky Deputy Knox."

Carley choked on her last sip and tried not to spit the rest of her coffee out as she sputtered, "M-me and Knox?"

Susan pressed her fingers to her mouth. "Oops. Sorry," she said, although she didn't sound sorry at all. "I know it just happened, and no one is supposed to know, but I'm just so happy for you."

"Thank you," she said again, not sure what other response was appropriate. She prayed she was talking about the fact that they may have been seen together or maybe she some-how heard that they were going out on a date—and not that thing with the dryer. "So…how did you hear about Knox and me? Already?"

"Oh, I heard it from Lisa, the dispatcher down at the sher-iff station, who heard it from Janice, Knox's admin. I guess he was talking about it at the station. And either he told her, or she overheard him talking about you. I'm not sure which."

He was talking about her…about *them*…down at the sta-tion? Oh, was he ever going to get it.

And he could forget about her going out with him now.

"Well, thanks again, Susan," Carley said, not knowing what else to say. All she wanted to do was get out of here. She fumed as she tossed her drink in the trash, then hurriedly scanned her few items through the checkout. Then she mut-tered and fumed some more as she stomped all the way back to the shop.

Who did he think he was?

She pushed through the door of the salon, then pulled up

short as she spotted the object of her consternation standing in the center of the salon.

"Your three o'clock is here," Danielle told her, gesturing to Barb Howard, and her cohort, Nancy. The two women were in their mid-sixties and had been friends for years. They often accompanied the other to the salon, visiting with each other and Carley throughout the appointment.

Carley gave the women a quick nod, then her glare returned to the deputy. "Well, hello, Knox," she said, her greeting carrying her level of irritation.

He turned around, his expression already telling her that he knew he was in trouble.

"Oh, Carley," Barb said before Knox could get out a word. "We were just talking to Knox and telling him that we're so happy for you both." She said it as if she were speaking for the whole salon in general.

"Well, you don't have to be because there's nothing—"

Knox cut off the rest of her sentence as he interjected, "There's nothing that would make us happier than your good wishes." He crossed to her and wrapped an arm around her waist as he leaned in close to her ear. "Can I talk to you, please? In private?"

"Oh, you have them," Nancy said. "You two are such a cute couple." She gestured to herself, Barb, and Danielle. "We were just talking about you before Deputy Garrison arrived, and we think you're going to make *such* a beautiful bride, Carley."

She blinked at the woman. "B-bride?" she stammered.

"We know it was supposed to be a secret," Nancy kept on

as if she didn't hear Carley's strangled question. "But we were just dying to tell you congratulations on your engagement."

Engagement?

Her eyes widened as she peered up at Knox.

"I *swear* I can explain," he said in a low voice.

"Well, *someone's* gonna be dying if you don't do it quickly," she said back in an equally quiet tone. "And it's either gonna be me because I'm having a heart attack, or you because I murder you."

"Sorry, ladies," he said to the women in the shop as he pulled Carley toward the back room. "I just need to borrow my *fiancée* for a few minutes. You know, wedding stuff."

"You take all the time you need," Barb called back.

"*Fiancée?* What in the heck is going on?" Carley whirled on him the second they stepped through the curtain and into the back room.

"Keep it down," Knox whispered. "I told you, I can explain."

"You better start talking fast. Why in the world do those women think we're engaged?"

He offered her a pained look. "Well, you see…"

Her mouth fell open as the odd incidents of the past few hours fell into place. "Wait a minute. I've had weird things happening all afternoon. Women stopping in the shop to tell me their family members handled wedding preparations, and just now, I was in the grocery and ran into Susan what's-her-name, who's friends with your dispatcher down at the station. She said she'd *heard* about us in this totally cryptic voice and wanted to tell me *congratulations*. I thought she'd heard we were going to go out on a date—not that we're *engaged*." She took a step back and grabbed the side of the counter for support. "Does the whole town think we're getting *married*?"

"Probably not the *whole* town," he said, cringing. "Not *yet* at least."

CHAPTER 8

KNOX TOOK OFF HIS STETSON AND SCRUBBED A HAND through his hair as he tried to figure out a way to tell Carley that he'd royally screwed up.

She stared at him, one hand planted on her hip, as she waited for an explanation.

He should just start with the facts—he'd completely goofed up and he was an idiot—then go from there. "Listen, Carley, first of all, let me just say that I know that I'm a total knucklehead and I absolutely screwed up, but you gotta know that my heart was in the right place." His heart and also his ego. "It's just that guy Paul—he's such a douche canoe. But I shouldn't have let him get to me."

Her lips quirked a little. "I agree with your adept description of Paul, but what does my ex have to do with the fact that half the town thinks we're engaged?"

"Because I told him we were." He hung his head and waited for her to blast him.

"*You?* You're the one who started this? Why?"

He let out his breath in a huff. "Because he came to my office to ask me what was going on between us. At first, I told him it was none of his business, but then he started getting all territorial and saying he came back to town to claim what was his, and that just needled me because I didn't think he had any claim to you anymore."

"You're right. He doesn't."

"That's what I thought. Look, I know what I did was stupid, but I sometimes tend to get overprotective when I care about someone, and so I was trying to stick up for you and tell him you were over him and somehow, I ended up telling him that we were dating."

She nodded slowly. "I can understand that. He has a way of getting under your skin. And I can even appreciate you wanting to stick up for me, but how the hell did you get from us *dating* to us being *engaged*? And how the heck does half the town know about it?"

He pressed his fist to his forehead. "Yeah, well that's where things got a little out of hand. When I told him we were dating, he scoffed at me."

"*Scoffed?*" Who the hell says *scoffed*?

"Yeah, you know, like he just kept huffing and acting like there was no way that a girl like you would go out with a guy like me. And believe me, Carley, I'm well aware that you are completely out of my league, but he just kept razzing me and also acting like you somehow still belonged to him, and I maybe got a little jealous, and a little defensive, and then all my protective instincts kicked in and I just wanted to defend you *and* take that guy down a peg. And I guess I was thinking that if he thought you were taken, he would lay off and not try to come after you. I swear I did not mean to say we were engaged. The situation just escalated, and it somehow popped out of my mouth."

She narrowed her eyes as if trying to deduce the truth of what he'd told her. "I get it. Believe me, I understand that he has a way of making you say and do crazy things. And part of me is a little flattered that you were trying to protect me, even if it was a totally screwball way to go about it."

"I know. I'm still not exactly sure how it happened."

"I'm not exactly sure how half the town already knows about it."

"Ugh. I'm pretty sure that's my fault too. My office door wasn't closed all the way, and I think my admin must have heard our conversation. Then I got called out before I had a chance to ask her not to tell anyone."

"You know how this town is. All she had to do was tell *one* person and the news would have spread like a wildfire on a windy day."

"I'm really sorry. I feel like such an idiot. But I can fix it."

"How?"

"My ego got us into this mess, it can dang well get us out. We'll just tell everyone that you broke things off with me."

"No way. Then I look like an idiot for breaking things off with the hot deputy."

A grin tugged at his lips. "You think I'm hot?"

She pressed her lips together as if trying not to smile, but in the end she failed. "Yes, of course I do. Remember our moment on the dryer?"

"Darlin', to my dyin' day, I will *forever* remember our moment on the dryer."

She shook her head. "You *are* an idiot."

"I know." He hung his head, then peered up at her. "Can you forgive me?"

She blew out her breath. "I guess. But forgiving you and wanting to marry you are two very different things."

"I understand. I do. But I'm still worried about that little weasel ex of yours. I just think he's up to something. And I don't think it's anything good."

"No, neither do I. Tell me again what he said about coming back to get what was his."

"That's all he said. But it was *the way* he said it, so possessive, and a little threatening. I tried to press him, but he changed the subject."

The jangle of the bell sounded from the front of the shop followed by a low murmur from the customers, and something set his spidey senses off. He leaned his head back to spy through the gap in the curtain. "Shit. Speaking of the douche canoe. He's here."

"What? Paul's here? What the hell is he up to?" Carley pressed against him to see through the curtain, and more than his spidey senses went off. Her body was just so curvy and lush, and he wanted to forget about her stupid idiot ex-husband and block out the rest of the town and focus on exploring those curves and showing her how sorry he was and how much she already meant to him.

"You want me to ask him to leave?"

"I'd rather you just shoot him," she said, then held up her hand. "I'm just kidding. Sort of. No, really, I'm kidding."

"I could start by having a talk with him, then I could consider shooting him later."

"I would say that's a good idea, but the last time you had *a talk with him*, we ended up engaged. I think I'd better talk to him this time."

She pushed through the curtain. He followed, his arms out and his shoulders back as if his body were already preparing for a fight.

———————

Bile rose in Carley's throat at the sight of the man who'd spent three years essentially destroying her self-worth. Just having him in the salon brought back so many anxious feelings, and she pressed her hands against her thighs to keep from tidying up the fashion magazines spread over the table in front of the hair dryers.

She could feel his judgment as palpable as if it were a thick fog leeching through the air as his critical gaze roamed over the shop, then ricocheted from her to Knox, then back again. His tongue flicked out and wet his lips, reminding her of a lizard. *Or more like a snake.*

He did an exaggerated eyebrow raise as he gave her a sanctimonious smile and held out a box of chocolates. "Hey, sweetie pie. I brought you a box of your favorite chocolate-covered cherries. Just like I used to. I know how you've always loved them."

She bristled but tried not to let him see her cringe. What the hell did he have to be smug about? And why was he standing in her shop acting like he owned the place and had every right to be here? "First of all, those were always *your* favorites, not mine. I don't even *like* cherries. And I told you to stop calling me that."

"Oh, yeah, I guess that's not real appropriate now that you're all engaged to the deputy here. That's what I heard at least. Thought I'd come by and see for myself if the rumors were true." He set the chocolates on the counter, completely ignoring the fact that she said she didn't like them, then took a few steps closer to her and lowered his voice. "Come on, Carley. We all know that the reason you haven't dated anyone since our divorce is because you haven't gotten over me."

"*What?*" she asked as her eyes almost popped out of her head. Surely, she couldn't have heard him correctly.

"It's okay," he said as if placating her. "I get it. We had something special, and I can understand why you'd want to try to win me back. But this little attempt to make me jealous? Come on." Even though Knox had six inches on him, Paul still managed to peer down his nose at him. "With this guy? Really?"

The nerve of this man. How had she been fooled into *marrying* him? How had she not seen how arrogant he was until it was too late?

She looked up at Knox. He was a thousand times more of a man than Paul could ever hope to be. His comment came back to her about him thinking he was out of her league— that was crazy. Knox Garrison was in a league of his own. He was handsome, charming, thoughtful, smart, and sexy as all get out. Any woman would be lucky to marry this guy. Except she wasn't looking to get married again. Ever. And the reason why was standing right in front of her.

But she couldn't let Paul know that. Or let him think that he and his ridiculous comments could get to her.

"Yeah, really, Paul," she fired back at him. "Knox and I *are* getting married. And it has nothing to do with you. In fact, he's ten times the man you are." She took Knox's arm, and felt his chest puff out as he stood taller next to her.

Take that, jerkwad. Score one for the deputy. Zero for the douche nugget.

"Yeah, right," Paul said, huffing out a laugh. "You keep telling yourself that, honey." She suddenly understood what Knox meant when he said Paul had *scoffed*. "But tell me this, if you two are all set to be hitched, how come no one in this town seems to know that you two have even been dating?"

"Just because I don't feel the need to broadcast my love life all over town doesn't mean that I don't have one," she said.

"And I already told you," Knox interjected, putting his arm around her. "We were waiting to announce our engagement until her sister got back in town."

Oh, good thinking, Knox. That made perfect sense. See, handsome *and* smart.

"And I suppose that's also why you didn't buy her a ring?" he sneered, then narrowed his eyes at them. "Something doesn't add up here. I don't know what it is, but I'm going to find out. This feels like either some kind of ploy to make me jealous or to throw me off the scent of what's happening with this building and the revenue of the salon."

Panic tightened Carley's chest. The *revenue* of the salon? Why would he mention that?

"It's none of your concern what's happening with the salon. Or this building. This is *my* business."

He huffed again and looked down at her as if she were a child. "Oh honey, don't you know that *your business* has always been *my business*?" He turned and sauntered toward the door, hollering over his shoulder as he pushed through the door. "You can't get anything past me, sweetie pie. I've always got my eye on you."

Carley's stomach twisted with nausea as she looked up at Knox. "What did he mean by that? Like he's keeping tabs on my personal life? Or did he mean the salon? Could he be snooping into my customers, or do you think he's saying he has some kind of *legal* right to the earnings of my business?"

Knox shook his head. "I don't know. It mainly sounds like he's just trying to unnerve you or throw you off balance."

"Well, it's working."

"Don't listen to that idiot," Barb told her. She gestured to herself and Nancy. "We know you aren't still carrying a torch for him. We think you and Knox are a great couple."

"Thank you," Carley told them. She'd almost forgotten they were still there. "I'd better get back to work," she told Knox.

"Yeah, of course," he said.

"I'll walk you out." She touched Barb's shoulder as she passed the salon chair. "I'll be back in just a minute to get you started."

"You take all the time you need, hon," Barb told her.

She followed Knox out to the sidewalk. "What do we do now?"

He shrugged. "What do you want to do?"

"I *want* to throat punch my ex-husband."

"I'll arm-wrestle you for the opportunity."

She laughed, even though her stomach was still unsettled. "He's just so unpredictable. And so arrogant. How can he possibly think I haven't been dating because I'm still hung up on him or that there is any possible chance in hell that I would want to get back together with him? Now that he's acting like you and I being together is such an impossibility, all I want to do is prove to him that we *are* engaged."

Knox nodded. "Me too." He ducked his head. "Thanks for that stuff you said about me in there."

She nudged his chest. "It was true. You *are* ten times the man he is."

"Thanks."

She chewed on her bottom lip. "Do you really think he's spying on me?"

"I wouldn't put it past him."

"He does have a point about no one in town knowing about us."

"Well, then, apparently we need to be seen around town as a couple." He tilted his head. "Think you might still be up for that date tonight?"

"I don't know. I thought I was, but now I'm not so sure. Seeing Paul again just makes me think going out with you, with *anyone*, is a bad idea."

"Then don't think of it as a real date. It's just two friends grabbing some dinner together."

"While trying to convince a whole town that they're so madly in love with each other that they can't wait to get married."

"There is that. But we'll cross that bridge when we come to it. What do you say? You up for a fake date with your new fiancé?"

She had to laugh. This whole thing was just ridiculous, but it would be worth it if it got Paul off her scent. "I have been wanting to try that new pizza place out by the highway. If we're getting hitched, I may as well get a pizza out of the deal."

"That's the spirit. Text me as soon as you're done with your last client. I'm off duty now, so I'm gonna run home and get my animals fed and haul some hay for my cows out to the pasture. Then I'll get showered and changed and be ready to swing by and pick you up when you're finished."

"Sounds good. See you in a bit." He leaned down as if to kiss her, and she automatically pulled back. "What are you doing?"

"Oh sorry," Knox said. "I figured since we're supposed to be engaged, that it would seem normal for me to kiss you goodbye."

"Oh yeah, right. Sorry." She looked up and down the street and took in the few locals going about their business in town. "It's just that we're standing out on the sidewalk. And we're in front of my work."

"I know. That's why it seemed like a good idea. If more people see me give you a casual goodbye kiss, then it will lend to the legitimacy of our engagement." He leaned a little closer to her ear. "And Barb and Nancy practically have their eyes glued to your front window."

"You're right. Of course. I just wasn't prepared." She smoothed her hair and rubbed what was left of her last application of gloss between her lips. "Okay. I'm ready. Go ahead."

"Geez. Now it feels weird. Like I'm applying for a job or something."

"You are. And no pressure, but the position of Carley's fiancé has been vacant for a long time. In fact, the position had previously been eliminated, as far as I was concerned. And management wasn't quite prepared to have it resurrected like this."

He chuckled. "You make me laugh. Which is good—it's helping with my nerves. But now it seems like it's been too long. Maybe we should say a fake goodbye again."

"Oh, just do it," she said.

"Okay, okay." He leaned down and tilted his head to the right to go in for the kiss. Unfortunately, she also tilted to the right. Their noses collided instead of their lips. Then they both over-corrected, tilting the other direction, which resulted in another nose crash and another near miss of their mouths. "Oh, geez, hold still," he whispered before plunging back in and landing a quick kiss on the side of her lip.

"That's good enough," she said, taking a step back.

"Yeah," he agreed, lifting his hand in a wave. "Text me later."

"I will. See ya," she said, reaching for the door handle of the shop and hoping no one saw their awkward attempts at a kiss.

"Hey, Carley," he said, his voice low and coy enough that it had her turning back around.

"Yeah?"

"That'll go better next time. I think we just need a little more practice."

CHAPTER 9

CARLEY WAS WAITING OUTSIDE THE SALON WHEN KNOX drove up that night. He parked and jumped out to circle the front of the truck and grab her door before she'd even made it to the curb.

"You look nice," she told him, seeing he'd changed into clean jeans and a button-down blue shirt. The ends of his hair were damp and curled slightly under the brim of his cowboy hat. The scent of his soap and a masculine cologne surrounded her as she climbed into the truck. "You smell nice too."

"Thanks. So do you."

She'd tried to focus on paperwork after she'd called him to tell him she was ready, but couldn't help herself, and ended up touching up her makeup and adding a few extra curls to her hair. Not that she was trying to look good for him, or anything.

But it was still nice that he'd noticed.

"You hungry?" he asked, pulling out and heading toward the highway.

"Starving. I can't wait to try this place."

Apparently, Carley wasn't the only one excited about trying out the new pizza spot. The parking lot was full of cars, and through the front glass window, they could see most of the tables were full.

"Um, I didn't expect it to be so crowded," she said.

"Yeah, looks like half the town's in here. But the good news is that if all these people see us together…you know… as a couple, then surely a few rumors will start flying and one of them will have to get back to Paul." He offered her a grin. "This is our chance to be seen together. We'd better make it good."

"What are you suggesting we do? Swipe the parmesan and napkin holder off the nearest table and start making out on it?"

He chuckled. "No, but I'll keep that idea in mind for another time, when we're in a more private setting." He held out his open palm. "Why don't we start by just holding hands?"

"I can do that," she said, resting her hand in his. Warmth flooded her at the way her hand fit perfectly in his as their fingers intertwined. She kept her gaze trained on the menu board as they entered the restaurant and approached the counter.

She was all too aware of the stares they got and the soft whispers she heard as they walked past, but she focused on holding her chin up and hanging on tight to Knox's hand.

"There's a booth over there in the corner," he said, after they'd placed their order. He put his arm around her waist and guided her that direction.

Her body felt like a bundle of energy, and she crossed her legs after they'd sat down to keep from bouncing her knee. "I don't know why I'm so nervous," she whispered.

He leaned forward and reached for her hand again, holding it across the table. "If it makes you feel any better, I'm a little nervous too."

"What's the big deal? We're just having a pizza."

"Yeah, but *I'm* having it with a gorgeous woman who makes my head spin and my knees a little shaky."

Her lips curved up as she smiled at him. "You do say some of the nicest things."

"You smilin' at me like that isn't doing anything to stop my knees from shaking."

She squeezed his hand as her smile widened. He had a way of making her feel good about herself, and she hadn't had that feeling in a long time. It felt both good and a little scary. "Tell me about the rest of your day. Did you get your animals taken care of?"

He nodded. "Yep. I even had time to do a little work on my tractor."

"You have a tractor?"

"Yeah. Why? Do you think tractors are sexy?" His thumb grazed over her knuckle and sent little shivers of heat swirling down her spine.

"If I do, are you going to offer to take me for a ride on yours?"

He laughed. "I would, but it would be a pretty short ride. And I don't think this one would fall anywhere into the *sexy* category. The thing hasn't run in years. It was my grandpa's, and it came with the farm."

"Are your grandparents still around?"

He shook his head. "No. I lost them a few years ago. That's what brought me back to Creedence—I moved here to take care of them and help out with the ranch. But then we lost my grandma, and Gramps just went downhill after that—it was almost like he lost the will to live after he lost Gram. They died within six months of each other."

"I've heard that happens quite often with couples who've been together a long time. How long were they married?"

"Over sixty years. I can only hope to someday have a love like that…" His voice got a little choked up, and Carley liked him even more for the obvious connection he had with his grandparents. "Anyway, I inherited my ranch from my grandparents, which was a really amazing gift, but that means not only did I get a bunch of animals, I also inherited a barn and several outbuildings full of what my grandpa liked to call his 'treasures.'" He ducked his head. "But my grandma just called it junk."

"What do you call it?"

"I probably fall somewhere in between. I did inherit my grandpa's love for tinkering, and I really enjoying fixing stuff. I like being able to take what seems like it's broken and make it work again."

"And all for the low, low price of a box of Twinkies," she said, remembering how Lyda Hightower had paid him for fixing her back gate.

"I'm pretty cheap labor," he said with another laugh.

"So what other animals do you have on your ranch?" she asked, enjoying hearing him talk.

"Oh, the usual. A pen full of chickens, a few horses, a dog or two, couple of barn cats, of course, and several hundred head of cattle."

"Several *hundred*? So, you're actually a real cowboy, huh?"

He chuckled and knocked the side of his cowboy boot lightly against her foot. "I don't wear these boots just for looks."

She tilted her head and batted her eyes, having a little fun flirting with him. "You do look good in them though."

His grin turned roguish, and he cocked one eyebrow. "Oh, yeah? You think so?"

She offered him an innocent shrug and nudged back at his foot. "Yeah. Maybe. A little."

Was she seriously playing footsie under the table in a crowded pizza place with a hot cowboy? How had her life changed so much in such a short time? A few weeks ago, she'd watched her sister get married, and as happy as she was for Jillian, and as fun as it had been to dance and flirt with the cute deputy at the reception, the whole thing had served to remind her what a colossal disaster her marriage had been. Her divorce had left her broken and filled with shame and self-doubt, and she'd renewed her promises to herself never to get married again.

So what the heck was she doing now? Not only was she out on a date, but it was a date designed to convince half the town she was *engaged*. A queasy feeling rippled through her gut, and she pulled her foot back under her side of the booth. "You said you have a dog *or two*. What does that mean?"

He laughed. "It's complicated. My real dog is Sadie, she's a golden retriever, and the sweetest dog you'll ever meet. She's not quite three, so she's still in her puppy phase and can cause a little trouble, but for the most part, she's great. I've even started bringing her to work with me sometimes. She loves riding in the truck. It probably sounds hokey, but she's kinda my best friend." He shook his head and laughed again. "And then there's Rodney. He's sort of like a dog, at least he thinks he is, and if you ask him, he'd probably tell you that I'm *his* best friend."

"I'm confused. How can he be *sort of* like a dog?"

"Like I said, it's complicated. You'll understand when you meet him."

His expression shifted, and Carley saw him go into cop-mode. His easy grin changed to an expression of alert caution as he turned his head and scanned the restaurant. She'd felt it too, a subtle shift in the air of the restaurant.

The noise level had dropped and a few more heads turned their way. It took them a second, but they both seemed to spot what had caused the shift and had even more curious expressions facing their way. Carley knew Knox had spotted him at the same time she did by the slightly tighter grip on her fingers, and she may have even heard a low growl come from the back of his throat.

Paul had just walked into the restaurant.

That queasy feeling returned with a vengeance as she watched him laughing and high-fiving people as he worked his way across the room. He had so many people fooled with that good ol' boy charm he portrayed—they had all thought he was such a great catch. She prayed he would be so absorbed in catching up with the locals that he wouldn't spot them tucked into the back corner.

Knox tugged on her fingers. "You want to get out of here?"

"Yes. But I want to eat more."

He laughed. "Why don't you grab us some sodas from the cooler, and I'll have them box our pizza up, and we'll take it to go. I know a spot where we can eat in peace and no one will be staring at us, except for maybe a few squirrels."

"Sounds good to me. And I prefer the company of a few squirrels to that jerk anytime." They slid out of the booth, and he took her hand again as they walked back to the front, both acting as if they hadn't even noticed Paul or that they didn't give a hoot that he was in the restaurant.

A tall cooler stood by the counter, filled with bottles of pop and water. She grabbed a couple of bottles and held them up for the cashier to see as Knox covered the check. They handed him a pizza box, and he followed her out to his truck.

The pickup was blessedly quiet after the hubbub of the pizza place, and the cab filled with the rich scent of garlic and tomato sauce as Knox set the box on the seat between them. "I thought we'd drive up the canyon and find a spot by the creek to eat," he said as he turned out of the parking lot and headed toward the mountains.

"Perfect. Although I may have to sneak a piece before we get there." Now that they'd left the restaurant, and gotten away from Paul, the queasiness in her stomach was replaced with hunger.

"Only if you pass me a piece too."

"Deal."

She pulled a couple of slices out and passed one to him before taking a bite of the other. She groaned in appreciation. "So worth it. This pizza is amazing."

Knox ate his as he drove up the canyon, passing several small picnic and camping spots along the creek. He must have recognized the one he liked, because he pulled off the highway and into a clearing nestled in evergreens with a picnic table and firepit set up next to the water. "This is one of my favorite spots. It's set back off the road a bit and has enough trees behind it to almost make you forget there's even a highway there. Plus, it has a great view of the creek." He grabbed the pizza and came around to her side of the truck to open the door for her.

"It's gorgeous," she said, taking their sodas and the stack of napkins she'd picked up on their way out of the restaurant and following him to the picnic table. The air cooled as they got closer to the water and smelled of pine trees and damp earth.

They sat next to each other, facing the stream, as they each took another slice. "Not a bad place for a date," Knox said, nudging her shoulder.

She caught herself smiling up at him. "No, not a bad place at all."

"Even though no one's here to witness our deep abiding love for each other as we prepare for our wedded bliss?"

She'd almost forgotten for a second that they weren't on a "real" date. Knox was so easy to be with. She was having fun with him. Not to mention the coils of heat that swirled through her belly as his thumb had traced circles around her knuckles while he was holding her hand. "Speaking of wedded bliss, maybe we should come up with a plan for how we want to do this."

"This?"

"Ya know, this fake engagement thing. How are we supposed to convince Paul and half the town that we've been secretly dating for long enough that we've fallen madly in love with each other and want to get married?"

He shrugged as he gave her a sideways glance. "It might not always take that long to fall in love with someone. Sometimes you meet someone, and you just know right away that you have a connection and that they're something special."

She swallowed. Was he talking about her? Even if she didn't like admitting it, she *had* felt like they'd had a connection, the way they seemed to get each other's jokes and feel so at ease with each other. Did he think she was someone special? She swallowed again at the sudden burn in her throat. It had been so long since she'd felt special to someone. Other than her sister and her nephew.

Paul had acted that way at first, like he'd won the million-dollar jackpot when she'd agreed to go out with him. Their relationship had burned so bright in the beginning, all passion and heat, like a flash in a pan. Which was why she'd agreed to marry him so quickly, why she'd jumped into a relationship, believing that the fire of their love would stay strong. But like a cheap birthday candle, their flame quickly died, leaving Carley burned and used up and feeling like she'd been anything *but* special.

Thinking about Paul again and the way he'd been so attentive and devoted at first, then so quickly lost interest after she'd married him was like a splash of cold water to the face. A wake-up splash that reminded her she couldn't let herself fall for that kind of thing again. No matter how cute or thoughtful the cowboy in front of her might seem.

"Have you felt that connection before?" she asked, trying to get the focus and her thoughts off her and her relationship with Paul. "You already know I've been married, but what about you? Ever been married?"

He shook his head, his bright smile diminishing a little. "Nah. Came close once though."

"How close?"

"Pretty close. Or at least I thought we did. It happened fast—but I'd thought it was the real thing. I'd ask her to marry me, she'd said yes. We'd even moved in together and gotten a dog."

"What was her name?" Carley asked, trying to ignore the funny feeling in the pit of her stomach as she tried to imagine Knox in love with someone else.

"Who? The woman or the dog?"

"The woman."

"Her name was Kimber."

Carley wrinkled her nose. "*Kimber?* Ugh. I don't like her already."

A grin tugged at the corner of his lips. "Jealous?"

"No," she said, a little too quickly. "So, what happened?"

He shrugged again, the ghost of a smile disappearing. "She got spooked, I guess. Or maybe she just realized she wasn't that into me. Our relationship got real serious real fast, and I think getting the dog together was somehow the tipping point for her. She took off, split one day while I was at work, left a "Dear Knox" note, but took the television and the dog."

"Wait. What? She took the dog? Without even telling you?"

"Yep."

"Now I really don't like her. What kind of person does that?"

"One I didn't want to be engaged to, I guess. She'd come from a broken home and had some trust issues, so I probably should have seen it coming, but I didn't. I guess I'd thought I was enough to fix all that for her, but apparently, I wasn't. I was pretty torn up for a while, then I sort of realized that I missed the dog more than I missed her, so I dusted myself off and got on with my life. It wasn't too long after that that I moved to Creedence."

"I'm sorry."

"It is what it is. I was probably a fool for believing things could happen that fast."

"I don't know. My dad took off when we were young, and Jillian and I were raised by a single mom, so I'm pretty jaded about marriage. But you told me earlier that your grandparents had such a wonderful marriage, so I'm sure that played into it for you. When you grow up seeing a great example of what marriage should be like, maybe you tend to believe in it more."

"I might have seen my grandparents' happy marriage, but that's far from the example I grew up with. Our dad took off when we were young too, and I wish my mom would have raised my little sister and me on her own. We would have all been better off. But instead, she got remarried—and he wasn't such a bad guy at first, or at least not when he was sober. But he was a mean drunk, and my mom took the brunt of his temper. I never understood why she stayed. We begged her to leave him, but she just covered up the latest shiner he'd given her and soldiered on. I understand now that as a mom with two kids, she maybe thought she didn't have a lot of options, or she thought she was doing it for us, to keep a roof over our heads. But I would rather have slept in a cardboard box and eaten out of a garbage can if it meant he could never touch her again."

He'd been staring hard into the water as he'd been telling her the story, but he leaned back and shook himself, as if fighting off a shudder or shedding the memory. "Sorry, didn't mean to get so dark on you and make things all awkward."

"It's not awkward," she said, suddenly having a better understanding of Knox's protective nature and his constant need to "fix" things. "It's just real."

He squeezed her hand and she looked down at their entwined fingers, not sure when she'd taken his hand, or he'd taken hers. But it felt nice. Right.

And she wasn't ready to let go.

———

After their "date," Knox had dropped her off at her car, then insisted on following her back to the ranch, just to make sure she got home okay.

"I'm all good," she said, getting out of her car and turning to wave at him from the porch steps. Maybe if she ran inside real quick, then he wouldn't have time to get out of his truck and then they'd both be saved from that awkward moment of trying to figure out how to end the night—shake hands, quick kiss on the cheek, or…gulp…quick kiss on the lips. "Thanks for tonight. It was fun."

Too late, dang it. He was already getting out of his truck and sauntering toward her. "I was thinking on the way out here…," he said as he stopped in front of her. "That was a pretty clumsy attempt at a goodbye kiss earlier this afternoon. If we were really a couple, don't you think that would come a little more naturally?"

She shrugged, all too aware of how close he was getting, the scent of him wrapping around her like a warm coat. "I don't know. I guess."

"What do you think we should do about that?"

She shrugged again, suddenly unable to form words because her mouth had gone as dry as the Sahara.

He stepped in closer still and raised his hand to cup her cheek. "Like I said earlier, I was thinking maybe we should practice. You know, just until we get the hang of it. Or at least figure out how not to have our noses bump."

"How do we do that?" she was finally able to say, although her voice came out as barely above a whisper.

"I think we just take it real slow and keep tryin' 'til we get it right."

———————

Knox might have sounded all calm and cool as he told Carley they should practice kissing goodnight, but now that his hand was on her cheek and he was leaning in for the kiss, he found himself as nervous as a long-tailed cat in a room full of rocking chairs.

Take it real slow.

He'd just said that. Now he needed to take his own advice. But the anticipation was killing him. He'd kissed her before and knew the sweet taste of her mouth, so all he wanted to do was pull her to him and ravish her. But this was about more than a kiss, this was about trust. And earning hers.

Which meant taking it slow. Even if it killed him. Although he had a feeling if this kiss was what did him in, it would still be worth it.

She peered up at him, her eyes wide.

"You sure have pretty eyes," he told her. "They remind me of a mountain lake the way they change from green to blue depending on the light and what you're wearing." Tonight she had on jeans and a turquoise tank top, and he touched the edge of her collar. "This shirt brings out the blue. Makes me think of the blue sage wildflowers growing up the side of the mountain behind my ranch."

She blinked twice, then she ducked her head, lowering her gaze to his shirt. "I don't even know how to respond when you say sweet things like that. Am I supposed to just say thank you, or 'I know,' or tell you that you have nice eyes too? Because you do."

"You don't have to say anything." He tilted her chin up

to look at him. "I think our 'practicing' needs to have less talking and more kissing anyway."

"I'm not sure we even need to practice. We seemed to have kissing pretty well figured out the other day on the... with the...you know, in the laundry room."

He grinned. "Yeah, we did. But there has to be a happy medium between *that* and smashing our noses into each other. I can't be ravishing you and wanting to rip your clothes off out on the sidewalk in front of the beauty salon. Well, I can *want* to, but I think we'd start a whole different kind of rumor in town about us if I did."

"All right. You make a valid point." She tilted her face up toward his. "So shut up and kiss me."

He laughed, but it came out throatier than he'd intended. He was trying to make this light and fun, but he was having a hard time keeping his hands off her. All he wanted to do was touch her—to run his knuckles over her bare shoulder, to let all that hair slip through his fingers, to pull her close and feel her against him. But he knew he needed to take this slow.

Hell, they were already engaged, it seemed a little late to be thinking of slowing things down. But this was important.

"We've got all the time in the world, darlin'." He leaned down and brushed his lips across the tender spot of her neck, just below her ear, keeping his voice low as he told her, "And I'm a patient man, so I'm committed to stickin' with it 'til we get it right."

He smiled as he felt her shiver, then pressed a soft kiss to the side of her throat. She tilted her head back and made a soft kitten sound that almost did him in. Another tender kiss, this one on the underside of her jaw. One more, this time just grazing the corner of her lips.

He was forcing himself to take his time—getting to this one kiss was killing him—but it was the most delicious kind of torture.

A soft catch of her breath as he barely brushed his lips over hers—so tempting to slant his mouth over hers and take what he wanted—but he held back, drawing away and aching inside as this time she drew closer. That one slight movement toward him, and the firm pressure of her fingers pressing into the side of his arm were the only indications that she wanted this as much as he did.

One more soft graze, then he tenderly pressed his mouth to hers, holding back his own sigh…her lips were so damn sweet…then he was finally kissing her, and the taste of her only made him ache for more.

She pressed into him, kissing him back with a hunger that made him want to lift her up, carry her into the bunkhouse, and then toss her into bed and ravish her until they were both sated and spent.

With incredible willpower, he finally pulled away, his breath ragged, as he peered down at her. "I think we may have passed the sweet goodbye kiss zone and moved into the wanting to rip your clothes off arena."

She let out a small shuddering sigh and melted into him. Her tone was flirty and coy, but he could still hear the need in her words. "Then I guess we'd better keep practicing."

Her soft, pliant body pressing into his, her heavy desire-filled eyes, begging for more kissing practice was about to undo all the patient resolve he'd been working so hard to show her she could trust him.

He stared at her kiss-swollen lips and ached to taste them again. He pressed his forehead to hers, the scent of her filling his senses, as he struggled to do what he knew was the right thing. Taking her by the shoulders, he lifted her away as he took a step back, the night air cooling the space between them.

"Sorry darlin'," he said, his voice coming out scratchy and rough. "I don't think I can handle any more practice."

CHAPTER 10

THE NEXT FEW DAYS, CARLEY DID HER BEST TO STAY BUSY, but she couldn't get Knox out of her mind. Not after she'd made such a fool of herself the night of their pizza date. She kept telling him she wasn't interested in something real, yet when he'd "practiced" kissing her, she'd practically thrown herself at him. No wonder he'd backed away.

He'd told her good night, then it had seemed like he couldn't get away fast enough, as he hurried to his truck.

She probably wouldn't be seeing him again for a while. Which was what she'd wanted, right? So why had she been taking extra care the last few mornings with her hair and makeup just in case she *happened* to run into him?

This morning, she'd planned to run into the salon and do some errands downtown, so she'd put on the black slender-fit ankle-cropped pants and the white gauzy top outfit that Jillian had told her looked great on her last time she'd worn it. She normally paired it with a chunky necklace and rows of bangly bracelets but couldn't wear them at work—not with as much as she did with her hands and the last time she'd tried a big necklace, she'd almost whacked her client in the head with it when she'd leaned over to wash her hair. So instead, today she'd chosen a delicate silver chain with a sterling-wrapped pearl pendant layered with a longer simple necklace that fell into the open neckline of her blouse.

She wasn't even supposed to be at the shop that day. Thursdays were normally her day off, but she had a bridal party scheduled for the next day and the bride was a friend, so she wanted to stop in and make sure she had everything prepared and ready.

Lifting her keys toward the door, she stepped onto the pink welcome mat and water seeped over and into her shoes.

"What the heck?" she muttered as she pushed through the door and saw water pouring down the wall separating the beauty shop from the yoga studio. She waded through several inches of water, despair flooding her as well as she noted the magazines and debris floating over the floor. A pink foam roller bounced off her foot, and she pushed a plastic trashcan out of her way as she tried to figure out the source of the water. All she could think was that a pipe must have burst. She could hear water gushing, but wasn't sure where it was coming from.

She had to turn off the water. *Where the hell is the shutoff?* She couldn't remember.

Think! The basement? The crawlspace?

She splashed through the water, running toward the back of the salon. Her foot hit a wet magazine, slipping on the slick surface and she went sprawling forward. She let out a shriek of pain and frustration as she banged her knee and splashed herself with freezing water as she put out her hands to break her fall.

Half crawling, half stumbling through the water, she

pushed past the curtain and into the back room. A half-door in the back of the supply closet led to the crawlspace. A bulk package of now bloated and sopping paper towels blocked the opening. She shoved them out of the way and yanked the small door open. The water main sat just inside, and she jerked the lever to the closed position. The loudest gushing sound stopped, but now she heard constant *drip, drip, drips* falling all around the shop.

She swallowed back the despair filling her throat and wished for the thousandth time that week that Jillian was back. As if on auto pilot, she pulled her phone from her pocket and tapped the screen, not even thinking about who she was going to call.

He answered on the first ring.

"Hey, Carley. Would you believe I was just thinking about you?"

"Knox." Her voice broke as she tried to speak, and she took a shuddering breath. "I need you."

His voice changed immediately from casual to concerned. "Where are you?"

"The shop."

"I'm already heading to my truck. I'll be there in three minutes."

Blinking back tears, she stared at her phone. He hadn't even hesitated. All she'd said was, "I need you," and he came running. She'd heard his boot heels hammering the sidewalk and his truck door slam before he'd hung up.

She didn't know what to do now. Feeling overwhelmed and helpless, she peered around her beloved shop, water

darkening the pink wallpaper and dripping onto the receptionist desk. Shampoo bottles and hair-care products floated
past her feet, her cute sneakers now completely soaked
through. She still hadn't moved a few minutes later when the
door flew open, and Knox burst in.

"Carley, are you okay?" He hurried toward her, splashing
through the water.

And again, she didn't think, her body just reacted as she
ran toward him and threw herself into his arms. He grabbed
her and pulled her close, but it wasn't until he said, "It's okay,
darlin'. I've got you," that the real floodgates opened, and she
sobbed into his shirt.

He held onto her, keeping his arms tightly around her as
if holding her together. As her breathing slowed and the tears
lessened, he finally asked, "What happened?"

Inhaling a deep breath, she tried to pull it together as she
loosened her grip on him. He kept one arm secured around
her waist as she took a step away. "I don't know. I just got
here, and I found it like this. Well, not like *this*. When I
walked in, water was gushing down that wall. I turned off the
main water line, then I called you."

"You did the right thing."

"I didn't really even think about it. Yours was just the first
number I thought to call."

"No, I meant by turning off the water."

"Oh, yeah. Of course."

"You did the right thing by calling me too."

She looked up at him and offered him a teary smile.
"Who else would I call? You are my *fiancé*."

He grinned down at her and then pulled her back in for another hug. "That's right, I am. And don't worry, I can fix this."

———————

Carley had dried her tears, found her gumption, and she and Knox spent the next few hours working side-by-side. As she tried to salvage what she could from the floating wreckage, he was on the phone, calling in favors with the utility company, a plumber friend, someone he knew who did flooring. In between calls, he'd found a broom and swept out as much water as he could, then he'd taken a mop and bucket and gone to work sopping up the rest from the floor.

"I know it looks bad," he said. "But your insurance is gonna cover most of this damage. And they can get someone in here to replace the drywall and lay in new floors."

"Maybe, but that all takes time," Carley told him. "And what am I supposed to do in the meantime? I've got a bridal party of five women coming in here tomorrow morning to get their hair done for an evening wedding."

"Yeah, that's bad," he said, gazing around the shop as if the answer would appear in one of the puddles. "But it's okay, I can fix this too." He wiggled one of the stylist chairs. "This doesn't seem to be stuck to the floor. Why don't we load my truck up with whatever you need, starting with this chair, and we'll set up a temporary shop for you at the bunkhouse?"

She thought for a minute, then nodded her head. "That's

not a bad idea. These chairs are portable, and we could bring a couple of roll-arounds," she said, pointing to a set of drawers on wheels. "I could manage with some basic tools and a small supply of product. I've got a portable shampoo sink in the back that I sometimes take to a client's house if she can't make it into the shop." She beamed a smile his direction. "I think we could make it work."

"That's my girl."

———————

Carley was ready the next morning when the bride, Chloe Bishop, arrived with three of her bridesmaids in tow. She and Knox had worked together the whole day before and into most of the night moving what they could from the shop to set up a temporary salon at the bunkhouse. In between moving, she'd called all her clients to give them her new location, and fielded calls with her insurance agency, Evelyn, various repair companies, and Autumn, who had about the same amount of damage in her yoga studio next door.

Knox had made his share of calls too, calling in more favors to get the repair work done quicker and at a better price. A ripple of pleasure had swept through her every time she heard him ask someone if they could do something to help out his "fiancée."

She knew it wasn't real. Heavens—she didn't even *want* to get married again. To anyone. But there was just something about the way the word sounded in his mouth that had her lips curving into a grin every time he said it.

"Thanks for being so adaptable and willing to come out to the ranch," Carley told the bride.

"Oh, no problem," Chloe said, pulling the hairdresser in for a hug. "This works out fine. And the Triple J is practically across the road," she said, referring to the ranch her fiancé, Colt James, and his brothers, Mason and Rock, ran. "It was just a hop, skip, and a jump to get here."

Carley had met Chloe a year or so ago when she'd stopped in her shop one afternoon on a whim and asked Carley for a new look. She'd cut and colored and given her a new style, but she was pretty sure Colt had been smitten with the kind schoolteacher before Carley had even touched her hair. But the new do had seemed to have given Chloe a little more confidence, and that was the part of the job that Carley loved and took such pride in.

"So, what's your handsome groom up to today?" Carley asked as she ushered the women inside.

"His mom's got him and his brothers running around picking up flowers and chairs and working on setting things up for the ceremony and reception."

"I swear Vivi and I have been cooking for a week," Quinn James, Chloe's new sister-in-law, said as she flopped onto the sofa. "I'm not complaining. I love to cook, and we're lucky we have such a great mother-in-law, but I think I got carpal tunnel from frosting three hundred cupcakes yesterday."

"Vivi knows not to let me near the kitchen," said the dark-haired woman who plopped down beside Quinn. Tessa Kane was a journalist who was dating Colt's other brother. "Not after she heard how Mason had to use a fire extinguisher to put out the flames of my last attempt at frying bacon."

"Well, I'm thankful for both your talents," Chloe said, smiling down at the women. "Tessa, you may be a disaster in the kitchen, but the invitations you designed were wonderful. And Quinn, I'm still having trouble imagining three hundred people are going to show up for my wedding tonight. I'm getting butterflies just thinking about it." She pressed her hand against her stomach. "I know it's a lot of work, but I'm so glad we get to have the wedding at the Triple J. I'm just praying nothing goes wrong."

"Nothing will go wrong. It's going to be beautiful," Carley assured her. "And so are you." She looked around at all the women. "You all will be gorgeous."

"Thanks to you," Chloe said.

Carley gestured to the kitchen island where she'd set out mini quiches, fruit, yogurt, and a mimosa bar. "Before we get started, you all make yourselves some plates. And I've got orange juice and champagne if you all want mimosas."

"I'm down for that," the third bridesmaid, whom Carley didn't recognize, said, as she strode into the kitchen and grabbed the bottle of alcohol. Already gorgeous, with her long blond hair pulled up in a ponytail, she wore a bright teal Western-cut shirt, jeans tucked into tall, embroidered cowboy boots, and a rhinestone-studded belt held together by a large, shiny rodeo championship buckle. "I may not be able to make fancy invitations or frost a million cupcakes, but I make a mean mimosa that will either land you on your ass or in the lap of a hot cowboy, and I'm making one for all of you."

Chloe nudged Carley. "That's Stacey, Colt's cousin. She's a barrel racer, and the rumors you've heard about them are true."

"But you love me anyway," Stacey said, then let out a whoop as she popped the champagne cork.

"Yes, we do," Chloe agreed, laughing with her. "But I've already got my cowboy, and the last thing I need is to land on my tush tonight, so make mine light on the champagne."

Carley laughed, even as she couldn't help thinking about how she wished all it would take was a mean mimosa to land her in a certain hot cowboy's lap. "I want you all to have a good time this morning. Chloe and I have talked through some style ideas for your hair, but feel free to look through my idea books and let me know if you find something new. I'll do Quinn's and Tessa's hair first, then work on the bride's, and then finish with Stacey's."

"Oh, and Colt's Aunt Sassy will be stopping by too. I'm sure you know her."

Carley grinned. "Yes, I think everybody knows, *and loves*, Aunt Sassy." Cassandra James, or Aunt Sassy, as the majority of the town knew her, was the real-life aunt of the James brothers and the adopted aunt of Bryn, Carley, and the rest of their gal-pals. She was a spitfire eighty-something-year-old and just as feisty as her name implied. It had been a few weeks since Carley had seen her, and she was glad to hear she was coming today. "And I'm used to doing her hair. It won't take me but twenty minutes to get her all gussied up and ready for the wedding."

"Perfect," Chloe said, accepting one of the mimosas Stacey was handing around.

"Here's to the bride," Stacey called out, holding up the last glass. "Now, let's get this party started."

———————

Carley had finished styling Quinn's and Tessa's hair and was starting on Chloe's when the front door opened, and Knox walked in. He held up two boxes of Twinkies. "Who needs a little sugar?"

"Oh, my word," Stacey squealed as she bolted off the sofa and charged toward him. "Chloe, you little devil. You got us a stripper." She circled around Knox looking him up and down as she went. "And *da-amn*, is he ever a good-looking one." She gestured to his service weapon. "Hey handsome, are you going to show us your big gun? Is it already *cocked*?"

"What? No…I mean…this is a real gun," Knox sputtered, putting his hand protectively over his holster.

"I'm sure it is, baby," Stacey crooned, leaning forward and giving him a little shimmy. "How much extra for a lap dance? Because I've got an hour still to get my hair real mussed up, and I've got money to burn."

"Stacey. Stop it," Chloe said. "He's *not* a stripper."

"Good try," Stacey said. "Look at those muscles. I know a stripper when I see one." She gave Knox the "Matrix come forward" gesture with her fingers. "Come on, baby, show us what you got."

Knox looked at Carley, as if hoping she'd save him. She'd never seen the deputy so tongue-tied, but he seemed completely flummoxed as he held up the cardboard boxes. "I just brought some Twinkies."

"We know. And we want to see 'em." Stacey hooted, then let out a long wolf-whistle.

"Listen now," Knox tried again. "I'm a deputy sheriff, and this is my official uniform."

"Great," Stacey said. "Now take it off. Then can I touch your gun?"

"What did I tell you?" Chloe said, shaking her head. "Barrel racers. You can't take 'em anywhere."

"Sorry, ladies," Carley heard herself say as she stepped around Chloe and in front of Knox. "This one's mine."

Mine? Since when did she consider this man *hers*? Apparently as soon as some hot barrel-racer started flirting with him.

Knox stepped forward and wrapped his arm around her waist. Either her declaration or the steadiness of his hand holding her hip must have given him some of his composure back because his voice changed back to his normal charming tone. "Yep, that's right. I belong to this one. Sorry, ladies. Carley's the only one I'm stripping for." He grinned down at her. "Too much?" he asked quietly, before turning back to Stacey. "And she's the only one who gets to touch my gun."

Carley barked out a laugh, then covered her mouth. "I knew I shouldn't have had a mimosa."

"I haven't had nearly enough," Stacey said, heading toward the kitchen. "I'm making another round. You in for one, Mr. Official Deputy Sheriff?"

Knox shook his head. "No thanks. I just stopped by to bring you all some snacks and to offer to help."

Carley's heart melted a little. "Aww. That's so nice of you."

"I was worried you would be having a rough time being out of your normal element and thought maybe I could do something. You already know my skills at washing hair. Do you need me to shampoo anyone?"

"No thanks," Carley said. "I appreciate the offer, but updos work best when you start with dirty hair."

"I've got dirty hair," Stacey piped up. "In fact, I'm real dirty. So, you can shampoo *all* of me."

"Stacey, seriously dude, you have to stop," Chloe scolded. "Knox is Carley's fiancé. He is *not* a stripper."

"What?" Aunt Sassy asked from behind them as she pushed through the door of the bunkhouse. "You all got a stripper? I didn't know you were getting a stripper. I would've skipped my dentist appointment entirely and come straight here if I'd known. Did he start yet?" She snapped open her handbag. "I know I have some cash in here. Do I need one-dollar bills, or do you think he can make change?"

Chloe raised an eyebrow at Stacey. "See what you started?" Then she called out to the other woman. "Sorry, Aunt Sassy, there is *no* stripper."

"Dang," she said, snapping closed her purse. "Is it too late to get one?"

"I had no idea this was what happened at these shindigs," Knox said, squeezing Carley's hip. She noticed he hadn't taken his arm from around her, and she tried not to think about how much she liked it. "I thought you just talked about hair and stuff."

"Oh, we talk about plenty of stuff," she assured him. "You are very sweet for stopping by."

"I really was hoping I could do something to help. You sure you don't want me to sweep up or something?"

"That's nice of you, but I'm just doing updos so there's really nothing to sweep up." She looked around the make-shift salon. "If you're really offering, there is something you could do that would help me a ton."

"Name it."

"I'm almost out of bobby pins and was thinking I'd take a break and run into the salon and grab a new box."

"Easy. It will take me ten minutes to get there and back. What does the box look like?"

She passed him her shop keys from the counter, then stepped over to one of the roll-arounds and held up a light pink box. "In the cabinet above the sink, on the left side, there should be several boxes stacked up that look just like this one. I thought I'd grabbed a full one yesterday, but this one had already been open and half used. You'd really be helping me out if you could get me a new box."

"Consider it done. I'll be back before you can sip another mimosa." He gestured to Stacey, who was raising her champagne glass and wiggling her eyebrows at him. "Well, maybe not that one. She looks like she could swallow that in two swigs."

"What, baby?" Stacey called to him as he tried to make his escape. "Did you ask if I swallow?"

He couldn't get out the door fast enough, and Carley laughed as the screen slammed shut behind him.

Knox pulled up in the alley behind the salon figuring it would be easier to quickly grab the supplies from the back room then head right back to the ranch. He was lifting the key to the lock when he saw it—a light moving around inside.

Slowly inserting the key, he carefully turned the lock and slipped quietly inside. He held the edge of the door and let it shut softly behind him. Resting one hand on his service weapon, he crept across the back room and peered through the gap between the curtains.

Someone was definitely in there. He could hear their footballs as they walked across the salon and see what looked like the small beam of a phone's flashlight flicking back and forth across the room. He tilted his head, listening intently to try to pinpoint their location and discern what they were looking for. A jingling chime followed by the thump of the cash register door popping open told him all he needed to know.

He took a deep breath as he pulled his weapon from the holster, then hit the light switch at the same time he called out to the man standing next to the receptionist desk, "Police. Hold it right there."

CHAPTER 11

THE MAN HAD HIS BACK TO KNOX, AND THE DEPUTY automatically catalogued his height and weight, and noted his black jeans, T-shirt, and cap as he held his hands up in the air and shouted, "Don't shoot."

"Turn around. Slowly," Knox instructed and gaped at the man who turned to face him. "Paul?" he asked, then followed with the same question Carley had asked him when she'd first seen him in the salon. "What the hell are you doing here?"

Paul squinted against the overhead light. "Well, if it isn't Deputy Dog. Do they even give you bullets for that thing?" he asked, nodding toward the gun.

"I'm not sure. Why don't you take off running, and we'll find out?"

"You're a funny guy."

"Yeah, a funny guy with a gun *and* a badge. So, I'll ask you again, what are you doing here?"

"Relax, Deputy. I'm not robbing the place, if that's what you think."

"Oh no. Why would I think that? You're just standing next to the open cash register."

"I didn't open it. I was looking for a light switch, and I accidentally bumped into it, and the drawer popped open."

"Yeah, that seems likely." Knox narrowed his eyes. "Even if you're not robbing the place, you're definitely trespassing."

"Look, this is just a misunderstanding. And I have every right to be here. It's not trespassing when you own the place."

"That's true. Except you *don't* own this place. Carley does."

"She only owns her half. For now. And she only has that because she duped me into giving it to her in the divorce. But the other half belongs to my grandmother, and we're working out an arrangement for her to sign it over to me."

Hmmm. That didn't sound like Evelyn. But Paul *was* her grandson, and family meant a lot to her. "I know Evelyn, and that seems unlikely."

"Oh. What now? You know my grandmother better than me too? First my wife, and now my grandma. I suppose you're *engaged* to Evelyn too?"

"Not hardly. But I have known her for a while now, and I don't think she'd do that to Carley."

"What would she be doing? Besides setting her up with a great business partner who could actually turn a profit with this place."

"I think Carley's been doing fine on her own without your help." He'd caught Paul's muttered *for now* when he'd mentioned Carley's half of the building, and he didn't like the sound of that one bit.

"Doing *fine* is not the same as doing *well*. I didn't realize how valuable this place was when I let her talk me out of it. With my help, we could make some real money with this hunk of junk piece of property."

No, Knox didn't like the sound of this at all. "Like I said, Carley's doing fine on her own. And I don't just mean with the business. She's doing fine without any help from you." He should have stopped there but he couldn't help himself. "And she's got me now, if she needs anything."

"Like I said, *for now*." Paul wiggled his fingers. "Can I put my hands down now? I don't think you can arrest me when my grandmother gave me her key and asked me to check in on the place. Damn shame about this flooding mess."

Knox's ego fell away as his cop-sense went back on high alert. Had there been something more sinister in Paul's tone with that last comment? Could he have had something to do with the burst pipe? Carley had suspected him, but Knox hadn't thought the guy would stoop that low, until now.

He gave a curt nod as he holstered his weapon. "Yeah, you can put your hands down. And I'm not gonna run you in." His excuse for being there was plausible. It made sense that Evelyn might ask her grandson to check out the damage. "But you've seen the place now, so just for grins, why don't we go ahead and walk out together."

Paul shrugged. "Sure. Why not? I've seen enough of the damage to know it's gonna be pretty costly to try to repair it all. You should tell her she'd be better off just selling the place."

―――――

Thanks to Knox's time-saving bobby pin delivery, Carley finished all the hair of the wedding party right on schedule.

He'd acted a little funny when he'd gotten back, but she hadn't had time to ask him what was wrong. He'd spent the last hour taking his favorite rescue horse for a trail ride while she'd been finishing up the women's hair but had come back to say goodbye as the group had been filing off the porch and loading into Chloe's SUV.

"Okay, we'll see you both at the wedding tonight," Chloe said, giving them each a careful hug so as not to mess up her hairdo. "And don't worry, even though you both RSVP'd separately, now that the word is out about you two anyway, I moved you to a table together."

"Thanks. We appreciate it," Knox told her. But Carley hadn't even considered that he'd been going to the wedding.

"What word is out about these two? About what?" Aunt Sassy asked, coming up behind them.

"About them being engaged," Chloe explained.

"*Engaged?*" Sassy practically screamed. "When the hell did that happen?"

"It's…a recent development," Carley said, avoiding Sassy's eye. There wasn't much that got past the older woman and considering she saw her almost every Tuesday at their weekly girls' night get-together, she was right to be suspicious. What with Jillian being out of town and their other friends being busy as well, they hadn't gotten together in weeks, but still. News like Carley getting engaged or even that she was dating again was not something that would have gone undiscussed in the tight-knit group.

"Uh-huh," the older woman said, followed by a nod and a knowing, "I see." Her narrow-eyed gaze bounced from Carley to Knox then back again, then her expression softened, and she pulled them both into a hug. "Well congratulations, of course. Couldn't happen to a nicer couple."

"Thanks, Aunt Sassy," Carley said, squeezing the other woman close.

"We'll talk later," Sassy whispered into her ear, before pulling away.

Yeah. They weren't fooling her for a second.

Chloe beeped the horn and hollered out the window. "Come on, Aunt Sassy. You'll see them in a few hours, you can talk then. But I've got still got a wedding dress to put on and flowers to arrange."

"I'm coming," Sassy said, skedaddling off the porch and heading for the car. "See you all at the wedding."

Carley and Knox waved as they drove off, and she couldn't help thinking this is what it would be like if they were a real couple, standing on their front porch waving goodbye to their guests. She sighed as she pushed that thought out of her head. This wasn't *their* house. And they weren't a *real* couple.

"I hadn't even thought about the fact that we'd both be going to this wedding," Knox said. "You okay with us going together?"

"I think we'd better. Now that Chloe's put us at the same table for the reception. You don't want to mess with a bride's seating arrangements on the day of the wedding."

"Good point." He walked the few steps off the porch. "I'm gonna run home and feed my animals and do a few chores at the ranch, then I'll be back to pick you up in a few hours. Will that work for you?"

"Sure. Sounds good to me." She watched him head toward his truck, the pensive expression he wore telling her he still had something heavy on his mind. And the fact that he hadn't tried to "practice" their new goodbye kissing only confirmed that it wasn't her.

———————

Two hours later, Knox pulled back up to the bunkhouse. Zane's truck was gone so he figured he and Bryn had probably already left for the wedding. Fine by him. He didn't need an audience for what he was about to do.

The gate of Tiny's enclosure was open, and the pig lumbered over to greet him. He patted her snout, thinking he could handle an audience if it was only the lone swine. Maybe the cheery pig could offer him some support. He pressed a hand to his pocket, feeling the weight of its contents and praying he was making the right decision as he headed toward the steps.

He'd been pondering the decision all afternoon, ever since he'd caught Paul in Carley's shop, and the more he thought on it, the more he felt like this was the right thing to do.

The screen door opened, and Carley walked out onto the porch, and then he couldn't think at all. She looked beyond gorgeous in a soft blue dress that was shorter in the front then lay in longer flowy layers in the back. Her shoulders were bare except for two tiny straps that didn't seem strong enough to hold up all that shimmery fabric. Her tan legs looked about a mile long, the cherry-pink color of her toe-nail polish just visible in the cutout toe-box of a pair of suede ankle boots. Her long hair was loose and lay in soft curls, and dangly silver earrings sparkled from somewhere within the shiny blond locks. The early evening light caught tiny sparkles on her skin, and she seemed almost to glow.

He'd stopped in front of the porch and couldn't seem to move. He could only stare up at the vision she was. "You look stunning," he finally managed to say, his voice hoarser than he'd intended.

She offered him a smile. It was the kind of smile that took all his willpower to hold back from charging up the steps, taking her into his arms, and kissing all that glistening pink lip gloss from her mouth. "Thank you," she said. "You clean up pretty well yourself."

He'd debated wearing a suit. It was a wedding, but since it was being held in a barn instead of a church, he'd settled on jeans, his good boots, and a dress shirt and coat. Granted, the barn did belong to the wealthiest family in Creedence, and knowing Vivi, the matriarch of the three James brothers, she'd probably had the floorboards scrubbed so shiny they could eat off them, but he still couldn't bring himself to don a tie.

"Shall we go?" she asked. "Or are you planning to just stand there and stare at me all night?"

"Oh sorry," he said, busting out of his beautiful-woman-induced stupor. "Yeah, we should go, but I was hoping to talk to you about something first."

"Uh-oh. Are you breaking our engagement? Because I

spent a lot of time getting ready and I'm planning on still going to this wedding, with or without you. Table arrangements be damned."

He laughed and climbed the steps to stand next to her. "No, it's nothing like that. In fact, it's kind of the opposite of that."

She gave him a quizzical look. "What could be the opposite of breaking up? We're already fake-engaged." Her eyes went wide, and she took a step back. "You're not going to suggest we actually get married, are you? Like having a double wedding tonight?"

He laughed again. "No. It's nothing like that." Although it was a little something like that. He gestured toward the glider. "You want to sit down a sec?"

"Okay, sure." She shooed the yellow and white cat off the seat and sat down on the edge. "But you're making me nervous, so just spit it out. Whatever it is, I can take it."

"You think you're nervous?" he said, wiping his palm on his thigh before reaching into his pocket and pulling out the small box.

Her eyes got even wider, and she pulled further away. "Um, Knox, is that what I think it is?"

"Yes. No. I mean, probably. But not exactly," he stammered. "Aw, hell, I knew I'd screw this up." He felt as nervous as if this were the real thing, as if he were really asking the woman he was falling in love with to marry him.

But this wasn't an authentic moment. His feelings were real enough, but he wasn't planning on popping the question.

"Listen." He swallowed and started again, feeling the

sweat on his forehead. "Something happened this afternoon. I had a bit of a run-in with Paul."

Her expression went from wary to concerned. "What kind of a run-in?"

"I'll tell you all about it, but it made me feel like this guy is planning on really coming after you. But he's going to have to get through me first and that's not about to happen. Regardless of all this fake engagement business, I care about you, and I'm not gonna let him hurt you or ever make you feel 'less than' again."

"Oh," was all she said, all traces of teasing aside.

"I also got to thinking about what Paul said, how you didn't even have a ring. And sometimes the strongest defense depends on having a strong offense, so I brought you this." He held out the box.

She held her hands up as if the box were on fire. "I'm not sure what all those sports metaphors meant, but if there's a ring in that box, I'm not taking it."

"It's not a *real* ring. Well, it is a real ring, it was my grandmother's, but what I mean is, it's just on loan. I don't have the time or the cash to go out and get you the kind of ring you deserve, so I thought this one could work in a pinch." He opened the box to reveal a diamond solitaire set in white gold with a circle of smaller diamonds surrounding it. The band was worn thin with wear, but the diamonds still sparkled.

Carley pressed her hand to her chest. "Oh, Knox. I couldn't."

"Sure you can." He pulled the ring from the box and held out his hand for hers.

She kept her hand pressed against her, squeezing her fingers into a fist. "I don't know what kind of ring you think I deserve, but I've never worn anything so beautiful."

He furrowed his brow. "Didn't numb-nuts buy you a ring?"

She huffed out a laugh, but it was hard and brittle. "He did, but it was nothing like this. He bought me the cheapest ring he could find at a thrift shop, promising to buy me something better when we could afford it. Which he never did. That ring didn't even have a stone in it, and if the green stain around my finger were any indication, it wasn't even gold. Although now that I think about it, that cheap-ass ring lasted longer than our marriage." She leaned forward to sneak another glance at the box in his hand. "It's a gorgeous ring, but I just can't, Knox."

"Let's just see if it fits, then we can decide." He took her left hand and eased it toward him. Slipping the ring from the box, he slid it onto her finger. It fit perfectly. "How about that? It fits like it were made for you." He looked up to see tears glistening in her eyes, and his heart felt like it was being squeezed in a vice. "Oh, hey now, darlin'. I didn't mean to make you cry. You don't have to wear it."

She closed her fingers around his hand. "You're a good man, Knox Garrison. Better than I deserve."

"You deserve everything," he whispered, the emotion stealing his voice.

She brushed away the lone tear that had slipped down her cheek and forced a shaky laugh. "I'm okay. Really. It just got me for a minute. This is how I'd always dreamed it would be. A handsome guy with a heart as big as Montana putting a gorgeous ring on my finger. But that's all this is. Just a fantasy."

CHAPTER 12

CARLEY'S WORDS, AND THE ANGUISH THEY WERE SPOKEN with, made Knox's heart ache even harder. How he wished this *were* the real thing. He couldn't say he'd dreamed of a proposal, but lately every time he imagined his future, Carley was in it. And he was starting to think that he couldn't see a future *without* her in it.

Maybe he should just tell her that he was having real feelings for her. Surely, she could tell that this wasn't all pretend for him. Not with the way he looked at her, or the way he was constantly finding ways to touch her.

She held the ring up in front of her. "I do see the logic of wearing it. Having this on will have to convince Paul, and anyone else who sees it, that we're really engaged. I just had to get through the step of putting it on. Are you sure your grandmother would be okay with me borrowing it?"

He grinned. "She'd love it. My Gram was always coming up with harebrained schemes to get us to do stuff with her, and I know she would have gotten a kick out of being part of this one. Plus, she would have fallen in love with you."

Just like I'm starting to.

The words were on the tip of his tongue, but she stood up before he had a chance to say them, and the moment was lost.

She held out her hand, the diamond sparkling as it caught a glint from the porch light. "Come on, handsome. Take me to this wedding. I've got a beautiful ring and a gorgeous fiancé to show off."

———————

She probably shouldn't have had that last glass of prosecco, but Carley was having such a fun night, she didn't want the celebration to end. Everything about the evening had been magical—from the moment Knox had slipped that ring on her finger, she'd felt like her night had been a dream.

Chloe was a beautiful bride, and there wasn't a dry eye in the barn when she and Colt had exchanged their handwritten vows. Knox had held Carley's hand through the entire cere- mony, and she'd never once felt the urge to pull it away. For such a big muscular guy, his touch was often tender and even though she'd seen his hard-as-steel side in his role as deputy, the tears she saw glistening in his eyes when Colt choked on his vows told her his heart was just as broad as his shoulders.

Word had definitely gotten around about them, and sev- eral people had noticed and commented about the gorgeous ring that sparkled on her finger. It was easier to accept the congratulations of people she didn't know as well, but harder to meet the eyes of the women she called friends. She could always explain later, but she didn't like the feeling of having to lie to them. Although she imagined her closest friends would know something was up and assume she'd explain later, just like Aunt Sassy had.

The one person she'd really wanted to talk to was Evelyn, but she'd arrived with Paul, and he hadn't left her side for most of the night. He'd tried to catch her eye a few times and had even dared to ask her to dance once, but Knox had stepped in and told him to back off.

Thankfully, the reception was attended by hundreds of people, which made it easier for her and Knox to say hello and be seen without having to hold any deep conversations. And the strangest thing was that every time someone congratulated them or flicked a glance at her left hand, she felt an odd prickle of joy, like a sense of pride at being chosen as Knox's fiancée.

Being with him was starting to feel so natural, and the knowing looks and quick smiles they shared when she knew they were thinking the same thing had started happening so often, it was easy to forget they weren't a real couple.

Or maybe it was the silvery strands of the moonlight, or the warm summer air, or the twinkling fairy lights strung through the trees and around the barn, or the soft strains of the band playing one love song after another as Knox glided her around the dance floor. Or maybe it was just the prosecco.

But all of it combined made her feel like happiness was possible and maybe she just might deserve a good guy like Knox. At least for tonight, she could fool herself into believing that were true.

"You up for one last dance?" Knox said, coming up behind her and sliding his arms around her waist. His breath tickled her ear as he asked, "Or are you ready to get out of here?"

She let herself lean back against him, relishing the feeling of being folded in his embrace, her back against his chest, his strong arms wrapped around her. Even if this was all for show, and their fake relationship stopped tomorrow, she felt like she was his for tonight. And she wasn't ready for that feeling, or this night, to end.

"One more dance," she told him, setting her glass on the table. She followed him out onto the dance floor and slipped easily into his arms. Her body fit perfectly against his and instinctively knew to follow his lead as he all but floated her around the dance floor.

"I can't believe I get to dance with the most beautiful woman at this wedding," Knox said, his voice deep and low, as it caressed her ear.

She pulled back and offered him a teasing smile. "I didn't see you dance with Chloe."

"Good try," he said with a laugh that hummed through her chest. He bent his head as he swirled her around, his hand riding low on her waist and his lips brushing her neck, both sensations sending delicious shivers of heat down her spine. "The bride looked gorgeous, but she doesn't hold a candle to the way you shine tonight."

His words filled her with happiness, a giddy feeling that bubbled inside her as dizzying as the wine. She wanted that feeling to last. And she really wanted to feel his lips on other parts of her than just her neck.

Her skin heated just thinking about it. What if she gave in to him? Just this once?

"This night feels like a dream," she whispered against his

neck. She wasn't sure if it was her or the wine talking as she dropped her voice even lower, speaking so quietly, she was sure he couldn't hear. "What if I don't want to wake up until after you've taken me to bed?"

His hand stilled on her back, and his feet faltered for the first time. Then he pulled her closer and spoke against her ear, the hunger and need evident in his voice. "Say that again."

Their cheeks were pressed together so she didn't have to look at him, and that somehow made it easier to speak the words a second time. The rest of the room fell away. "I know this is all supposed to be pretend, but what if just this once, just for tonight, it was real. This feels real to me. And I don't want this feeling to end."

He pulled back, searching her eyes, then his gaze dropped to her lips. "It doesn't have to end." He took her hand and led her off the dance floor. "As far as I'm concerned, it never has to end," she thought she heard him say, but his words were swallowed up in the sound of the music.

It took them less than five minutes to say their goodbyes to the bride and groom and head out. Carley heard her name being called as they ducked out the barn door and turned to see Chloe running toward her, waving the bridal bouquet over her head. "We took a vote and decided we wanted you to have this. Catch," Chloe called, pitching the bouquet directly at her.

Without thinking, Carley caught the flowers against her chest. She let out a groan as it dawned on her what catching the bouquet meant.

She was next.

Then she stopped thinking as Knox leaned down and brushed his lips against her neck. She held her breath, waiting to hear one of the sweet nothings he'd been teasing her with all night. "I'm dying to take you home, darlin', but is there any chance you remember where we parked the truck?"

She busted out laughing as he grabbed her hand like it was the most natural thing in the world, and then they were running through the field where all the cars had parked, cracking each other up as they searched for Knox's truck.

"I know I parked it here somewhere," he said, craning his neck to see over the sea of cars. "Damn, how many people did they invite to this wedding?"

"It had to be half the town." And they had all seen her dancing with Knox. Holding his hand, sneaking a kiss, all the motions of a real couple.

"There it is," she said, pointing to the pickup in the next lane over. She stumbled over a clump of dirt, but his steady arm caught her, holding her up. "You okay to drive?" She hadn't seen him drinking anything all night, but she still felt compelled to ask.

"Yes, for sure. All I've had tonight was a few swallows of champagne with the toast," he told her. "But something about being with you tonight is still making me feel a little drunk. Or maybe just stupid-happy. Like I want to howl at the moon or something."

"You're crazy," she said.

"Crazy about you." He followed her to the passenger side of his pickup, but instead of opening the door, he circled his arm around her waist and pressed her back against it, his mouth crushing hers in a hungry kiss of desire. He laid a warm trail of kisses along her jaw and down her neck. A surge of heat shot through her as he dragged his teeth over her earlobe at the same time his hand cupped the rounded circle of her butt.

"I've been wanting to do that all night," he told her, his voice husky against her ear.

"Do what?" she teased. "Kiss me or grab my ass?"

"Yes," he said, pressing another kiss to her neck. "And sooo much more." He pulled her to him, then reached for the truck handle behind her and yanked the door open. "Get in. If we don't get out of here, I'm gonna take you against the side of my truck. And as much as I'd enjoy that, I've got so much more in mind."

"Promises, promises." She climbed in, letting him slam the door behind her and laughing as he ran around the front of the truck and almost dropped his keys in his haste to get the engine started. He wrapped an arm around her, pulling her across the bench seat to kiss her once more. Then he tucked her against his side, dropped the truck in gear, and drove out of the field.

Thank goodness the horse rescue ranch was practically across the road. The drive took less than three minutes, and she kept her hand on his thigh the whole way there. Except for the porch lights, the farmhouse was dark, but Zane's truck was parked next to the house, so Carley assumed they'd already come home and gone to bed.

Knox parked in front of the bunkhouse, and still holding

the bouquet, she slid out his side of the truck and into his waiting arms. He lifted her up, cradling her against him, as he carried her inside.

"I can walk," she said. "I'm not that drunk." Although she loved the feeling of him carrying her.

"I know you can, but this way I can get you into bed faster."

"That's what I like about you, handsome *and* smart," she muttered.

He laughed as he stopped inside the door to toe off his cowboy boots. "It would take too long for me to tell you all the things I like about you."

He didn't turn on any lights, didn't need to. The brightness of the full moon shined a silvery glow into the bunkhouse and through her window as he carried her into the bedroom and set her gently on the bed.

The folds of her shimmery dress cascaded around her thighs as she raised her leg and pressed her foot into his chest. "Help me with my boots?"

"When it comes to undressing you, I'm always willing to help." Setting his hand on her thigh, he drew it slowly down her leg until he reached her boot and then pulled it off. He repeated the process on the other leg, teasing his fingers over her skin as he made his way down again. His lips curved into a roguish grin as his gaze raked over her body. "What else can I help you take off?"

She offered him what she hoped was a seductive grin. It had been a long time since she'd played this particular game, but Knox made it easy...and fun...and she was enjoying the hell out of it. She pushed to her feet and reached for the lapels of his shirt. "My turn."

Releasing the top button of his dress shirt, her fingertips brushed his skin as she slid her hands down to the next one, and she loved hearing the soft catch of his breath. Another button free, and this time she leaned in and pressed a kiss to the spot on his chest she'd just exposed. Another button, another kiss. Then the anticipation was too much for her, and she pulled the tucked part of his shirt from his pants and fumbled the last few buttons free.

As she slid her hands inside his open shirt, he leaned down, cupping her cheeks between his palms and took her mouth in a tender kiss, a soft touch of his lips to hers followed by another, this one more insistent. Then another.

They stood like that, just kissing for several minutes, but it was more than *just* kissing. It was testing and teasing and learning each other. It was offering promises of what was to come and whispered soft assurances of trust and possibilities.

He finally pulled back, his breath ragged as he peered into her eyes. He didn't say anything, didn't offer a funny quip, but instead, he took her shoulders and turned her away from him.

Confused for a moment, a frisson of fear raced through her that he was changing his mind, then her pulse quickened as his fingers found the zipper of her dress and slowly pulled it down. She shivered as he ran his knuckles up her back to slide under the thin spaghetti strap and ease it off her shoulder. In the same way she'd done to him, he pressed a kiss to the spot where her strap had been, then another at the base of her neck, then one more in the hollow spot under her ear.

The only sound in the room was the soft murmur of silk as her dress slid from her body and landed in a shimmery pool at her ankles on the floor. With her back still to him, another delicious shiver ran through her as his palms skimmed over the bare skin of her shoulders and down to her waist. Then his fingers hooked the delicate lacy band of her thong panties, and he eased to his knees behind her, pressing another light kiss to the small of her back as he drew the fabric down.

His movements were slow, measured, designed to draw out the anticipation. He made her feel like a gift he was unwrapping, a treasure to be cherished. His palms skimmed back up her legs, teasing along her skin and drawing out another shiver as he stood and pressed his chest to her back.

His breath was warm as his lips swept over her shoulder, then leaned closer to her ear. "You are perfect."

"No, I'm n—" she started to say but he cut her off as he turned her to him.

"Yes," he said, looking into her eyes and making her feel seen in a way that no one else ever had. "You are. In every way."

She pushed onto her toes and crushed her mouth to his, kissing him fiercely, trying to convey the depth of her feelings without having to say the words. Or maybe even acknowledge them to herself. Still kissing him, she pulled him back onto the bed with her, desperate to feel his skin against hers, his weight on top of her.

His hands, which had been gripping her arms, released her and she heard the jangle of metal as he undid his belt. He pulled away to yank off his shirt and shimmy out of his jeans then he was back, kneeling over her, his gaze raking over her body.

His eyes paused at her chest, squinting in the dim light as he did a slight tilt of his head. "What the hell are those?"

Hmm. Not exactly the reaction she was hoping for as he peered down at her girls. "Boobs," she said. "I thought you'd be familiar with them."

"I am familiar with them. And I was looking to get to know yours much better. But I wasn't prepared for them to be wearing flower stickers."

She looked down at her chest then laughed at his description of the petal-shaped silicone nipple covers she'd stuck on earlier. "They're my petal pasties."

"Pasties?"

"Yes. I couldn't wear a regular bra with that dress, and strapless bras are torture devices that are either too tight or not tight enough to stay up, so these are like silicone stickers that keep my headlights from shining through my dress if I get cold." She offered him a flirty smile. "Or if a hot cowboy turns me on."

His lips tugged up in a grin. "I'm turned on just thinking about your headlights, even if they do have flower stickers on them." His grin turned wicked. "Are they shining right now?"

She pushed up on her elbows, giving him an even better view. "Peel off the petals and find out."

He slid his fingers around the edge of one, lifting it carefully to break the seal to her skin. "Will it hurt?"

She shook her head, her nipples already tightening with need. A soft cry escaped her lips as he peeled it off then bent his head to circle her pebbled tip with his tongue before drawing it into his mouth. The scrape of his teeth combined with the soft tug of his lips sent darts of heat and desire straight to her core, and she squirmed her hips beneath him.

He deftly peeled the other pasty away and kneaded her breast as he continued to tantalize and tease her nipple. Every lick, every caress sent pleasure coursing through her, and she arched her back, willing him to take more.

Biding his time, he tasted and sampled, kissed and nipped, caressed and teased, as he savored the contours of her body, learning what she liked, what made her squirm, and what made her hands grip his shoulders as her body arched into him for more.

The pleasure he brought her seemed to amplify his own enjoyment, and she loved the way his smoldering gaze raked over her when he touched her, encouraging her responses. She thought she would die from his touch, and relief swept through her as he leaned off the edge of the bed and fumbled for his wallet in his jeans. Pulling out a foil packet, he ripped it open, lost his boxer briefs and then covered himself before settling back into the spot between her legs.

Leaning down, he kissed her again and she moaned into his mouth, drawing him closer and inviting him in, relishing the weight of his body on top of her. His hips ground against hers, and she tightened her legs around him, the sensations of the friction between her legs making her light-headed and breathless.

He pulled back, just enough to brush her hair from her face and peer into her eyes. "Are you sure this is what you want?" he whispered.

The quiet question, tinged with concern for her, brought the sting of tears to her eyes. "Yes. I want you," she whispered back, holding his gaze as he moved with her, setting the pace, starting slow then increasing the tempo with desire and demand.

Her body was all nerve endings, all sensation as desire sparked through her. She clutched his back, matching his rhythm, taking everything, then giving it back, holding on, savoring the sweet torment as he drove her higher and higher.

It was delicious torment, but it was more than just heat and sensation. Somewhere along the way, in the glow of the moonlight and clutched between the hard muscles of his body and the soft flannel of the sheets, she let herself go. For just that moment in time, she let herself trust Knox, with her body and her heart, and surrendered herself to him.

Pleasure ricocheted through her, heightened with every caress, every sweet nothing he spoke against her hair. She hung onto him as he took her to the very edge of control. Then with the whispered sigh of her name on his lips, she let go.

Throwing her head back, she clung to him, crying out and giving herself to the exquisite sensations as the waves of pleasure erupted through her. His grip on her tightened, pulling her closer, as his muscles constricted. His teeth grazed her shoulder, and a low growl hummed against her skin as he tensed and shuddered, moving with her as he matched her release.

Letting out a shaky breath, he collapsed next to her and

dragged her to him, wrapping her in his arms and nuzzling his chin into her hair. She pressed a kiss to his chest, right above his heart, then let out a sigh as she laid her cheek against the spot.

For two people claiming to be faking a relationship, everything about tonight had felt all too real.

CHAPTER 13

THE SPARKLY GLINT OF THE DIAMOND ON HER FINGER WAS the first thing Carley saw when she woke up the next morning. But it wasn't the first thing she *felt*.

There were too many sensations at once, she thought as she catalogued each feeling. She was spooned against a broad, muscled chest, a heavy arm was wrapped securely around her waist, and a large hand palmed her left boob. The sight of Knox's long fingers stretched over her bare breast made her nipples tingle, another sensation to add to the list.

All her good ideas from the night before came rushing back to her, and most of them didn't seem so great in the light of day. What the hell had she been thinking?

She held back a groan as she spotted the bridal bouquet propped up on her nightstand. Last night had been amazing, like everything she'd been dreaming of, but that's all it had been—a dream.

She realized the gravity of what they'd done. And now half the town was involved in their lie. She needed to slow this engagement train down before someone got hurt. Especially since she already knew it was going to be her.

"Good morning, beautiful," Knox said, nuzzling her neck.

"Morning." She breathed out the word, all thoughts about the town and their engagement train forgotten as his thumb grazed back and forth over her nipple, tightening the tender bud with an achy need that surged straight through to her core. As if they had a mind of their own, her hips ground back against him, and what she felt there removed any doubt that his thoughts were in the same place as hers.

A slow smile curved her lips. "Did you bring your gun to bed, Deputy? Or are you just happy to see me?"

"Oh darlin'," he said in that low sexy drawl of his. "I'm beyond happy to see you, but make no mistake, my gun is definitely in the bed with us."

She laughed as she turned in his arms and reached her hand down between them. "I seem to recall you saying something yesterday about me being the only one who gets to touch your gun."

"I do recall saying that," he said with a roguish grin. "But I have to warn you, a gun can be dangerous if you don't know how to handle it."

"Oh, I'm pretty sure I know how to handle it."

"Yes, ma'am," he said, with a quick catch of his breath. "I believe you do."

Last night had been like a dream, but it was one she wasn't ready to wake up from. Not just yet. Not when she had Knox in her bed, and in her hand, and the nerves in her body were zinging with arousal and hunger. They'd already pulled the trigger, so to speak, the night before.

It couldn't hurt to be together just one more time, she thought, right before Knox slipped his hand between her legs. Then logic and reason escaped her, and she couldn't think anymore.

═══════════

Two hours, and two more times—once in bed and once in the shower—later, they finally made it into the kitchen where Knox drew her to him and kissed her neck while the coffeepot brewed. Which could have ended in a third time if they hadn't already emptied his wallet of protection.

"Do you want me to make you some breakfast?" she asked when they'd finally pulled away from each other and she'd poured them both a cup of coffee.

"Thanks, but no," he said, opening the refrigerator and passing her the creamer she loved. "I've got to get to work. Although how I'm ever going to concentrate today is beyond me."

"I know the feeling," she said, pouring the creamer into her cup and stirring it into the dark liquid.

"I've got a ten-hour shift today and a ton of things to catch up on tonight at the ranch. But I get off early tomorrow afternoon, and I'd like to come back over. If you're up for it, I've got something I'd like to show you."

"Really? I feel like I've already seen your best stuff."

His eyes widened at her dirty reference, then his lips curved into that sexy grin. "That was just the opening act. I've got way more than that up my sleeve."

The night before, and this morning, had been amazing. Some of the best sex of her life. Her toes curled at the thought that that was only the beginning of his skills.

"I can see you're thinking about it."

She nudged his arm. "Get out of my head."

"Seriously, can I take you back to my place when I get off work tomorrow? Just for a little bit? I want you to meet Sadie."

"And don't forget Rodney. I'm dying to meet your *sort of a* dog."

"Believe me, I could never forget Rodney. But I should warn you to keep your expectations low." He leaned down and brushed a kiss against her lips. "I think we're getting better at this."

She tilted her head. "I don't know. Maybe you'd better try again, just to be sure."

A low chuckle sounded in his throat as he swept his arm around her waist and pulled her to him. "I told you, I'm nothin' if not thorough." Leaning her back, he slanted his lips over hers, *thoroughly* kissing her with an intensity that had her forgetting everything else except considering dragging him back into bed again.

She blinked as he pulled away and set her back on her feet. A little unsteady, she kept hold of his arms, understanding for the first time the meaning of being kissed senseless. It seemed like hers had completely flown the coop. "Wow," she said, as she breathed out.

"Yeah, I think we may be gettin' the hang of it." He grinned again. "But let's work on it some more tomorrow, just so we don't fall out of practice."

Knox had been gone less than hour, and Carley had just finished cleaning up her breakfast dishes when she heard a light knock on her front door. Her pulse quickened at the hope that he was back.

Gah. Where did that come from? It was more likely Otis butting his horns against the door, stopping by to see what she'd made for breakfast and if there were any leftovers.

"Hello? Anyone home?" a female voice called.

So *not* Knox.

"Oh, hey, Bryn," she called back, ignoring the small flicker of disappointment in her stomach as she recognized the voice of her friend and new landlord. "Come on in. I'm in the kitchen."

Bryn came through the door, holding a foil-wrapped plate aloft. "I made some cookies this morning. Thought you might want some."

"Oh, wow. You didn't have to do that."

"I could take them back," she said, pretending to head for the door. "But they're still warm."

"Okay—you twisted my arm," she said, already grabbing the milk out of the fridge. She held up the carton. "Join me for one?"

Bryn smiled. "All right. If you twist *my* arm."

Carley poured them each a glass of milk while Bryn peeled back the foil on the plate. The scent of vanilla, chocolate, and butterscotch rose in the air, and Carley inhaled a deep breath. "Oh, gosh, they smell heavenly." She took a bite of one and groaned as the warm, gooey cookie melted in her mouth. "Mmm. They taste heavenly too."

"Thank you. They're my grandmother's recipe. She used a chocolate chip cookie dough, but at the end, she always mixed in an extra cup of butterscotch chips. They're my favorite and always make me think of her."

"They're amazing. And it's totally the butterscotch that makes the whole cookie," she said, already reaching for another one. "And now these will always make me think of you and what a sweet gesture this was for you to bring these over to welcome me to my new place."

Bryn raised her shoulder in an offhand shrug. "This is nothing. I still feel bad that I didn't bring a meal over for your first night here."

Carley waved away her concerns. "Don't even worry about it. Besides, Evelyn brought over a lasagna, so we definitely didn't go hungry."

Bryn tilted her head. "*We?*"

"Yeah," she said, cursing her cheeks for getting warm again. "Knox Garrison helped me move my stuff out." She tried to keep her tone light, despite the evidence of the blush she was sure was on her face. And she knew Bryn would notice.

"Knox has been out here quite a bit helping us take care of the brown mare he and Cade and Nora rescued last month. In fact, he must have come over pretty early this morning to check on her," Bryn said, an impish grin on her face. "I noticed his truck was outside already when I got up."

Carley avoided her gaze as she wiped at a cookie crumb on the counter. "Oh?"

Bryn let out a soft laugh, and she knew her innocent act

wasn't fooling her friend. "I've always thought that you can tell a lot about a person by the way they treat animals and horses, and I like Knox. He's a great guy. And cute as all get out." She leaned a hip against the counter. "I know you've been flirting with each other, and you two looked pretty cozy at the wedding last night, but I was a little surprised to hear that you're already engaged."

"Yeah, I was gonna tell you." Carley shook her head, hating that she couldn't just confess to Bryn that it was all an act. "It's complicated."

"I can imagine. Want to talk about it?"

"Not yet."

"Well, I'm here if you need me. If you want to talk or if you just need more chocolate."

"Thanks. I appreciate it. And I'll tell you all about it soon. I promise."

"I can wait." She pushed off from the counter. "I'd better go, but I also wanted to tell you that Zane and I are going to have to take off again for a few days."

"You just got back."

"I know. But we've got someone down in Durango who wants to adopt that little pony we rescued last month for their ten-year-old daughter, and we said we'd bring him down there. And my cousin, Holt—Cade's brother—lives down there so we said we'd drop in to visit for a few days afterwards. We may be gone as long as a week, but don't worry, we'll get someone to take care of the chores around here. We won't leave you without knowing you're in good hands."

"That's good, but what do I do if someone wants me to rescue a horse?"

"I can't imagine they will. It's not like rescues arrive on a daily basis. But if one does, just find a place in the barn for them and we'll deal with them when we get home. I haven't turned away an animal in need yet."

―――――――

For a temporary setup, Carley still stayed busy with clients that day and the next. And it seemed like everyone in town suddenly had a reason for stopping out at the ranch and popping their head into the makeshift salon. Whether it was to purchase hair products or under the guise of dropping off a housewarming gift, they all wanted to sit and visit a while and they all seemed to find a way to bring Knox or their engagement into the conversation. A few of her customers didn't even try to be sly about it.

"We heard there was a ring, and we had to see it," Nancy told her when she and Barb dropped in the following afternoon.

"It's gorgeous," Lyda Hightower said. She'd dropped in for a blowout, and Carley was halfway through styling her hair and couldn't help noticing the gleam of the diamond on her finger every time she twisted the flat iron around a lock of Lyda's hair. "It belonged to Knox's grandmother. Isn't that so sweet?"

She wasn't a fan of being the center of everyone's attention, but she liked having the shop full and the sale of the extra product was nice too.

One person Carley hadn't expected to see was Paul. A hush fell over the customers seated around her living room when he pushed through the door, a cheap grocery store bouquet of flowers in his hands.

"Hey, sweetie pie," he said, holding up the flowers. "I just wanted to drop in and tell you how sorry I was to hear about the flood and give you these to brighten up your day."

The wilted carnations and dried out daisies weren't going to do much in the way of brightening up anything. She could see the yellow clearance sticker on the plastic from there.

"Oh, how thoughtful," one of her customers said. She had only moved to town in the last year and probably hadn't had the grand opportunity to get to know Paul's charms yet.

Thoughtful was not the word Carley would have used. More like *calculating*. She just couldn't figure out what he was up to.

"That's me. Always thinking about others," he said, smiling at Carley as he set the flowers in the kitchen. She noted the way his eyes scanned over the counter and his head tipped slightly toward the screen of her open laptop, silently snooping into her business. "Speaking of which, did Deputy Dog tell you I stopped by the shop the other day? Just wanted to see how bad the damage was to our investment property. Didn't look so great in there. You should maybe consider selling."

Selling? Was that his game? Although she wasn't sure how he would stand to benefit from a sale since the shop belonged to her and his grandmother. "First of all, it's *my* shop and that building is not *our* investment property. Evelyn and I are the ones who own it. And we have no interest in selling it."

He shrugged. "I'm just looking out for you both. Somebody's got to. My grandmother is too generous. She's always doling out cash to stupid charities and squandering all her money on donations."

You mean squandering your inheritance.

"And you're practically giving away your services here," he continued. "I've checked out some of your prices, and they don't compare to half of what some of the high-end places are charging for the same stuff down in Denver."

What the fridge? Why was he checking into her prices?

"We aren't *in* Denver," she told him, angry at herself for even rising to the bait, but unable to hold herself back from explaining. "And my shop is about more than making money, it's about building confidence and creating community."

His lip curled up in an obvious sneer. "Confidence doesn't pay the mortgage."

"You do realize the women who are paying for those services are sitting right here, don't you, Paul?" Barb asked, saying his name like it was another word for *dumb-ass*.

He offered her one of his most charming smiles. "Nothing personal, Barb. You know I'm just offering my wife a little advice. She might be a wiz with those little curling iron things, but she's never really had a head for numbers."

How dare he?

Fury and embarrassment burned Carley's throat. She had a successful business that may not make a ton of money, but it made enough to support her. And he was making her sound like an imbecile *in front* of her customers.

She searched her brain for a witty comeback that would really put him in his place, but she was coming up with nothing. How could he still have this hold over her where he could destroy her confidence with a few sentences?

Her phone dinged with a notification of a text, saving her from having to say anything. It was sitting on the island between her and Paul, and he leaned his head to the side to read the message along with her.

A smile tugged at her lips as she read the words.

Hey gorgeous. Just checking in on my beautiful wife-to-be. Hope you're having a great day. See you tonight. He'd added four little emojis of a flame, a diamond ring, a heart, and a couple dancing, drawing out her smile even more.

Paul raised his head to glare at her, a scowl covering his face. "Guess that's my cue to go."

Your cue to go happened the second you walked in here, she thought. But all she said was, "Yep. See you later. I mean, hope *not* to see ya later."

It was pretty lame as far as witty comebacks went, but at least she'd said something instead of just sitting back and taking his jabs. And that felt like progress to her.

"*Dipshit*," murmured Barb as the door slammed shut behind him.

Carley laughed and went back to styling her customer's hair with one of those "little curling iron things." She couldn't have agreed more.

Knox picked her up a little after five. He was still in his uniform, and Carley had to admire how well he wore it. The crisply pressed shirt hugged his broad chest, and even though it was paired with jeans and cowboy boots and a hat, he still looked official and hot as heck.

She'd been finishing off an iced coffee and sitting in the glider on the porch, the yellow-and-white cat curled in her lap, when he'd arrived.

He'd leaned down to press a quick kiss to her lips, then pressed a second one, as if he couldn't help himself. "Hi, honey, how was your day?" he asked, teasing as he sat down next to her and put his arm around her shoulders.

She laughed. "Good. Busy. Funny how many people stopped in just to chat or to grab one thing or set an appointment then nonchalantly found a way to bring our engagement into the conversation." She decided not to mention Paul's visit just yet. Why ruin a nice moment by talking about the douche-canoe?

"Sounds like our fake engagement is good for business."

It seemed to be good for a lot of things. Like the serene feeling she was having sitting on the porch with him after a long day's work. "I got a ton of compliments on the ring. Everyone thought it was just gorgeous." She'd been petting the cat's back, but she paused to straighten her fingers and admire the ring. "It is very pretty. And I've been very careful with it."

"I'm glad you like it," he said, then nodded to the feline stretched across her lap. "You've been feeding that cat, haven't you?"

"Um, well, just sometimes. But just when she meows at the door to be let in."

"Which is how often?"

She shrugged innocently. "Not that often. Just at night. Anndd in the morning. But she's so sweet."

"So now you have a pet cat?"

She shook her head. Her nephew's goofy retriever mix puppy had lived in her apartment with them, but she'd never had a pet of her own before. "No, I think this cat probably likes the bunkhouse more than she likes me. She's not my pet."

"What's her name?"

"I've been calling her Nala, because her tawny color is like a lion, and because she kind of acts like she's the queen of the house."

"And where does she sleep?"

"Wherever she wants."

"What about at night?"

Carley averted her eyes. "Sometimes at the foot of my bed." Sometimes curled next to her.

Knox laughed. "You feed her, you named her, and she sleeps in your bed. Honey, you've got yourself a pet cat."

She scratched Nala's neck as a ghost of a smile tugged at her lips. "Maybe I do."

"Being a pet owner looks good on you." He nudged her leg. "You ready to go?"

"Yep. Just let me put my cup inside." She transferred the cat to her spot on the glider, ran her glass into the kitchen, then followed him to the truck.

They'd been on the highway for about ten minutes when Knox pulled up to a four-way stop. "I have kind of a surprise for you," he said, activating his blinker.

"Oh good. I love surprises. Does it have anything to do with what's under that tarp in the back of the pickup?"

"Sort of. I've been holding out—couldn't decide if I should bring you to my house or not, but now that we're 'engaged,' I figured you should probably know where I live."

"Hmm. Why are you making it sound so mysterious? Are you embarrassed or something? You've totally got my imagination running wild. I can't figure out if you're secretly rich and you live in a mansion. Or wait, now I'm picturing you living in a cave in the side of a mountain, or maybe you live in a camper behind the barn." She narrowed her eyes. "I don't get why seeing where you live is such a big deal."

"You will." He turned onto a smaller road and drove about a mile before slowing at a driveway lined on one side by tall evergreen trees. "This is it. This is where I live."

She gasped as he pulled into the driveway, and she caught her first glimpse of his house. "No. It can't be." She looked from the house to him, then back to the house again. "Did you know?"

He pulled to a stop, letting her take in the view of the blue two-story Victorian-looking log cabin farmhouse with dormer windows, a wide wraparound front porch *with* a swing, big pine trees next to it, and a bright red door.

The pine trees had grown taller and there were no rocking chairs on the front porch, but otherwise, it looked exactly the same as she'd pictured it in her mind. "I can't believe it.

This is the house I remember from when I was a kid." She choked a little on the emotion clogging her throat. "The one I imagine when I think of *home*." Her hand rested on the seat between them, and he put his on top on hers and squeezed. "Why didn't you tell me?"

He shrugged. "I don't know. I guess I wanted it to be a surprise." He jerked a thumb toward the bed of the pickup. "And I've got one more surprise for you under that tarp."

She'd noticed the tarp earlier but had forgotten to ask about it as they'd driven up to the house and shocked recognition had dawned. "What could be more of a surprise than this?" she asked, sliding out of the truck.

"When you were telling me your vision of home, you described the house to a tee. Except for one thing. There haven't been rocking chairs on the front porch since my grandparents passed away. So I thought I'd better remedy that today." He pulled back the edge of the tarp with a flourish, revealing two gleaming white rocking chairs.

"Oh, my gosh," she said, pressing a hand to her chest. "They're perfect."

"You're perfect." He leaned down to kiss her but laughed as she shifted from one foot to the other. "What's up with you? You got ants in your pants?"

"No, I just drank a whole iced coffee on the way over here, and I've got to go." She hopped back to the other foot. "I really want to help you unload these, but I need a quick pit stop first."

"I got this," he said, grinning as he handed her his keys. "The gold one gets you in. Bathroom is down the hall and to the right. I need to give the horses some oats, then I'll be right in."

"Thanks," she said, already hurrying up the porch steps to unlock the door. She caught just a glimpse of a farmhouse kitchen to her left and a large stone fireplace as she went running down the hall. When she came out a few minutes later, she took her time looking around the tidy living room. Neat stacks of firewood sat to the right of the hearth, and a large landscape of the mountains hung above the mantle. The tan overstuffed sofa and recliner sat at forty-five-degree angles from each other, both facing a large-screen television on the wall. A stack of books sat on the floor next to the recliner and she inched into the room, curious as to what he was reading.

A thud sounded from the kitchen followed by the sound of toenails against wood. Assuming it was Sadie, she hurried across the room, anxious to meet the golden retriever who Knox claimed was his best friend.

She pulled up short as she rounded the wall of the kitchen and let out a tiny yelp at the small creature perched on the counter, one small paw crammed inside a bag of corn chips. Its round eyes stared at her from behind a black furry mask as it pulled out a chip and nibbled the edge.

"You must be Rodney," she said, trying to get over her initial fright at finding a raccoon sitting on Knox's counter calmly eating a tortilla chip. She'd never seen one up close, and this one didn't seem frightened of her at all. In fact, it seemed a little miffed that she'd interrupted his afternoon snack. "I'm a friend," she told it, inching a little closer and reaching her hand out to pet it.

"Stop right there, Carley," Knox's stern voice commanded from behind her. "Lower your hand and step away from the raccoon."

She did as he said, responding to the cop-sounding directive of his voice. "What's wrong? I was just going to get better acquainted with Rodney. Doesn't he like to be petted?"

He let out a soft chuckle. "Darlin', that is *not* Rodney."

CHAPTER 14

"*What?*" Carley whipped around to see Knox standing in the doorway of the kitchen.

He pointed to the small black-and-white calf pressed against his leg. "*This* is Rodney."

"Then who is that?" she squeaked, pointing to the racoon as she took a cautious step backward.

"I have no idea."

"Then why is it in your kitchen, eating your chips?"

He seemed way too calm as he offered her a shrug. "My best guess is that he must have come in through the doggie door with Sadie."

Her eyes widened, and she skittered behind a kitchen chair. "You mean that's a *wild* raccoon? And I was about to try to pet it?" She jumped up on the chair. "Oh, my gosh, do something."

"What do you want me to do? Get him some salsa to go with those chips?"

"This isn't funny."

"It's a little bit funny." He slowly reached over to open the utility closet next to him and eased out a broom.

"What are you going to do with that?"

"Well, I thought I'd shoo him back outside, then sweep up any of the chips he missed."

The raccoon hadn't moved from his spot on the counter. He'd just been nonchalantly shoveling chips into his mouth as he casually watched them.

"You just stay put on that chair," Knox told her as he took a small step forward.

The real Rodney must have been worried Knox was leaving without him because he let out a mournful bawl. The raccoon's chin lifted, and his paw froze midway into the bag of chips at the sound.

"Easy," Knox instructed, his voice low as he took another step forward and slowly raised the broom. "Everybody stay calm." A soft whirring sound came from what appeared to be a mudroom off the back of the kitchen. Then "Oh, shit," was all he got out before all hell broke loose.

The whirring was followed by a whine, then an excited yip as toenails scrabbled across the hardwood and a tawny-colored golden retriever bounded into the room.

"Sadie, get back," Knox yelled. But he was too late.

The dog and the raccoon spied each other at the exact same time, and Sadie let out a sharp bark as she shot forward. The raccoon took off across the kitchen counter, his round butt waddling back and forth as he headed for the refrigerator. In an impressive feat, he jumped from the counter to the top of the fridge, knocking off a box of Cheerios but still holding tight to the tortilla chips.

Carley shrieked, Sadie barked up at the raccoon, Rodney scrambled behind the kitchen table, and Knox swore as he waved the broom toward the masked bandit.

The cereal box hit the floor and Cheerios exploded out,

rolling across the hardwood, and creating enough of a diversion as Sadie went into a frenzy trying to lap up all the tiny O's, that the raccoon saw its chance to escape and jumped from the top of the refrigerator straight toward Carley.

It landed on the table, then jumped to the floor and went racing toward the mudroom as Carley jerked away, her feet slipping on the slick wooden seat of the chair as she fell backward. Her arms pinwheeled as she cried out, but instead of hitting the floor, she landed in the strong arms of the deputy.

"I got ya," he said, setting her feet on the floor, then tearing after the raccoon. He must have hit a manual switch because she heard the whirring sound again followed by a whoop of victory.

He came back in, a big grin on his face. "Crisis averted. Just another day at the Garrison ranch. Casualties include one bag of corn chips and half a box of Cheerios."

"And possibly one baby cow," she said, pointing to where Rodney had gotten his gangly legs tangled up in the rungs of the kitchen chair as he leaned out his neck to try to reach some of the spilled Cheerios. He let out an annoyed moo as his long pink tongue stretched out of his mouth in an attempt to lap at a lone piece of cereal that had rolled under the table.

"You goofy cow," Knox said, cracking up as he crouched down to untangle the calf's legs. Then both the puppy and the cow took advantage of the fact that he was on the floor and tried to scramble into his lap, the dog frantically licking his ears and chin.

"I can't believe you have a pet cow," Carley said, laughing as Knox tried to push both animals out of his lap.

"It's a hell of a lot better than a pet raccoon." He finally managed to stand up and shoo both animals out the front door. The screen door slammed behind them, and he turned and leaned against it. "Whew. I worked up a thirst. You up for having a glass of iced tea and testing out those new rocking chairs with me?"

In all the excitement, she'd almost forgotten about the rocking chairs and the fact that Knox lived in her dream house. "Sure. Can I help?"

"Nah, I've got it." He pulled two glasses from the cupboard and filled them with ice and tea from a jug in the fridge. "Have you eaten? I was gonna make a turkey sandwich. You want one too?"

"Sure."

"I'd offer you some chips, but I seem to be out."

She laughed as she watched him put together a couple of sandwiches. His hands were big, his movements strong and sure, and she couldn't help but remember the way those hands had felt as they stroked down her skin. She swallowed and looked around the kitchen, trying to focus on anything other than his big hands and long fingers. "You sure I can't do something to help?"

He nodded to a set of cupboards behind her. "You can grab a couple of paper plates out of that cupboard."

She turned and pulled open the cupboard, then let out a shocked gasp just as he said, "Not that one, the other one."

"Too late," she said. "I've already seen your dirty little secret." She stared at the several shelves stacked full of white boxes of yellow snack cakes. "Holy cream filling—how many boxes of Twinkies can one man eat?"

"It's not what you think. I haven't bought a box for myself in months. But when it got around that I accepted Twinkies for helping someone out, suddenly I had more boxes than I could count. Most of those are from Lyda. I swear she gives me a new box every time I see her."

"It suddenly makes more sense why you brought over some Twinkies to share while I was doing Chloe's bridal party's hair."

He cringed. "Oh, geez. Don't remind me of that disaster. You're welcome to one if you want. Or heck, you can take a whole box."

"I'm good, thanks." She closed the cupboard, opened the one next to it, then grabbed out two paper plates and passed them to Knox. He put a sandwich on one and passed it and a glass of tea back to her.

She took them and followed him out to the porch, where he'd set up the two chairs so they were turned slightly toward each other but still faced out enough to the take in the view of the ranch. She settled into one of the rockers, giggling as Sadie and Rodney came racing back up the porch steps and tumbled over her feet. The calf wasn't much bigger than the dog. She reached out to scratch each of their heads, surprised at how soft the fur on the calf's forehead was. "I don't think I've ever petted a cow before."

"He's hardly a cow. He barely even registers as a calf."

Sadie scrambled over to Knox while the calf settled down by Carley's legs and rested his head on her foot. "Aww." She took a sip of her tea and leaned back against the slats. "Okay, I'm dying to hear the story. How did you end up with a pet calf?"

"He's not really a pet. At least he's not supposed to be. I told you it was complicated, and it's actually a pretty sad story."

"What happened?"

"I might seem tough on the outside, but I don't do very well when one of my animals is hurting, and I had this momma cow who was in a bad way. I didn't know it until it was too late, but she'd wandered off into a mess of trees and was stuck back there when she went into labor. I don't think she'd been eating, and her breathing was already labored by the time I got to her. The calf was already kind of sickly when I pulled him, but I just kept fightin' to save him. I tried everything I could to help them both, but unfortunately, his mom didn't make it."

Carley pressed a hand to her mouth. "Oh, no."

"I was on horseback when I'd found her, so I ended up wrappin' the calf in my shirt and cradling him to my chest to be able to get up on my horse and bring him back to the barn to try to bottle-feed him. But the silly thing had the hardest time takin' the bottle and kept bawlin' every time I tried to leave him, and you have to understand, at this point, I'd been up half the night with him, and I was exhausted and cold, and it just seemed easier to bring him into the kitchen to keep trying. And somewhere in all that mess, the dang thing must have imprinted on me."

"Aww. That's so sad. And so sweet."

"I agree with the sad part, but it wasn't so sweet when I tried to leave him in the barn, and he bawled so hard and scratched up his body trying to get out of the pen that it about broke my heart. Then the only time he would eat was when I brought him into the kitchen. He and Sadie bonded like they were siblings, and now I can't convince the darn fool that he's a cow instead of a dog. Sadie's even got him house-trained. The two of them curl up together to sleep, and half the time I come home from work and find them standing on the porch together, like they're just waiting to welcome me home."

"That's so cute."

Knox shook his head. "It may be cute now when he's a ninety-pound runt, but it's not gonna be so cute when he's nine *hundred* pounds and standing in my kitchen begging for a dog treat."

She let out a loud laugh. "Oh, my gosh, I can just picture that."

"So can I, and it's not the least bit funny," he said, but then ended up laughing with her.

"Thank you for bringing me here," Carley said when she finally stopped laughing. "I love it. It's so peaceful. And the view is gorgeous."

"It sure is," he said, but he was looking at her instead of out at the mountains.

And the look in his eyes had heat warming her cheeks, but she couldn't tear her gaze away. Something about this man was getting to her, and she was finding herself dreaming about a life that she had no business imagining. She'd learned her lesson about marriage and falling in love the hard way, and she wasn't about to let herself fall into that trap again. But sitting here on the porch of the house that had been in her dreams and staring into the eyes of this handsome cowboy who made her laugh and feel safe and protected was wearing down the thick wall of defense she'd built around herself. The past week of pretending to be a couple had her heart longing for that imaginary relationship to be real.

"Ma-a-a-a." The calf bawled as he butted his head into her leg, bringing her back to earth and away from the starry-eyed gaze she and Knox were sharing.

"Sorry about that," Knox told her. "It's dinnertime for these two, and neither one of them ever lets me forget." He ruffled the neck of the golden retriever, who had stood and was resting her head in his lap. "Have you ever bottle-fed a calf?"

She laughed as she shook her head. "No, I've barely ever bottle-fed a human."

"Do you want to help me feed this guy?"

"Sure." She followed him through the kitchen and into the utility room, the two animals scrambling around their ankles to get there first.

"I usually wait to put Sadie's food down until I've got Rodney's ready. Otherwise, they just try to eat each other's." He lifted a dog dish onto the counter and dumped a scoop of kibble into it, then took a container out of the drying rack on the sink. "The calf gets fed a couple of quarts of this milk replacer twice a day. I start with warm water and fill it to this line in the container, then dump in a level scoop of milk replacer, then whisk it all up so you don't have any lumps. Then we'll pour it into that two-quart bottle and screw on the nipple cap."

"Wouldn't it be easier to just dump it all in that bottle to begin with and shake it up?"

"You'd think so. But this stuff isn't like making gravy where you're just shaking up cornstarch and water. There's a lot of science involved. You have to get the water just the right temperature and you want to make sure you get exact measurements of milk replacer because screwing it up can affect the health of your calf." He stuck a thermometer on the side of the container he was filling with water. "I've been doing this long enough that I'm usually pretty close just by feel, but I always check it before adding the powder to make sure it's around a hundred and ten degrees, then by the time we mix it and fill the bottle, it should cool to about a hundred and two, which is just right for feeding." He dumped in the milk replacer, then handed her a whisk. "Here you go. And remember, it's not like pancake batter—you want to make sure you get all the lumps out."

"Who knew feeding a baby cow was this precise?" she said, alternately whisking the liquid and scraping the bowl for any excess powder. "I think I got it, but you'd better check," she said, passing him the whisk.

"You did great," he told her after a couple of whisks. He poured the mixture into the two-quart bottle, screwed on the lid with the nipple attached to it, and passed it to her. "Now you just tip it up by his head and try to hold on." He pointed to the bench seat under where his coats and cowboy hats hung. "It's probably easier if you sit."

"You're making me nervous," she said, taking the warm bottle and trying to sit on the bench as Rodney clambered around her legs, bawling and stretching out his neck toward the bottle. "Hold on, dude," she told the calf. "It's coming."

"Tip it up," Knox said. "He knows what to do."

She turned the bottle over and pointed the nipple toward the calf's mouth. He latched on and suckled with gusto, milk replacer foaming and dripping around his mouth, as he sucked then head-butted the bottle toward her hand. She grabbed it with both hands so he didn't knock it loose. "Gah. Why is he doing that? Am I holding it wrong?"

Knox chuckled. "No, you're doing it just right. When baby calves suckle from their mom, they butt their noses against her udder to get more milk to come out, so that's all he's doing."

"So he thinks I'm his mom?" She grinned as she wrinkled her nose. "I don't know how I feel about that."

"I know I'm smart enough to keep my mouth shut regarding any comment you make about comparing yourself to a momma cow."

"You *are* smart." She laughed with him, then nodded to the calf's rear end. "Look at his tail. The more he eats, the more it keeps going up, and it's wagging like crazy. This calf *does* think he's a dog."

"I told you. Except most calves actually do that. It's pretty cute though."

"You are cute, aren't you boy?" She scratched the calf's head and neck, then pulled her sneakered feet back against the bench to avoid getting dripped on by the excess milk. "He's quite the sloppy eater. Do you have like a burp rag or something?"

"Not hardly. And I'm not planning to lean him over my shoulder to burp him either. He does make a mess though. That's why I started feeding him in here. Or sometimes I can get him to eat in the back yard."

She smiled up at him as the calf greedily sucked at the bottle. "It is kind of fun though."

He gave her one of his teasing grins. "Bottle-feeding a calf is just one of the thrilling things you get to look forward to as a rancher's wife. After this we'll go out and give the horses some hay."

Even though he was playing with her, a little thrill still swirled through her stomach at his words, and at the thought she'd just had at the other thrilling things she'd get to do with the rancher if she really were his wife. And none of the things she was thinking about involved a baby calf. Although one of them had involved rolling around in some hay.

———

"That was all kinds of fun," Carley said, an hour later when they'd cleaned up the mess of Rodney's bottle and finished feeding the rest of the animals. Knox had introduced her to his two horses, and each had eaten a sugar cube off her hand. It had not escaped her notice that the one Knox rode the most was white. Of course he would ride a white horse. "But I should probably get back."

"Yeah, sure. Just give me a few minutes to grab my stuff. I've got it all packed." He left her on the porch while he disappeared inside.

She wasn't sure what kind of stuff he needed, and definitely wasn't prepared for him to come back out a few minutes later carrying a large duffle bag, his pillow, and a crate filled with dog food and all the equipment to feed Rodney. "Umm, did I miss something?" she asked, half-teasing as she gesturing to all the stuff he was holding. "Are you planning on moving in with me?"

"Yeah," he answered, with no humor in his voice. "Last night was so amazing, and since we're already engaged, I figured we might as well shack up. I already packed my toothbrush. And now you've met Sadie and Rodney, so we're good, right?"

CHAPTER 15

KNOX HELD HIS FACE STRAIGHT AS HE WATCHED CARLEY'S eyes go wide, then she blinked twice as she sputtered, "Um, gosh, I don't..."

He couldn't hold it any longer and busted out laughing. "I'm just teasing you," he said, nudging her in the side. "You should see your face though. You looked terrified. But you can relax. I'm not moving in with you. But I am moving in *next door* to you. At least for the next few days."

"You are? Why? Because of our engagement? Because I don't think we have to get that extreme."

"No, it has nothing to do with that." He pressed a hand to his heart. "Although that does hurt a little that you're so opposed to the idea. It has nothing to do with us. Bryn asked me to look after the horses and the animals at the rescue ranch while she and Zane are gone. She said I could stay in the other side of the bunkhouse," he told her, referring to the duplicate apartment on the other side of the bunkhouse from her. "And since I have a hired hand who can help out around here, I figured it would just be easier to be on site for the next few days."

And to be closer to you.

He didn't think he could say that now. Not with the look

of shock on her face she'd displayed after his joke. What was he expecting? For her to jump into his arms and cheer for the idea? That reaction probably would have terrified *him*.

"Sorry. I didn't mean to overreact. And I wasn't *that* freaked out. Terrified seems a little dramatic. I was just more shocked by the idea." She shook her head. "I'm not making this any better. Let's forget your stupid joke and load this stuff into the truck," she said, reaching to take the crate of animal gear.

"Good idea," he said, hauling his bag toward his pickup. "But just so you know, Sadie and Rodney both like to ride shotgun."

She laughed as they loaded his things and then all piled into the cab of the truck. Sadie took the center between them, and Rodney sat on the floor, his head on Carley's knee. "Just so *you* know," Carley told him, buckling in as he started the engine. "Just because I'm not ready for us to *shack up*, doesn't mean I don't think it will be fun having you next door for a few days."

He couldn't help his smile as he pulled out of the driveway and headed toward the rescue ranch.

———

It didn't take him long to unload his things into the bunkhouse, then he and Carley sat next to each other on the front porch steps to watch Sadie and Rodney, who were having a ball sniffing out the new area and racing around the barnyard. The calf was a little more timid, but the golden retriever zoomed from one side of the yard to the other, taking in every scent, then running to the next spot. Tiny came out of her pen to say hello, and she and Sadie sniffed at each other's noses. Otis stayed in the corral with the horses, but he and Shamus kept an eye on the newcomers and the mini-horse came to the fence to snuffle at Sadie's outstretched nose.

"They're having so much fun," Carley said, laughing as the calf tried to make friends with Nala, who was keeping watch over everything from her perch on top of the porch glider. The cat playfully swatted at the calf's ears. "You may need to take them to sleepovers more often."

He raised an eyebrow in her direction. "Oh? Is this going to be a sleepover?"

"Well, you're sleeping over at the ranch, I mean."

"I love the way your cheeks turn the slightest pink when I tease you. Especially when I tease you about S-E-X."

He loved a lot of things about her, especially the way she laughed and looked so at ease as she sat next to him on the steps. She was dressed casually in sneakers and jeans and a faded denim button-down shirt, yet she still managed to make the outfit look sexy as hell the way it hugged her ample curves. Her shirt was unbuttoned just enough to offer him an occasional glimpse of her creamy skin and show off a slim silver chain that dipped to the exact spot where he kept imagining placing a kiss.

"Oh my gosh," she said, pressing her fingertips to her cheeks. "That is so not true. I can handle talking about sss… you know…S-E-X."

He chuckled and slipped an arm around her waist to

pull her tighter to his side. He leaned closer to her ear and lowered his voice. "I'd much rather be having it than talking about it."

"I'll take that under consideration," she said, her coy grin telling him she'd definitely be considering it.

Raising his hand to cup her neck, he drew her closer, then pressed his lips to hers, a soft kiss, just to test her reaction. She pressed back, her hand reaching up to his chest and fisting a handful of his shirt as she pulled him closer. She let out a soft kitten murmur, somewhere between a sigh and a moan, and the sound of it had heat and need surging through his veins.

He wasn't sure if he pulled her there or she twisted herself around, but suddenly she was straddling his lap and torturing him with every move of her hips as she deepened the kiss.

He wanted to taste her, to touch her, to rip her clothes off, then slowly explore every inch of her naked body. With one hand still behind her neck, he slipped the other underneath the back of her shirt to grip her waist and pull her closer. His mouth roamed from her lips down her neck and into the open collar of her shirt. She arched back, offering him more freedom to nibble and kiss her neck.

His hand slid down and freed first one button then another, giving him a glimpse of her plump breasts overflowing a lacy pink push-up bra. A guttural groan escaped his throat as he dipped his head to graze her skin with his lips.

Her body, languid and loose as she seemed to revel in his attention, suddenly stiffened as she sat upright and raised her voice to a stern command. "Stop it. Let go of me."

Without a second's hesitation, Knox pulled back and raised his hands in the air. He was confused as hell, but he knew "no meant no" and would never overstep that boundary. "Okay, no problem," he said, although he couldn't quite control the problem her hips were currently lodged against.

"Not you," she said, pushing her torso toward him again.

He shook his head as he started to lower his hands.

"Get off me," she said again, her voice even louder and more commanding.

"*You're* the one sitting on *me*," he said, even more confused.

"I'm talking to *him*," she said, jerking her thumb behind her. "Help me. Before he rips my shirt."

Knox peered around her to see Otis, his teeth clamped around the bottom hem of Carley's shirt. His front legs were planted in the dirt, and he was pulling at the fabric. The goat must have snuck up on them while they were otherwise occupied and grabbed her shirt. Knox reached around her and swatted at the goat's head. "Get back, Otis!"

"NO. If he goes back any further, he'll rip my shirt off."

"You're not making a very convincing argument for me to try very hard," he said, chuckling as he had both hands around the goat's jaw now, trying to pry his mouth open.

"Just get him to let go," she said, bumping up and down on his lap.

"Hold still, woman," he told her. "You wigglin' around on my lap is sorely messing with my concentration. And making me think I should just let the goat *have* your shirt. And your pants too."

She swatted at his arm, then let out a shriek as the goat moved closer. "Ack! I just felt his hairy chin touch my back."

The goat's grip must have been slipping because he opened his jaw just enough to get a better bite, but it was the break Knox needed to yank the fabric free. "Got it. No, go on, Otis. Go find your own gal to nibble on. This one is mine."

The goat didn't move, just stared at him, holding his gaze for a full minute before letting out an annoyed bleat and trotting back toward the barn.

"You're free," Knox told her, chuckling as she collapsed against him.

"Talk about a mood breaker," she said, laughing against his shoulder.

"Yeah, I was so *in the mood*, I didn't even notice him coming up to us."

"Neither did I. Not until I felt him grab my shirt and pull." She sat back up. "And he was super sneaky about it. At first, I thought it was you tugging on my shirt, until I realized one of your hands was gripping my waist and the other was deftly unbuttoning my top."

They both looked down at her chest where even more of her lacy bra was showing, thanks to the goat yanking her shirt from the back. A roguish smile curved Knox's lips as his gaze raked over the lavish display of cleavage. "You can't blame the guy for wanting to rip your shirt off. And *his* hijinks definitely worked in *my* favor."

Instead of tugging the shirt closed to cover herself, as he thought she'd do, her actions had him falling even harder for her as she offered him a seductive smile then unbuttoned the remaining buttons and let the shirt fall completely open. She wrapped her arms around his waist, the motion pushing her breasts even higher. He groaned as she wiggled closer to him, brazenly teasing him with a delicious display of skin. "Now where were you before we were so rudely interrupted? I think you mentioned something about nibbling on me…"

He laughed, the sound sinful as it came from deep in his throat, as he bent to press a kiss to the lacy edge of her bra. "If I recall, I think I was about here." He slid lower, pressing another kiss closer to the center of her cleavage. "Or maybe it was here."

"Mmm-hmmm," she murmured, squirming in response to the heat of his warm breath and lips on her bare skin.

"Blleat!"

She jumped and grabbed the back of her shirt, pulling it tight against her back as the goat bellowed behind them. "Oh, no, you don't. Not again."

Knox sighed. "I think he's telling us he's hungry."

"Ignore him. He's always hungry." She licked her lips as she gazed at his mouth. "And right now, I'm the one who's hungry for the hot cowboy whose lap I'm currently occupying."

He grinned and leaned in for another kiss but stopped as one of the horses in the corral let out a whinny as they trotted up and down the fence. He groaned as he leaned back and scrubbed a hand through his hair. "Seems like Otis is the spokesman for the whole farm. So, as much as I am enjoying this moment—and make no mistake, darlin', I am *immensely* enjoying this moment—I think I'd better go feed all these critters before more of them decide to revolt."

She sighed as she hung her head. "You're right. And it's probably for the best. Someone had to save me before I uttered another corny comment like that last one."

He smiled. "I loved that comment, and believe me, I'm just as starving for the hot beautician who is in my lap."

She groaned as she twisted off his legs and covered her face with her hands. "Oh, gosh, it sounds even dorkier than I thought."

He laughed as he pushed to his feet. "Good thing I'm kind of a dork then." He gestured toward the barn. "It won't take me that long to feed and water all the animals. Hold that thought?"

She uncovered her face and gave him one of those flirty grins of hers that he loved. "It will take even less time if I lend a hand. Got anything I can do to help?"

"I like the way you think." He took her hand and pulled her to her feet. "Although I'm having trouble thinking at all with your shirt hanging open like that. I'm going to need you to keep an eye on me, so I don't accidentally give the pigs' food to the horses."

She pulled the edges of her shirt together, eliciting another groan from him. "Wait," he told her. "Leave it. We can start a new tradition—topless chore night? I'll take my T-shirt off too."

She broke out laughing, a loud, bawdy laugh that had his grin spreading from ear to ear. Dang, but he did love her laugh. Especially when he caught one like this, where her mouth was open and mirth sparkled in her eyes. She flashed her shirt open and jutted out one hip in a teasing stance. "Aren't you worried we'll get arrested for indecent exposure?"

He shook his head. "Nah, I've got connections in the sheriff's department." He reached behind his head, hooking the neck of his T-shirt and started to pull it over the back of his head.

"Gah. No." She grabbed the bottom of his shirt, pulling it back down and at the same time, sending waves of want coursing through him at the touch of her fingers against his abs. "I'm just kidding. We are *not* having topless chore night."

"Fine," he said, dropping his shirt back down. "But for the record, I think this is a great idea, like we could start a new trend."

She laughed again as she rebuttoned her shirt. "As much as I've always dreamed of being a trendsetter, I still think I'll be more comfortable feeding the horses in my shirt rather than my bra." She grabbed his hand and led him toward the barn. "Now, tell me what I can do to help."

"First, I'm going to need you to fill up that tub with water," he told her, pointing toward a black rubber tub in front of the horse's stall.

"To give to the horses?"

"Eventually," he said. "But I think I need you to dump the first one on me. Closest thing I can think of to a cold shower."

She nudged his arm. "Don't tempt me."

"All right. I'm teasing. Mostly. But you can fill all the tubs with fresh water for the horses in the barn while I get them some grain and fresh hay. Then I need to take a few bales out to the horses in the corral, and I'm assuming your friend, Otis, will want in on those."

"He's no friend of mine. Especially after he tried to steal the shirt off my back," Carley said.

There were only a few horses in the stall inside the barn, and Knox gestured to the brown roan mare who had come forward to lean her head over the stall door as he approached. "When I'm around, I usually try to give Sienna a little extra attention. I sneak her a few sugar cubes and try to give her a good brushing every day or two."

"You really love that horse," Carley said. "And it's clear she loves you."

"Yeah, I do. I don't know why—but I've just really bonded with her. She was in such a bad way when Cade and Nora and I found her and rescued her, she about tore my heart out. She'd obviously been neglected and abused, and the bastard we took her from was taking her to be killed, but she's a fighter, and she's really come back from that trauma."

Just thinking about that night and remembering how they'd found her tied inside a vile trailer standing in inches of manure and filth, had his blood pressure rising and fury building in his chest. Carley rested a hand on his arm, the weight of it somehow settling the anger inside him.

"It's a good thing you all got there when you did," she said softly. "You were obviously meant to save her."

"I wanted to take her home with me that first night. But as much as I wanted to, I knew she needed Bryn and Zane's help more than mine. They know more about this stuff, the trauma and neglect, and could give her the round-the-clock care she needed."

"It obviously helped. She looks amazing. And way better than she did before."

"Yeah, she does." He patted the horse's neck, and she nuzzled her nose affectionately into a shoulder. "You are a beauty, aren't you, girl? I'm gonna talk to Bryn and Zane when they get back about me keeping her."

"You want to adopt her?"

"Yeah, I guess."

"Well, you already feed her, and you told me you're the one who named her. According to your earlier assessment, all you've got left is to let her sleep in your bed with you and she's yours."

He slid his arm around her waist and pulled her close. "Too bad the extra spot in my bed is already reserved for someone else I'd like to make mine."

Carley stilled in his arms and stared up into his eyes. Damn, he'd pushed it too far. Making fun flirty comments, even ones about S-E-X, could still fall under their fake relationship scheme, but this was different. Yeah, they were still teasing and joking around, but he'd just declared he wanted to make her *his*. That was a much more serious statement that claimed he *actually* wanted to be with her.

She held his gaze as he held his breath. He did want to make her his. This fake nonsense may have started out as a way to get Paul off her scent, but he was starting to have real feelings for. And not just the kind of feelings brought on by seeing her sexy pink bra. He'd liked her from the first time they'd met, but this was more.

She studied him, and he waited to see how she'd react. Would she play it off as a joke or would she press up on her toes and kiss him senseless and tell him she was already his?

She broke her gaze and wiggled her ring finger, the light in the barn glinting off his grandmother's diamond. "Lucky for you, we're *already* getting married."

So, the joking route it was.

But maybe he could still convince her. He leaned down to kiss her but paused at the sound of an engine roaring down the driveway and pulling to a stop in front of the barn. "You expecting company?"

Carley shook her head as she stiffened in his arms, and he knew she was thinking it could be Paul. He hated that the guy could affect her emotions like that and buckled down on his conviction to get him out of Carley's life.

The engine turned off, replaced by the sound of a slew of barking dogs, and Carley relaxed in his arms. "I don't know anyone who has enough dogs to make that kind of racket."

Sadie and Rodney had been sleeping in the barn while they fed the animals, but they both came running toward Knox, then darted toward the barn door to see what all the commotion was about.

"Bleat." Otis slipped through the rungs of the fence of the corral to join the dog and the calf in their welcome committee duties.

Knox and Carley followed the animals out to where a dusty white Subaru Legacy was parked, the interior filled with a myriad of bouncing, yipping dogs. Carley could count as many as five, a mix of breeds and sizes, racing around the interior of the car.

A harried middle-aged woman with brown hair pulled up in a messy ponytail emerged from the car amidst a chorus of howling and barking. "Is this the Heaven Can Wait rescue ranch?" The windows were all down several inches, and she leaned toward one. "You guys, puh-leeze stop barking." They all seemed to ignore her as she turned back to Carley and Knox and raised her voice to be heard over the din. "Please tell me I'm in the right place."

"Yes," Carley assured her. "That's us."

"Oh, thank goodness, I made it," she said, her body sagging against the door. The dogs quieted a little, presumably from the nearness of her and the obvious emotion in her voice. She stared at Knox and Carley with pleading eyes. "You've got to help me. I think my husband is going to kill me."

CHAPTER 16

KNOX'S HAND AUTOMATICALLY WENT TO HIS HIP, searching for his service weapon. "Are you hurt? Did he follow you? Has he hurt you before?" His eyes scanned the highway beyond the ranch, searching for anyone in pursuit. "You're safe now, I'm a deputy. And don't worry, Creedence is small, but we've got a good shelter here."

"Oh, no, I can't take Cletus to a shelter."

"Who's Cletus?"

"He's my dog." She looked mournfully into the car. "Or he *was* my dog—one of them, at least. But I can't bear the thought of taking him to a shelter."

"No, ma'am," Knox assured her. "The shelter is for you. It's for battered women and children. You'll be safe from your husband there. I promise, he won't hurt you again."

"Hurt me? What are you talking about?" A realization dawned in her eyes. "Oh, my gosh. You thought...when I said my husband was going to kill me...oh no, it's not like that." She held up one hand. "Stand down, officer. I promise, I'm okay. My husband wouldn't *really* kill me. Gerald can barely bring himself to kill a spider. I'm sorry if I gave you the wrong impression." She pushed her mess of bangs away from her face. "Don't worry about me—I'm married to a darling sweetheart of a man. And he puts up with my need to save every stray dog I've ever met. But I think Cletus will be the straw that breaks the sweet darling camel's back. He's the eighth dog I've taken in, and I'm pretty sure *this* dog will break him."

The woman was talking too fast, and Knox shook his head as if to clear it. "So, just to be clear, you are *not* afraid of your husband?"

"Oh, I'm afraid all right. He's getting home from a business trip later tonight, and if he finds eight dogs in our house, I'll be sleeping outside in the doghouse with them. But no, I'm not afraid he'll hurt me."

Knox relaxed his stance. "I think you need to start from the beginning."

"Okay, yes." She leaned into the car and, using one hand to hold two dogs back, she pulled another out by the collar, then shut the car door as quickly as she could. "This is Cletus." She pointed down at a stout black and white bulldog. "This darling older woman at my church broke her hip and had to move into a care facility. She's hoping she'll only be there for a few months, but the place doesn't allow dogs. And Dottie, that's the woman's name, doesn't have any other family to help her. She said Cletus has been with her for over a decade, and he's like her best friend. So, when she practically begged for someone to leave her dog with at church last weekend, I just couldn't say no."

"Of course not," Carley agreed.

"But that was when my husband was out of town. He comes home tonight, and I thought about trying to trick him into thinking we had this one all along—like he might not notice the eighth dog—but he would notice this one. My Gerald may be sweet as all get out, but he's not stupid. You've got to help me."

Carley gave Knox a beseeching look. She lowered her voice and leaned closer to confer with him. "Bryn said if a rescue comes in to just take it, and then she'll figure out what to do with it when she gets back."

He glanced from the big bulldog with the sad eyes back to Carley. "Yeah, but that means you're in charge of this mutt for the next however many days they're gone."

"I can handle it. How hard can taking care of one dog be?" She shot a quick look at the woman by the car. "She takes care of seven. When you look at it that way, one seems totally doable. And it's only for a few days."

He shrugged. "It's your call. I'll be glad to help if you decide to take him. But it's your decision."

Carley walked toward the dog and bent down in front of him. He peered at her with big brown eyes and let out a soft whine. One of his bottom teeth stuck out over the front of his mouth making him look goofy and lovable. She held her hand out for him to sniff, then ruffled his neck. "You're a good boy, aren't you? You're just missing your momma." She stood and brushed her hand on her jeans. "His skin is loose, but I didn't know it would be that soft."

"He's really a sweet dog. No trouble at all. He's not a barker, and Dottie said he's a real lovebug, but so far, with me, he mainly just lies around."

"Okay, sure," Carley said. "Why not? We wouldn't be

much of a rescue ranch if we didn't take in those in need of rescue."

"Oh, thank you so much," the woman said, throwing her arms around Carley. "I've got all his things packed up, and I wrote out his feeding instructions and packed some food. I've got a page in his bag with my information on it, as well. Call me anytime." She pulled out a large tote bag and set it by the dog. Leaning down, she gave him a cuddle then turned back to Carley and Knox. "Your wife is just the most wonderful person. You all have no idea how this is going to help me."

Knox started for a second, not used to having anyone referred to as his *wife*. Then he stepped forward and wrapped an arm around Carley's shoulder. "Yeah, she's pretty great, isn't she?"

"You take care of each other. A good one is hard to find. Which is why I'm so thankful to you all. I've spent twenty years training my Gerald, I'm not about to let him divorce me and have to start all over just because I couldn't say no to another dog." She chuckled at herself as she opened the car door and pushed back a large black lab who was trying to escape, then slid into the driver's seat. She waved a hand out the window and hollered, "Take care," before driving off.

Knox and Carley looked at each other, then down at the dog—who had lain down in the dust, his skin pooling around him like a wrinkly puddle—then looked back at each other.

"I guess we'd better take him inside. Get him settled," Carley said. She called to the dog who slowly raised to his feet and waddled up to the porch with her.

Sadie and Rodney approached him cautiously, touching

their noses to his, before racing ahead of them to the porch, apparently deeming the bulldog as okay. Otis kept his distance, preferring to stand off to the side and warily keep his eye on things.

Carley stopped on the top step. "You ready to turn in for the night?"

He checked his watch. It was close to eight. Not that late. "I don't know. You?"

"Maybe. I'll probably watch a little TV. Do you wanna watch a show with me?"

He shrugged, acting as if it were no biggie when really his stomach felt like mini kangaroos were hopping around inside it. "Just to be clear, when you say watch TV, do you mean you really want to watch a show or is watching TV code for like 'Netflix and chill,' which is really code for…"

She held up her hand to stop him. "Yes, I know what it's code for. And I *really* meant watch television. Although I should warn you that I'm currently in the middle of a new season of *The Great British Bake Off.*"

"What's that?"

"Just what it sounds like. A reality show where people compete to see who the best baker is. They make things like…" She put on a British accent. "Biscuits and custard and choux pastry and other bougie-sounding British foods."

He had to smile at her accent. "So, you just *watch* them bake?"

"Yeah. I know how it sounds, but it's actually quite a fun show. They make these amazing creations and because it's a competition, someone gets booted off every week."

"What do they get if they win?"

"A cake stand and some flowers. *And* all the glory."

He shrugged again. "Okay, I'm in." He was acting like the premise of the show mattered, but the way he'd been feeling about her lately, he was pretty sure he would have watched paint dry with her. As long as he got to be with her.

"I'll pop some popcorn. The show always makes me hungry." She opened the door and waved him in.

"Great. I'll bring a barnyard full of animals," he said, ushering in Sadie and the calf, then held the door for Cletus to amble in behind them. Nala, the cat, snuck past him and scampered toward Carley's bedroom. "Lucky cat," he muttered then peered outside the door. "Are we expecting anyone else?"

"Not yet," she said, tossing a packet of popcorn into the microwave and pressing the button. "But Otis and Tiny seem to show up whenever I make popcorn. I swear they can smell butter a mile away."

"They're out of luck tonight," he said closing the door. "Can I do anything to help?"

"Nope, just turn on the TV and queue up Netflix. I've got wine, water, iced tea, or root beer. Pick your poison."

"Root beer sounds good. I haven't had one of those in a long time."

"I usually keep it around for Milo. But it's good with popcorn. I'll have one too." She popped the tops on two bottles and passed them to him. The scent of butter and popcorn filled the air as she took the bag out of the microwave and pulled the top open. Holding it by the corners, she dumped the contents into two bowls and carried them into the living room.

He set the bottles on the coffee table and picked up the remote, trying to act casual as he sank into the corner of the sofa. There was another chair in the room, but he was hoping she'd sit by him. He tried to hold back his grin as she settled in the center of the sofa, her leg almost touching his.

———

Carley drifted awake, then kept her eyes closed when she realized she had her head in Knox's lap. One show had turned into two, and she'd had a glass of wine after the popcorn, thinking she could use the liquid courage to hang out with him. And maybe also thinking the wine would be a good excuse for why she let herself cuddle up with him on the sofa.

But apparently her plan had backfired, and the wine had just made her sleepy. The television was quiet so the show must have ended. Darn, not only had she fallen asleep on Knox, but she'd also missed the Show Stopper and hadn't seen who got kicked off at the end of the episode. Add to that, the embarrassing worry that she might have drooled on Knox's leg, and her night was ending up just peachy. And now she had to figure out the best way to extricate herself from his lap.

She startled as she heard a deep rumbling snort, then chuckled as she nudged Knox in the side. "Wake up," she told him as she pressed herself up to sit beside him. "You're snoring."

"I'm awake," he said, totally clear-eyed. He nudged her back. "I thought that was you."

Another loud snore sound filled the room. She leaned forward to peer over the coffee table to where the bulldog was lying on his back, his back legs spread eagle, his front paws held crossed on his chest. "Oh, my gosh. He sounds like a freight train."

Then another loud sound followed the first, but this one came from the opposite end of the dog, and Carley pulled the collar of her shirt over her nose as a noxious odor filled the room. "Oh, my gosh. That is awful."

"That was definitely the dog."

"I know. Oh my gosh, I can't talk, or it will get in my mouth." She pressed her lips closed and then barely opened them to say, "We should open a window."

"Or at least light a match. Or a candle. Or anything that would give us a better scent."

"How can you stand it?" she asked, keeping her shirt over her nose.

He shrugged. "I'm a deputy sheriff *and* a rancher. Being around disgusting smells is part of my job description."

She laughed, then groaned as the dog let loose another round of snores followed by a toot. "Oh, my gosh. What is wrong with him?"

"Must be his food. With eight dogs to feed, I can imagine that woman might not have sprung for the most expensive dog chow."

"Remind me to remedy that tomorrow."

Her phone buzzed with a text message, vibrating against

the coffee table where it sat in front of them. "That must be Jillian," she said, picking up the phone.

But it wasn't her sister.

The message was from Paul, and the way she was holding her phone up to see it made it easy enough for Knox to read the message on the screen as well.

Just checking in on my sweetie. Wondering if you're free for lunch tomorrow? I'd love to take you out. Just to catch up, it read, followed by several heart emojis.

Knox stiffened and it was as if all their easiness and comfort with each other disappeared. He grabbed his boots from the floor by the sofa and pulled them on, then stood. "It's getting late. I should probably take off."

She peered up at him, confused by his sudden shift in behavior. "What's wrong?"

"Nothing. Like I said, it's just getting late, and I have to work in the morning. I'll head out and let you return your text."

She made a gagging sound. "You don't seriously think I'm going to text him back? Is that why you're upset? Because there is no question at all that I plan to ignore this text, just like I do all his other texts."

A scowl tightened his mouth. "I didn't realize you all texted each other that much."

"We don't text. He texts me, and I ignore them." She held up her phone. "You can look at them if you don't believe me."

He took a step back. "I'm not going to look at your phone or read your messages. Those are yours to do with as you want."

"I want them to stop. I have no interest in the guy. You *know* that."

"Maybe not, but maybe you like the attention of his messages."

Her eyes widened. She couldn't believe what she was hearing. She crossed her arms over her chest. "Maybe it *is* time for you to go."

He scrubbed a hand through his hair as he let out a rueful sigh. "I'm sorry. That was a dumb thing to say. I do know how you feel about him. It just annoys the hell out of me that he thinks he can text you whenever he wants. And I really hate that his text is the last message you get at night before you go to bed." He gave a shudder. "That guy just gets under my skin."

"You have my number too. If it bothers you, maybe you should text me. Then *your* message will be the last thing I see before I go to bed."

"Maybe I will." He whistled for Sadie and Rodney who were sacked out on the floor in the kitchen. "I need to put these guys out anyway."

Cletus blearily opened his eyes and lifted his head from the floor.

"You too, big guy," he told the bulldog as he opened the door to let all three of them outside. "You sure you'll be okay with Cletus tonight? He can sleep over on my side if you want."

If she were being honest with herself, she'd have to admit that what she really wanted was for her to be sleeping on his side of the bunkhouse with him too. But that wasn't going to happen. She'd just been reminded that this whole thing was a charade, just a ruse to fool her ex, who didn't seem to be getting the hint anyway. "No, I'll be fine with him," she said.

The bulldog shuffled back onto the porch, and Knox let him inside. He returned to his spot by the coffee table and lay back down. "Okay, goodnight then."

"Goodnight," she said. Then just like that, he was gone. Another stark reminder of how things always went with the men in her life, one minute they were there, the next they were gone.

A heaviness settled on her shoulders as she put their bowls in the sink, turned out the lights, then trudged down the hall to get ready for bed. It didn't take her long to get into her pajamas and do her nightly routine.

The cat was waiting for her, curled up on the opposite side of the bed, when she walked into her bedroom and Cletus had come down to lie on the rug at the end of the hall. She climbed into bed, gave the cat a cuddle, and lay her head on her pillow. But she couldn't sleep.

Her phone buzzed from where she'd plugged it into the charger on the nightstand and the light from the display lit the room. Annoyance filled her. If that was Paul texting her again, she wasn't going to ignore him this time. No, this time, she was going to tell him what to do with his lunch offer.

But the text wasn't from Paul.

It was from Knox. She smiled as she read his message. Just wanted my words to be the last ones you read before you went to sleep. Thanks for a fun night. And in case you were wondering, the guy with the funny accent was the one who got booted off the show.

She laughed as she typed back, All the guys had funny accents.

Then we'll just have to rewatch the show together. Do-over tomorrow night? I'll bring supper.

It's a date, she typed, then deleted the last word and changed it to plan.

Goodnight, beautiful.

Goodnight, she typed but held back from adding a heart emoji. What was she? Sixteen? But she couldn't stop herself from pressing the phone to her chest or hold back the grin that curved the corners of her mouth.

CHAPTER 17

CARLEY WAS SO SLAMMED THE NEXT DAY, SHE BARELY HAD time to think about anything other than the head of hair in front of her. She'd taken advantage of the extra attention around the shop and squeezed in a few extra bookings. Which meant she skipped any breaks she might normally have and only took a few minutes to shove down a protein bar somewhere around lunchtime.

Staying so busy should have been the perfect way to put her problems pertaining to a certain cute cowboy out of her mind. If only every client didn't feel the need to bring him up.

Some questions were innocuous or just curious like, "How's that cute fiancé of yours doing?" or "What's Knox up to today?" But others were just plain nosy, like "Exactly *how* long have you two been dating?" and "Why haven't you set a wedding date?" And one person even asked if he was good in bed. Then she'd laughed and pointed at Carley as she'd hooted and said, "He is. I can tell by your face. I knew it." Carley tried to ignore most of the questions, changing the subject or giving the client a new direction to bring the focus back to her hair.

The one guy she didn't seem to have to worry about was

Cletus. The bulldog lay stretched out on the rug at the far end of the hallway in what she'd come to think of as *his* spot, and he'd kept to himself most of the day.

She'd let him outside once about midday, and a couple of the women in the shop had tried to pet him, but he'd shied away and then returned to his spot at the back of the hallway once he'd taken care of his business and come back inside. Carley couldn't figure out if he was sad, lonely, or just antisocial.

He'd been friendly enough with her and Knox the night before, accepting their pets and neck ruffles, but when she'd gone to bed, he'd curled up on the hallway rug and stayed there pretty much ever since. He kept an eye on her, though, his gaze following her that morning as she'd moved around the bunkhouse getting ready for the day.

His big jowls drooped to the floor on either side of his mouth, giving him a sad-sack look, and Carley couldn't help but feel like he was missing Dottie. After a decade together, it made sense that he would be gloomy without her.

All the customers had finally cleared out by around four when Evelyn showed up for her weekly wash and set.

Carley hadn't really been able to talk to her since the big announcement of her and Knox's engagement. They'd spoken on the phone a few times since the building had flooded, but their conversation had been centered around insurance forms and what to do about the cleanup and repairs.

"How ya holding up, honey?" Evelyn asked, giving Carley a hug before plopping into the stylist chair.

"I'm doing fine," Carley assured her.

"What's happening with the building?"

"Nothing new. Just waiting to hear more from the insurance company." The insurance policy had been under Evelyn's name, so they'd both been fielding calls.

"I'm sure it will all be covered," Evelyn said, giving her hand a reassuring pat.

"I hope you're right." Carley hadn't let herself think too much about the expenses incurred from the building cleanup and repair, knowing it would send her into a tailspin if she thought insurance might not cover them. She tried to change the subject to a more positive one. "In the meantime, I'm just thankful Bryn let me set up my shop out here. I've been swamped all day."

To her surprise, while they'd been talking, Cletus had plodded out into the living room and sat on the floor at Evelyn's feet. He stared lovingly up at her before resting his chin on her knee.

"Oh, my word. Who is this handsome devil?" she asked before Carley could shoo him off her leg. "I used to have a bulldog as a kid. I just love their sad, droopy faces. They're so sweet."

"A woman dropped him off here last night. She said an elderly woman at her church broke her hip and had gone into a care home and needed someone to look after him for a few months until she could come home. This woman had tried to keep him, but she already had seven other dogs."

"Seven? Heavens. Who in their right mind would have seven dogs?" Her expression changed from horror to tenderness as she gently scratched the bulldog's head. "But that's awful about the woman breaking her hip and having to go into a care home." She shuddered. "One of my worst fears. And I'll bet this guy was her constant companion. She must be missing him terribly. What are you going to do with him?"

"I honestly don't know. Bryn's out of town, so I guess I'm just holding onto him until she gets back, and we can find a good temporary or possibly permanent home for him."

Evelyn's face lit up. "I could keep him for you. You know, just until you figure something else out."

"Oh, Evelyn, no. I couldn't possibly ask you to do that."

"You're *not* asking. I'm offering." She reached down and lifted the dog's saggy chin. "Just look at that adorable droopy face. How could I *not* want to take him home with me?"

"You're so sweet for offering. But this dog—well, honestly—he's got a few issues that make you might reconsider."

"Like what?"

"Like you'll never get any rest with him around because he snores like a locomotive."

Evelyn huffed out a breath. "Don't worry about that. So did my late husband. Believe me, if I can sleep through the racket of the way he sawed logs, I can sleep through anything. What else?"

Carley shifted from one foot to the other, not sure how to mention the other *issue* with the dog. "Well, I'm not sure how to put this delicately, but his snoring is not the only strong sound he produces." She wrinkled her nose. "And the other one smells a lot worse."

Evelyn chuckled. "Ha. That's another thing my husband did. So far, you haven't given me a single good reason why I shouldn't bring him home with me. If anything, you've only convinced me that I want him more."

"*More?* How can me telling you that this dog snores and toots in epic proportions make you want him even more?"

She laughed again and rubbed the dog's neck. "Because he'll make me feel like my husband is around again. What's this fella's name, anyway? I forgot to ask."

"Cletus."

Evelyn slapped her leg and let out a hoot. "Well, that settles it. Cletus was my late husband's middle name. So, it sounds to me like it was meant to be." She peered up at Carley. "Please, honey. Let me take him home. That big old house I live in can get awfully lonely sometimes. I think Cletus would be good company for me."

Carley lifted her shoulder in a shrug. "Okay. If you really want him, he's yours. But don't say I didn't warn you. And if he's making you crazy in a few days, bring him back, and we'll get Bryn to help us figure out what to do with him."

Evelyn's face beamed. "Thank you." She leaned down to nuzzle the dog's face. "Did you hear that, boy? You're coming home with me. We're going to have so much fun."

The dog let out a long groan and then plopped down on Evelyn's feet and proceeded to stay there until Carley had finished the elderly woman's hair.

Evelyn pulled her feet free as she stood. "Say, do you know what the woman's name is who owns Cletus? Or what church she goes to?"

"She didn't say what church it was, but I think the woman who dropped him off said her name was Dottie. She gave me her number. I could call and ask her."

"I might have you do that. But first, let me ask around. If I can find out where this Dottie is, maybe I can try to bring Cletus in to visit her."

"What a nice idea," she said, leaning down to give Evelyn a hug. "You are just the sweetest, most thoughtful person I know."

"Oh shoot, then you need to get out more," Evelyn said. Carley gave her the tote bag full of Cletus's things, then Evelyn called the dog and led him to the door.

Following her out, Carley was surprised and happy to see Knox coming up the stairs of the porch. He looked so handsome in his uniform, his jeans hugging his long legs and his brown felt Stetson riding low on his forehead. He carried a white paper bag in his hand.

"Honey, I'm home," he said, then leaned down to give Carley a one-armed hug and a quick kiss on the cheek. "How was your day?"

"Good," was all she could muster up to say, a little flustered at both the endearment and the soft brush of his lips against her face.

He set the bag on the table, then squatted down and scratched the neck of the bulldog. "How did this guy do today?"

"He was practically comatose—slept at the back of the hallway all day. That is, until Evelyn showed up then he ran over to her and practically crawled into her lap. She's taking him home with her."

"What? No way. That's great." His look of delight changed to a grimace. "Well, except for...did you tell her about how he...?"

"Yes," she said with a laugh. "I told her everything. And she still wants him."

He tipped his hat at the older woman. "Miss Evelyn, you *are* a saint."

Evelyn waved away his compliment. "Now, don't go starting that rumor. I'm as big a sinner as anyone. Why, just this morning I dropped the butter tub on my toe and let out a string of curse words that would make a sailor blush."

Knox laughed. "I would have liked to have heard that."

"I'm glad you're here, honey," Evelyn told him. "I wanted to tell you both that I'm planning to throw you an engagement party. This weekend. So, if you have any plans for Saturday night, break 'em."

"Oh no," Carley said. "Evelyn, we can't let you do that. It's too much."

"Nonsense. And you're not *letting* me do anything. I'm telling you that I'm doing it, and that's that. No arguing."

Carley looked over her head at Knox, who just shrugged. *Fat lot of help he was.*

Evelyn was already making her way to her car, Cletus trotting happily along at her heels. It was like he was a different dog around her. Carley hadn't seen him this happy since he'd shown up. Evelyn opened the passenger door, and the dog jumped onto the seat.

Carley caught up to her and took her arm as she leaned in and lowered her voice. "Evelyn, I love you, and it's so sweet that you want to throw us an engagement party, but the truth is..."

Evelyn held up her hand. "I *know* what the truth is. And I know why you're doing it. And I'm throwing you the party for the same reason. Paul is my grandson, and I love the jackass, but I love you too. And the sooner he leaves town and forgets about his big plans for you and that building, the better." She touched a weathered hand tenderly to Carley's cheek. "You are like a granddaughter to me, and I only want you to be happy. You may not really be in love with Knox Garrison, but I think you could be. If you'd only let your guard down and see what a good man he is." She narrowed her eyes as if studying her. "Or maybe by that little smile you just made when I mentioned his name, you already have." She nudged Carley in the ribs. "Plus, he's a real hottie." She leaned even closer and lowered her voice. "*And* I heard he used to be a stripper."

Carley let loose a loud laugh. "You shouldn't believe everything you hear."

Evelyn huffed. "*You* shouldn't take away an old lady's fantasy." She winked at Carley then blew an air kiss in Knox's direction. "See you soon, Deputy. Saturday night. Six o'clock. My house."

He looked at Carley as if for confirmation. She gave him a nod. "Sounds great. Wouldn't miss it."

"Bring your appetite."

"Always do."

They watched her drive away then Knox let Sadie and Rodney out of his truck. He'd taken them back to his house for the day and must have picked them up on the way back over tonight. The golden retriever raced around Carley's legs, then plopped to a sit in front of her, her hind end wiggling in excitement as she waited for Carley to lavish her with pets.

How could she resist?

"What's in the bag?" she asked Knox after cuddling both the dog and the calf. Never in her wildest dreams had she ever imagined herself showering a baby cow with affection, but Rodney was so dang cute, she couldn't help herself.

She was finding she had the same problem with his owner.

"Pulled pork sandwiches and mac and cheese. I stopped at the food truck after I picked these guys up."

She pressed a hand to her chest and groaned. "Oh, yum. Two of my favorites." She started to reach for the bag, then froze with her hand in mid-air. "Oh, wow. That was super presumptuous. Is this *your* supper or *ours*? And no worries if it's just for you."

He chuckled. "It's ours. I told you last night, I'd bring dinner home tonight."

She raised an eyebrow. "Wow, that sounded a lot like the kind of thing a *husband* would say."

"If the comment fits," he said, offering her a grin. "We might have to heat it up though. Let me get changed out of my uniform and then we can eat."

"I can do that while you change," she offered. "Okay if we eat out here on the porch?"

"Perfect."

That's the problem, she thought as she took the bag of food inside and assembled plates and drinks on a tray. This all felt too perfect. Like a life she had only dreamed of. Like it was supposed to have been with Paul. But the time she spent with Knox was nothing like the time she'd spent with Paul— they had fun together and Knox never made her feel like an idiot for something she said or did.

That's because this is all pretend. That's what a fake relationship is.

If they were really together, sharing a life, she was sure they would have spats and arguments. If Knox spent enough time around her, she was sure he would get tired of her and leave her, just like every other man in her life had.

"So, tell me about your day," Knox said, patting the glider next to him when she brought out the tray of food and drinks. "Tell me what exciting things happened in the world of beauty today."

She shook her head as she passed him a plate. "I can't think of a single thing. I was slammed all day, but I don't think anything too exciting happened. I mainly just washed, cut, and styled hair. Oh, and fielded a million questions about us and our impending nuptials."

"I got several of those too."

"Yeah, but women chatting in salons are different. They talk about *everything*. I doubt anyone asked you if I was good in bed."

His eyes widened. "No way. Someone asked you that about me?"

She nodded. "Yep."

"And what was your answer?"

She nudged his knee but couldn't hold back a grin. "I knew you were gonna ask me that the second I said it. I didn't give them an answer, but apparently, they made their own assumptions by the smile on my face."

He grinned. "Nice."

"How about your day?" she asked, picking up her sandwich. "What thrilling things happened in the world of law enforcement?"

"Not much, pretty ordinary day. Gave out a speeding ticket, responded to a fender bender, did some paperwork, and broke up a bar fight this afternoon."

"A bar fight? In the middle of the afternoon?"

"Well, it wasn't much a fight. It was between a husband and wife, who are both in their eighties, so no punches were actually thrown. Apparently, Fred and Mavis McGee stopped in to the Creed to have a margarita, or three, and got into a disagreement about a woman Fred supposably flirted with back in seventy-two. They were both three sheets to the wind, and I guess the argument got heated, and they were shouting names at each other, and a basket of chips and a bowl of salsa were allegedly dumped in Fred's lap. But still, I wouldn't have even been called if it weren't for the gun going off."

CHAPTER 18

"*GUN?*" CARLEY ASKED, HER SANDWICH MIDWAY TO HER mouth. "Wait, there was a shooting today too?"

"Yeah, well, sort of. That's the only reason I'm telling you the couple's names because I'm sure it will be all over town by tomorrow. And don't worry, no one was hurt. According to Mavis, she didn't even remember having the pistol in her purse when she walloped Fred in the shoulder with it and the gun went off. The shot went wide, but the noise of it startled Fred so bad, he fell off the barstool and whacked his head on the counter. And you know how head wounds bleed, so she tried to wash off the blood with the ice in her glass, but it still had margarita mix *and salt* in it, so it must have burned like a son of a gun, because old Fred howled and hollered like he was being tortured. By the time I got there, we'd had seven different calls about gunshots, a mass shooting, and a murder at the Creed."

"Oh, no." Carley almost choked on the bite she'd just taken, she was laughing so hard.

"Between the blood and the salsa, Fred looked like he *had* been murdered, and with all the fuss he was making, someone had called an ambulance. By the time the EMTs arrived, Mavis was contrite and the two of them had made up and she was fussing over him like an old mother hen. The ambulance took them to the hospital to stitch up his head, and I went back to the station and wrote up a heck of an entertaining report."

"That is too funny. Did you ever figure out why Mavis McGee was carrying a pistol in her purse in the first place?"

"She said she'd taken it to bingo a few nights before because the last time it had gotten a little rowdy during the blackout round, and then forgotten she had it in there."

"She took a loaded gun to bingo? The one for seniors down at the Methodist church on Friday night?"

He nodded. "I guess those seniors must get kind of crazy."

She finally stopped laughing. "You had a bar fight *and* a shooting. I'd say that trumps my day by a mile."

"Day's not over yet," he said.

She checked her watch. "It's almost six. I can't imagine anything happening in the next few hours that could top that."

As if on cue, a sleek black Maserati sped up the highway and turned into the driveway of the ranch. It braked to a stop in front of the bunkhouse porch and a blond woman who looked to be in her early thirties got out and looked around. She wore Lululemon tennis attire, although the amount of diamond jewelry around her throat and wrists suggested she hadn't been on the court that day, and bright white sneakers that probably cost more than Carley had made that entire month. "Is this the ranch with the salon?"

Carley stood to greet her. "Yes ma'am. I'm Carley, the salon owner, but I'm afraid we're closed for the day."

The woman had a sporty layered bob that Carley easily discerned as a high-end cut-and-color job, and a style like that had to be maintained every three to four weeks. It was obvious it had just been done, so Carley had no idea what the woman would need her services for.

"Damn. Damn. Double damn," the woman swore. "I knew I was going to be late. I drove up from Denver and got lost trying to find this place." She jerked her thumb toward the car. "Listen, my Desiree needs a cut so bad, and the last place I took her just annihilated her bangs. I heard you're a great stylist and it's so hard to find someone who offers your services. It shouldn't take too long to do her hair, she wears the new wolf cut, I'm sure you're familiar with it."

"Yes, I know the style," Carley said. The wolf cut was all the rage right now, but it was essentially just a mix of a vintage shag and a slight mullet. She squinted into the car to see what she was dealing with but couldn't see through the dark tinted windows.

"I'll pay you extra for your time. Double even. Name your price," the woman said. "My girl has a show next weekend, and she's got to look great."

A show? Was her daughter a model? Or an actress? She'd have to be a child actress because the woman didn't look old enough to have an adult daughter. The thought of doing the hair of someone famous both excited and terrified her. But the woman had driven all the way up from Denver. And with everything that was going to have to be replaced at the shop, Carley could certainly use the money.

"Sure. Okay. I'd be glad to take care of Desiree's hair."

"Oh, thank you," the woman said, rounding the car to the passenger side. "I'm Megan, by the way. And this is Desiree." She opened the car door, and a large beautifully groomed gray-and-white English sheepdog climbed out.

"Oh," was all Carley could think of to say. "Um…maybe there is some confusion. I'm not a dog groomer."

Megan huffed. "I should hope not. And if it's not obvious that Des has been recently groomed, then I'm paying her groomer too much. My girl doesn't need to be groomed. She needs a haircut. And you said you were the owner of the ranch salon."

Carley heard Knox stifle a laugh, and she turned to offer him a beseeching look. "Help," she mouthed.

"Don't worry. I can fix this," Knox whispered. He cleared his throat, then stood up next to her. "Carley is a gifted beautician whether she's working on people *or* animals. And your Desiree is one gorgeous animal. I'm sure you'll be pleased with Carley's work, but with the late hour and all, her fee is going to have to be a little higher." He named a price that had Carley almost choke. It was more than what she'd made on Chloe's entire bridal party's hair, including the generous tip they'd all included.

But she had to give it to him. Surely naming such an outrageous price would ensure Megan would load up her pampered pooch and drive away.

Megan narrowed her eyes at Knox then said, "Done. And don't worry, I'll also add in a lavish tip. Just for fitting us in without notice."

Carley couldn't believe it. For that price, she'd paint the

dog's toenails too. "Welcome to Carley's Cut and Curl," she said, sweeping her arm toward the bunkhouse door.

The dog padded up to Carley, stopped to peer up at her through too-long bangs, gave a quick lick to her hand, then entered the bunkhouse and jumped up into the stylist chair.

"You've got to be kidding me," Carley muttered as she followed her in and reached for a comb.

The dog was an absolute sweetheart and held perfectly still while Carley trimmed her bangs, then created lots of shaggy layers around her face. When she was done, she spritzed the dog with some of her best-smelling hair spray, and Desiree gave a little woof as if she approved.

A satisfied Megan led a newly wolf-cut Desiree back to her car, and Carley pocketed a hefty chunk of change and had a new story to add to her salon tales. "I can't believe that happened," she told Knox as they waved to Megan and Des as they sped away. "How in the world did she even hear about me?"

"I can solve that one. We were chatting while you were working and apparently her husband plays hockey for the NHL and is on Rock James's team. She said that she'd met Quinn at some function and had heard her talking about what a great job you do on hair and something about you being on a ranch. It's my guess she wasn't listening to the whole story and just made her own assumptions that you cut the hair of farmyard animals." He peered around the yard. "Have you seen Otis? He could probably stand a trim. At least give his beard a shave."

She nudged his arm with her elbow. "Very funny. I don't

think Otis could afford my new rates. Thanks for that, by the way. I owe you a free haircut for that one."

"I might just take you up on that." He smiled at her then his gaze dropped to her mouth, and a swirl of heat spun through her stomach. He leaned toward her, and she sucked in her breath, anticipating his kiss. Except instead of kissing her, he brushed past her arm to collect their plates and glasses from the table. "You still up for an episode or two of the Bake Off? I actually turned it off last night when I realized you'd fallen asleep, and I've been in suspense all day wondering who was going to get kicked off the show."

She laughed. "Yeah, I'm sure the Show Stopper was all that was on your mind today while you were dealing with a bar brawl and an errant gunshot."

The next day, Carley took the morning off to spend cleaning up the salon. She and Knox had done the best they could that first night, but she knew she would need more time to put things back to rights. They had laid out a lot of things to dry, and she hoped to be able to put things away and get reorganized.

Walking in, she could tell that the cleaning crews had been working hard, but thought she still detected a faint scent of mildew—not the smell anyone wants when they step into a beauty salon.

But the floors and the wall were no longer damp, and it looked like the drywallers had come in and replaced the worst sections of the wall that had been damaged. Starting in the front of the shop, she worked her way back, cleaning up and putting things away as she went.

She'd been working for a few hours when she heard a tap at the front window and looked up to see Autumn standing outside. She unlocked the door and let the yoga instructor inside. She was surprised when Autumn threw her arms around her neck and hugged her.

"Oh, Carley," she said. "I'm so sorry this happened. What a mess. I've been working on cleaning up the studio all week. Have you heard anything new from the insurance company?"

She shook her head. "No. And I have no idea how long this sort of thing takes."

Autumn chewed on her lower lip. "I've got considerable damage on my side too, and now I'm nervous that insurance isn't going to cover all of it."

"Why wouldn't they?"

"I don't know. Evelyn's grandson was here yesterday looking around, and he came next door to check on me. Or at least that's what he said, but I think there was more to it."

"Wait. Paul was here? In the salon? Did you let him in?"

"No. He had a key. I saw him unlock the back door when I was taking a load of trash out to the dumpster in the alley."

Alarm bells went off in Carley's chest. Alarm and anger— Paul had no right to come into her shop when she wasn't there.

"Anyway," Autumn continued. "He started talking about all the damage and how expensive it was going to be to have everything fixed, and he said sometimes insurance only covers *some* of the damage and that he thought there was a huge deductible on the policy. Then he said this really strange thing about how insurance wouldn't cover any of it if they found out that the damage had been caused deliberately or that our business had been sabotaged."

Sabotaged?

The alarms bells were really clanging now.

"Isn't that weird?" Autumn asked. "I mean, I know we've had our differences, but I hope you know I would never purposely do something to damage our livelihoods. And I don't think you would either."

"No, of course not. I would never. Is that what he was implying? That *I* flooded both of our stores to somehow hurt your business?"

Autumn shrugged. "Kinda."

Carley tightened her hands into fists as she seethed. "The nerve of that guy. That doesn't even make sense. Why would I do that? And my shop was flooded too."

"I know. That's why it seemed so weird. But if he wasn't referring to either of us, then who was he talking about? Who would want to intentionally mess with our businesses?"

"*Him*," Carley said. "I don't know what his game is, but something's going on."

"Has he told you anything?"

"No. I barely talk to him."

Autumn wrinkled her perky nose. "Really? Because he said he was working on you two getting back together. And that he might be helping you with the salon. He said he had tons of ideas for the shop, but that you all might be going in a new direction, and it might not be a bad idea for me to start thinking about finding a new place to rent." She nervously twisted a silver band around her ring finger. "I love my studio, and I hate the idea of leaving. But I'd rather know now if you're planning to evict me than get surprised later."

Carley scrubbed her hands over her face, then let out a deep cleansing breath in order to stay calm. "Oh, my gosh, I don't even know where to start with all of that. First of all, I am NOT getting back together with Paul, not now, not ever. And he has no say in what happens with this building or with our shops, and I can assure you that I have no intention of evicting you or asking you to leave. And I haven't heard Evelyn say anything about this either."

Autumn let out the breath she appeared to have been holding. "Oh, thank goodness. You don't know how relieved I am to hear you say that." She frowned. "But then why would Paul say all that?"

"I have no idea. I can't figure out what he's up to. But I think he's trying to get his hands on this building. He encouraged me to think about selling it the other day."

"But why? What does he want with our businesses?"

"I don't know." She thrummed her fingers on the side of the stylist chair as she tried to figure out what could be going on in Paul's pea-sized brain.

She was distracted by the sight of a man pulling up in front of the shop in an expensive looking car. She didn't recognize either the man, or the car, from being around here. He had dark hair, was dressed in jeans, loafers, and a polo shirt, and held a clipboard. He stood staring at the building for a moment, then began taking measurements of the front window and door.

"Look," she said, pointing to the man. "There's a guy with a tape measure and a clipboard outside now. Maybe he's the insurance adjustor, and he can tell us something."

Autumn followed her out and they approached the dark-haired man together.

"Hi, there," Carley called out. "We were hoping to ask you a few questions."

"Sure," the man said, pressing one end of a tape measure against the side of the building. "But can you hold this first?"

Carley pressed her thumb down where he instructed, and he pulled the tape out to measure the distance between the side wall and the front door. "We were just wondering if you have any information or updates on our claim."

"What claim?" he asked, marking down the measurement on his clipboard.

"Aren't you from the insurance company?" Autumn asked.

"No, I'm the developer," he said. "This is a great little downtown property. Perfect spot for a couple of loft apartments, and I think I can fit three businesses down here. We're talking about a vegan coffee shop, a tattoo parlor, and a gentleman's barber shop or maybe an artisan doughnut place. I've been working on a sweet deal with the owner of this building to buy it."

Carley lifted her thumb and let the tape measure zing back into the case. "You're working with Evelyn?"

He absently shook his head as he tried to pull the tape

measure back out and hook it to a crack in the sidewalk to measure the distance between the building and the street. "No, I don't know any Evelyn. I've been working with the guy who owns this place. His name is Paul. Paul Chapman."

CHAPTER 19

BILE ROSE IN CARLEY'S THROAT. *THAT LOWDOWN SNAKE IN the grass.* He *was* trying to sell the building.

"I hate to inform you—actually, I take that back," she told the developer. "I'm *very happy* to inform you that Paul Chapman is *not* the owner of this building. It is in fact owned by me, and Paul's grandmother, Evelyn Chapman. So, you can take your tape measure, and your clipboard, and your bougie hipster business ideas, and go back to California or wherever you came here from, because we are *not* selling."

She felt Autumn do a little wiggly dance next to her. "That's right. What she said."

The guy studied them for a moment, then tucked his tape measure into the front pocket of his jeans as he walked to where his car was parked at the curb. "I'll go. For now. But I think you need to get your facts straight. This Chapman fellow was pretty clear that he was the owner and that he was *very motivated* to sell."

"No, sir. I think *you* need to get your facts straight. His name is not anywhere on the deed." She said the words with conviction, but an inner niggling fluttered in her stomach. What if Paul had somehow swindled Evelyn into signing over her half of the building?

She felt nauseous as she and Autumn watched the man get into his car and drive away.

"Wow," Autumn said. "I'm so impressed. You really gave that guy what for."

"Thanks," Carley said, suddenly feeling drained and emotionally exhausted. "Well, now I guess we know what Paul is up to."

"Yeah, but I'm still stumped about what a vegan coffee shop is," Autumn said, scratching the side of her head. "I mean, I'm no expert, but isn't all coffee vegan? It's made from a bean. Or maybe the shop is only for customers who *are* vegan."

Carley shook her head, just as bamboozled. "I have no idea. And what the hell is an artisan doughnut anyway?"

———————

"He actually said that Paul was the owner of the building?" Knox asked Carley that night as she dished salad and a heaping spoonful of baked ziti onto his plate.

She hadn't cooked the dish in a while, not since Jillian and Milo had moved out, and she realized she kind of missed cooking for someone else. Or maybe she just liked cooking for Knox. They'd been having dinner together almost every night since he'd started staying next door and helping out with the rescue ranch. Carley had found herself looking forward to going home and thinking about recipes and ideas of what she could make for him. Which was a dangerous habit to get into.

"Yes," Carley told him as she filled a plate for herself. "And that he was working on a deal with him to sell it to him."

"That guy is unbelievable."

"*Unbelievable* is not the word I was thinking of using to describe him." She picked up her plate and followed Knox out onto the porch where they'd taken to eating their evening meals. She'd already set up a tray with glasses and a pitcher of iced tea, and Knox poured them each a glass as she settled onto the glider next to him. "But some of the stuff he said to Autumn has got me a little worried. What if he really did sabotage the building and cause the flooding?"

"Then I'll be more than happy to arrest him. In fact, I could bring him in for questioning right now, just on suspicion of insurance fraud."

"No way. I don't want to give the insurance company any reason to think that we even suspect any kind of foul play."

"That makes sense," he said with a sigh. "But I sure would love to arrest that guy for something."

"Believe me, I understand. But it makes me think I need to be prepared. Financially. Even if insurance does cover this, which I'm praying they will, I'll still need to come up with the deductible, and I know there will be odds and ends that I'll need to replace." She tapped her fork against her lip. "I need to brainstorm some ideas of ways that I can make extra money and quickly."

"Okay, I can help with this." He leaned back against the cushion, his expression pensive. "Hmm. Do our ideas have to be legal?"

She laughed, thankful she hadn't just stuck a bite of pasta

into her mouth. "Yes, I think they should, considering I'm engaged to a sheriff's deputy. I don't want to have to be the one you arrest."

"But we could have fun with my handcuffs."

She nudged his leg, but inside her stomach fluttered with unease. The words had slipped so easily out of her mouth— *engaged to a sheriff's deputy*. Sitting on the porch with him, eating supper as their knees touched and they playfully teased each other, it was so simple to imagine they were a real couple.

But they weren't. This was all pretend, a made-up scheme to try to keep her ex-husband away from her. And thoughts of Paul just reminded her why she didn't let herself get too involved. Men left her behind. No matter how much baked ziti she made them or how cute her hair was styled or how much she made them laugh. In the end, men did not stay. Not for her.

She set her plate down, no longer hungry, and stood up. She needed to put some distance between her and the handsome deputy that she, in fact, was *not engaged* to. That she wasn't even really dating.

"What just happened?" Knox asked, eyeing her warily as he set his plate down next to hers.

"Nothing."

"No. That was definitely something. One second you were laughing and at ease, then the next your body went stiff, you got that little frown line you get on your forehead when you're stressed about something, and you stopped eating."

"What are you? A detective?" She tried to play off his

words with sarcasm, but it unnerved her a little that he could read her so well. She rubbed at the spot between her eyes. Did she really get a frown line there when she was stressed? The fact that he knew that simple thing about her touched her more than she wanted to admit.

"Yes," he said. "I *am* a detective. And I'm trained to read body language, and yours just said you couldn't get away from me fast enough."

She shook her head as if dismissing his claim. "I just needed to stretch my legs." Her heart pounded against her chest as he stood and walked toward her.

He gently pulled her into his arms, then tenderly smoothed the spot on her forehead. "You can trust me, you know." He spoke softly, saying the exact words she ached to hear.

She didn't need platitudes or stupid pet names. She needed a man she could trust.

She fought against the emotions building in her as she stared into his gorgeous brown eyes, so full of care and conviction. "I do trust you," she whispered then lowered her gaze. "Just not with my heart."

He lifted her chin, forcing her to look at him, to see the sincerity in his eyes. "You can trust me with that too. I swear I won't break it." Locking her gaze, he drew closer, tipping her chin higher, then sliding his palm across her jaw to cup her cheek as he pressed a kiss to her lips.

As if separate from her mind, her arms automatically went around him, and she melted into his embrace. All those emotions came teeming to the surface as she kissed him back with passion and desperation. She wanted to believe him.

With everything in her soul, she wanted to put her faith in him, but she couldn't let that part of herself go. Not her heart.

But her body seemed futile to resist as he slid his arm down her back, then lifted her up and carried her inside. It was the same way he'd done the night of the wedding, except this time she was completely sober and there was a new fervor to the way they kissed, as if they were both trying to say things with their bodies and emotions that they didn't know how or couldn't put into words.

They could barely keep their hands, or their mouths, off each other as their clothes disappeared and they tumbled into Carley's bed. She yearned for him with a hunger she couldn't remember ever feeling for another man. Her body ached with need and impatience as he fumbled with the foil packet and covered himself, then she couldn't hold back the satisfied moan as he finally sank into her. He felt so good, so right.

They fell into a rhythm, slower as he lowered his head to taste her skin, to stroke and caress her breasts, then faster as he clutched her to him, holding her body tightly against his in an embrace that was both tender and possessive.

She may not trust him with her heart, but she gave him her body to do with as he pleased, and it almost broke her the way he alternately cherished it as if it were a treasure, then ravaged it with an insatiable hunger.

When they were done, she lay spent and shattered, her body limp, her arms thrown out across the bed. Untangling his legs from hers, he lay down next to her and pulled her body against his, nestling her head in the crook of his neck.

The top sheets lay in a jumbled mess, hanging halfway off the bed, and he reached for the edge of it and pulled it across their bodies.

She let out a contented sigh, snuggling in closer to him, basking in the afterglow and relishing the gentle affectionate circles he drew on her shoulder with the pads of his fingers.

They didn't speak, didn't seem to have to. And she didn't know what she would say anyway. Maybe if they didn't talk, she could pretend this was her real life. That Knox was truly her fiancé and that they were in love and going to get married. She could pretend that this was a life she could have. And hold onto.

So content, she'd almost drifted off to sleep when the sound of a truck engine coming down the driveway came through the open window of her room. She groaned against Knox's shoulder. "This place is busier than Grand Central Station. How's a person supposed to enjoy their after-amazing-sex nap when people keep showing up at their house?"

She felt the rumble of his laughter against her chest. "I can fix this," he told her, lifting her arm and slipping out of bed. "Stay here. I'll see who it is and get rid of them before you can even start to snore."

"I don't snore," she said, laughing as she tossed his pillow after him. "I told you that was the dog."

She tried to close her eyes and fall back into sleep but couldn't resist the temptation of watching him get dressed. His body was long and lean and tan in all the right places. She imagined him shirtless and riding his horse across an

open field—something she was sure he would never do—
but hey, they were her hot cowboy fantasies so she could
imagine him any way she liked. And right now, all she'd like
was to have those muscular arms he was pushing through the
sleeves of his T-shirt back in this bed and around her.

"Be right back," he said, shoving his feet into his boots
and hurrying out the door.

She heard the screen door slam then seconds later, the
cat sauntered in and jumped up on the bed, curling up in
the warm spot Knox had left behind. Carley stroked the cat's
back, feeling the hum of her purring under her palm.

And now all she could think about was the way Knox had
just made her purr a few minutes ago by stroking her back.

She heard Knox call out a greeting, then the sound of a
trailer door clanging. Her curiosity got the best of her and
dragging the sheet with her, she slipped out of bed and carefully tiptoed down the hallway to spy out the front windows.
She could see Knox and a man she didn't recognize standing
by a small trailer hooked to the back of a pickup, then she
spotted something else behind Knox and…

Oh my.

She was going to need to get dressed. And fast.

CHAPTER 20

"OH, MY GOSH, THEY'RE ADORABLE," CARLEY SAID A FEW minutes later as she peered into the back of the trailer. It hadn't taken her long to pull on her clothes and slip her feet into a pair of sandals. She realized too late that her cheeks were probably still flushed, and her hair was certainly sexmussed, but there was nothing she could do about it now.

And who could think about pillow-head when there were baby goats around. Close to a dozen tiny goats were inside the trailer—she couldn't count how many because they kept hopping over and scampering around each other.

"They might be adorable, but they are noisy as all get out," the man said, sticking out his hand. "I'm Jim Townsend. Good to meet you. I was just telling your husband here that my wife got a little carried away the last time she went to auction, and she came home with a baker's dozen of baby pygmy goats."

Why did everyone assume she and Knox were married? Did they give off a *couple* vibe? Or was the state of her hair and cheeks more obvious than she thought?

"I can see why," Carley said, marveling at the sight of the endearing little creatures. Most of them weren't much bigger than a house cat. "They're so cute. They'd be hard to resist."

"They might be cute now 'cuz they're just kids," the man said. "These are all around three or four months old. But once they get older, they turn into little fat eating machines that escape their pens and bleat until you pay attention to them. And more than a dozen goats are just too many to try to constantly pay attention to. My wife is beside herself, but even she had to admit, after keeping them for a few weeks, that thirteen is just too many. We differed on how many we could reasonably keep. I said two, but I was overruled, and I've still got five of the little buggers scampering around my place."

The baby goats were a multitude of colors, black, white, brown, tan, gray. There was one that was pure white and one that was all black with just a small white patch on his head and thin white socks, but most were a mixture of colors. The smallest one was light gray and white, and it came running over to nuzzle her palm when Carley put her hand down into the trailer.

"That one's the runt," Jim said, pointing to the adorable tiny goat who was now trying to climb out of the trailer to get to Carley. "My wife only paid for twelve goats, but because she's so small, they threw her in for free. They're all sweet and affectionate and get along like great friends, but she's the most loving and cuddly."

"I've never thought of goats as cuddly or affectionate," Carley said, thinking most of her goat knowledge was from the cantankerous Otis. And no one would want to cuddle him.

"Oh yeah, that one will crawl right into your lap and

fall asleep, like a puppy does. In fact, they share a lot of the same characteristics of puppies. They're playful, they sleep a lot, they can learn tricks, and my wife has even been potty-training them not to go in the house."

"You're kidding," Carley said. "I didn't even know that was possible."

"Oh yeah. These guys spend the majority of the day penned off in our kitchen, and I don't think we've had an accident inside with any of them in weeks."

"They are cute. I'll give you that," Knox said. "But we're a horse rescue ranch. I'm not sure we can take on this many goats. Or if we're even authorized to take on any at all."

"But we can call the owner and ask her," Carley said, jumping in.

"I'd sure appreciate it if you would. I'm at my wit's end with this bunch, and I drove all this way to bring 'em here because I heard you all were so good at finding homes for animals in need. And believe me, these animals *need* new homes. I can't bring them back with me."

"Give me just a minute," Carley said, then stepped away to try to call Bryn. Knox followed her over and stood beside her as she listened to several rings, then Bryn's voicemail picked up. "No answer," she told Knox. "But before she left, she told me that if we had any rescues come in, just to find a place for them in the barn and she'd figure out what to do with them later."

He shrugged. "Okay. It's your call." A grin tugged at his lips. "But it sounds to me like we're taking on a whole bunch of baby goats."

"Yeah, I think we are." They walked back to Jim. "We'll need to get some information from you, have you fill out a few forms, but we'll take them off your hands."

Jim's shoulders sagged with relief. "Oh, thank goodness. You have no idea how happy that makes me. And it will make my wife happy, too, once I tell her what a nice couple you are and how much you like the goats. These kids are great with human kids too. You two got kids of your own?"

"Nope," Knox said, and Carley noticed that not only did he not even try to correct him, he seemed to be enjoying the man's mistake. He even had the nerve to wink at her. "Not *yet* anyway."

Before Carley had a chance to correct him, Jim opened the door of the trailer and the young goats all tumbled out. They scampered in all directions, racing and bouncing around like little baby Tiggers.

"Don't worry," Jim said. "They'll all come running back as soon as I shake a can of food at them." He picked up a coffee can full of grain and shook it, and he was right. The goats all came darting back to him. "Where do you want them?"

"I guess we should put them in a couple of stalls in the barn," Carley said, leading the way. "Will two horse stalls be enough space for them? Or should we split them up into more?"

"No, that's good. I'd say you might want to put them all in the same one for the next few nights since they're in a new place. Like I said, they're all good friends and they get along real well. Plus, they're still babies so they like to sleep in big piles, and they'll stay warmer in a smaller space. As they get bigger, they'll need more room though."

As she helped Knox to spread fresh straw into a stall on the other side of the barn from the horses, Carley hoped they wouldn't be here long enough to get too much bigger. She got Jim's information and had him fill out Bryn's forms while Knox set the kids up with water and a trough of hay.

Twenty minutes later, after a relieved Jim had driven away, she and Knox sat side by side on the floor of the stall while the baby goats climbed over and around them and nuzzled into their chests. The little gray-and-white girl kid had curled in Carley's lap and had her head resting on Carley's thigh. Every few minutes, she'd let out a contented sigh as Carley scratched her adorable little ears. "Oh, gosh," she said, looking over at Knox. "I just realized we never asked Jim their names."

"Maybe they don't have any."

"They have to have names," she said. "But how are we going to come up with names for eight goats?"

Knox thought for a minute then asked, "Can you think of any groups, like rock bands or pop groups that have around eight people in them? There aren't enough Beatles names to go around, and it looks like there's four girls and four boys, so the members of NSYNC are out too."

"NSYNC? Are you serious? That's your go-to for a rock band?"

"What? They were really popular when I was a kid. I may have even had a hamster named Joey after Joey Fatone." He nudged her shoulder. "Come on. Don't tell me you didn't have a crush on at least one of the Backstreet Boys or the members of NSYNC?"

She shrugged. "Okay, I admit it. I did. And if it makes you feel better, I *still* have a crush on Justin Timberlake."

"I knew it."

"Okay, can we get back to the business at hand, now?"

"Yes, okay. So, no boy bands. What about characters from a television show? He did say they were all good friends."

"I like that," she said, looking around at the goats. "Let's name them after Friends. Those two gray and white girls who seem inseparable can be Monica and Rachel. And those three boys all have black fur on them somewhere, so they can be Ross, Joey, and Chandler. That whitish-tan one with the little tuft of hair on his forehead can be Gunther. And this little sweetheart in my lap can be Phoebe."

"Great. What about that last one? The brown and white one who won't stop bleating at the top of her little goat lungs?"

They looked at each other and spoke at the same time. "Janice," they both said, then busted out laughing.

They spent another thirty minutes playing with the goats, then finally decided to call it a night. As they walked back to the bunkhouse, Carley's anxiety ramped up over whether or not she should ask Knox to come in to talk or just invite him in for a sleepover. But he took the decision from her hands by saying he still had some chores to do and giving her a quick goodnight kiss before telling her goodnight.

She wasn't sure if she was relieved or disappointed as she cleaned up the supper dishes, then brushed her teeth and washed her face and changed into a pair of sleep shorts and a tank top. She'd just turned out the light in her bedroom when she heard a soft knock on her door.

Unable to help the smile that snuck across her face, she hurried to the door, her stomach already fluttering and her body stirring with arousal.

But when she opened the door, it wasn't Knox standing there.

CHAPTER 21

"WHAT ARE YOU DOING HERE?" CARLEY ASKED, LEANING down to pick up the tiny gray-and-white goat. Phoebe let out a bleat, then nuzzled into her shoulder. Carley cuddled her to her chest as she looked around outside, but the barn was dark and so was Knox's side of the bunkhouse. "You little escape artist. How did you get out of the stall? And the barn?"

The little goat bleated again, and Carley couldn't help herself. She was just so darn cute. She had to bring her into the house and cuddle with her for a bit on the sofa. After several yawns, she laid down on the couch and covered herself with the throw blanket, and the baby goat curled in a ball against Carley's stomach and zonked out. She figured she'd wait up in the living room for a little bit to see if Knox did decide to come over.

———

Carley blinked awake the next morning, squinting at the sunlight coming in through the front window of the bunkhouse. Ugh. She'd fallen asleep and slept all night on the couch. With a goat.

Not the ideal image of the night she'd hoped to have.

Phoebe squirmed and made cute little noises as she woke up, her tiny face looking so adorable as she yawned and peered sweetly up at Carley. She let out a small bleat that had to be goat talk for "good morning."

So maybe waking up with this goat wasn't so bad. Carley yawned and stretched, her back sore from sleeping on the sofa as she opened the front door to let the goat outside. Phoebe ran out to the lawn, did her business, and then bounced back up the stairs and into the bunkhouse. Nala, the cat, snuck in behind her.

How had her life turned into this? Living on a ranch, sleeping with a hot cowboy, and having a goat and a cat as pets. On second thought, maybe her life didn't seem so bad.

Knox's side of the bunkhouse was still dark, but she heard a yip and a moo come from inside, so she figured he'd be up soon. She was tempted to just let his animals outside but wasn't confident enough in her calf-roping skills to be able to handle if either the dog or the baby cow ran off.

In the shower, she mused over the night before, feeling a little stumped as to why Knox hadn't come over after he'd finished the chores. They hadn't made a plan for him to, and he hadn't been sleeping over, but after his "you can trust me" declaration and the amazing sex they'd had, she'd just assumed that he'd be knocking at her door hoping for Round Two.

Maybe the sex *hadn't* been that amazing. Or maybe he'd just said all that trust stuff to get what he needed and wasn't interested in her anymore. She sagged against the side of the shower, the tile cold against her shoulder, crippled with self-doubt as bubbles of shampoo slid down her neck.

Stop it! Stop doing this to yourself.

She took a deep shuddering breath, stood up tall and pushed back her shoulders.

I am worthy.

She repeated the mantra as she smoothed in condi-tioner and shaved her legs and by the time she was out of the shower, she'd talked herself down off the ledge. Just because Knox hadn't come over the night before didn't mean he wasn't interested in her anymore. Maybe he'd had a long day and was exhausted or maybe he was on call. She hadn't thought to ask him.

Stop borrowing trouble. Instead of worrying and fret-ting, she'd decided to take the proverbial bull by the horns, or in this case, the cowboy by the boots, and go to him instead of fretting and waiting around for him to knock on her door.

She had a can of cinnamon rolls in the fridge and popped them in the oven while she finished getting ready, all under the watchful eye of Nala and Phoebe, who had already become fast friends and were curled up in a corner of the sofa together. Dressed in jeans, sandals, and a light-pink Henley, she'd left her hair down and curled it in big soft waves. Swiping on a little lip gloss, she felt pretty good about herself as she grabbed a hot pad and picked up the pan of warm cinnamon rolls. Knox was always bringing her little things. He was going to love this.

She pushed out the door then froze, the smile falling

from her face as nausea swirled through her belly. A snake was in the chair on the front porch.

A five-foot-ten snake wearing a black cowboy hat and a smug smile. "Mornin' sweetie pie," the snake said. "Those cinnamon rolls sure smell good. Did you bake those for me?"

"No, of course not," she said, pulling the pan closer to her chest. "What are you doing here, Paul?"

"You haven't been answering my texts, so I just came by to see how you're doing. Say hello."

More likely he'd heard she and Autumn had run into the developer and he was here doing damage control. "Hello," she said. "Now goodbye."

He had the audacity to look hurt. "Come on now. Is that any way to treat an old friend?"

"I don't know. I'll let you know when I run into one." She scanned the farmyard and was more disappointed than she wanted to admit to see Knox's truck was already gone. And he'd taken the animals too. There was no way she wouldn't have heard Sadie barking at Paul if she was still inside the bunkhouse. And Knox had usually texted her by now. Just to say good morning.

Although he hadn't texted her to say good night the night before either. The self-doubt started to creep back in like the thin tendrils of bindweed that snaked through a garden choking out all the flowers with their clingy vines.

It didn't help that a real snake was sitting here looking at her with a mixture of pity and disgust. "Oh, sorry, your boyfriend left already. I saw him tearing out of here as I was coming in. Sort of like he couldn't get away from you…or here…maybe, fast enough. Didn't he tell you he was leaving?" He tsked. "And after you went to all that trouble to make him those nice cinnamon rolls."

"Shut up, Paul."

He reached out a hand, ignoring her comment. "I'm here, though. And those rolls smell mighty good. I'll take one."

She took a step back, her knuckles going white as she clutched the pan as if her life depended on it. Maybe not her life, but her sanity at least. "No. These aren't for you. I wouldn't give you a roll if you offered me a million dollars for it. But you don't have a million dollars, do you? Not yet, at least. Is that why you're trying to swindle our building out from under me and Evelyn? Are you broke? Again?"

A flash of something, annoyance, fury, crossed his expression, then he pasted his fake smile back in place. "Of course not. And selling that building is just good business sense."

"Good for *you.*"

"Good for you too. We'd share some of the profits of the sale with you. And what do you need that old musty building for anyway? Seems to me you're doing great running your little business from out here."

"*Little business?* Damn, Paul. Why does everything that comes out of your mouth have to be something that demeans me?"

"I'm not trying to make you feel bad. I'm trying to help you. I know that business sense wasn't always your strong suit."

"I've been running my business on my own for the last five years, and I'll have you know, it's very successful."

His ears perked up. "How successful?"

"None of your business."

"Actually, sweetie pie, it *is* my business. You share that building with *my* grandmother, and I stand to inherit it someday. But we've been having some real serious talks lately about me taking it over, so it sounds like you and me are about to be partners again. And I have lots of ideas of how to show you what real success is. So why don't we just play nice and try to get along?"

"Why don't you shove it?"

His brow furrowed, as if she'd finally broken through his fakey-nice facade. "Don't test me, Carley. We can do this the easy way, or I'm just as happy to do it the hard way. And the hard way would mean throwing you out on your ass. I don't need your permission—I can do anything I want with that building. And there's nothing you can do to stop me."

Her eyes flicked to Knox's door.

"And don't think Deputy Dog is going to be able to stop me either," he said. "Not like he would. He's not even here." He huffed out a scornful laugh. "Seems to me like he got what he wanted, then he took off. Like I said, he was going pretty fast when I saw him leave. Like he couldn't get away from you fast enough."

He'd already said that. But it seemed like his repeated words were like the hammer pounding in more painful nails of her insecurities.

Was that really why Knox had left this morning without even saying goodbye or sending a single text since they'd slept together? Had he gotten what he wanted, then just taken off?

A loud ruckus from the barn had her turning her head to see the baby goats had escaped their stall and were bleating and bouncing around as they raced toward her, Otis leading the charge. Her heart twisted as something told her the ornery goat may have been the mastermind behind the kids' escape.

"What the hell are those?" Paul said, cowering back as the goats scrambled up the stairs toward them. Two of them scaled up the side of Paul's chair while two more tried to climb into his lap. "Get them off me," he said, kicking out his legs.

"Be careful," Carley yelled. "Don't you dare hurt them. They're babies."

"They're menaces," he said, shoving his elbows at Gunther, who was sticking his furry white tufted head into Paul's jacket pocket. He came out with a crumpled piece of paper in his teeth and then jumped off the chair and bounced toward Carley, dropping the paper in front of her like it was a prized offering.

She'd been going to ignore the paper—it looked like a wadded-up piece of trash—if it weren't for Paul's reaction.

"Give that back," he shouted. "That's mine."

She snatched the paper from the ground, shaking it open, and spied her name at the top of the page. "No, it's not. It's *mine*. It's got *my* name on it."

"Get off me, you stupid things," Paul scolded the kids as he tried to get out of the chair and make a grab for the crumpled page.

But Carley was quicker. She'd recognized Knox's handwriting. Setting the rolls on the table, she smoothed the paper open and realized it was a note to her. From Knox. And from this morning. "Good morning, Carley. Sorry I had to rush out this morning without saying goodbye—got called into the station and needed to run Sadie and Rodney home before going in. Can't stop thinking about you and how amazing last night was. Supper's on me tonight. I'll bring something home." He'd signed it, "Your future husband, Knox."

Tears threatened her eyes. He hadn't ignored her or ghosted her or left without saying goodbye. She must have been in the shower or getting ready when he'd left this. He might have even tried to knock.

She blinked back the tears, her sentimental feelings replaced with anger as she shook the note at Paul. "You are such an asshole! You had no right to take this. You can spout nonsense all day about wanting to help me, but it's all a bunch of garbage. The only person you've ever wanted to help was yourself. You haven't changed a bit."

Paul sneered, all pretense of his Mr. Nice Guy routine gone. "Oh, and you think this guy does? Just because you're sleeping with him, you think that means he cares about you?"

"What is wrong with you? It's like you get off on hurting me. I finally found a guy who I can trust, who doesn't constantly make me feel bad about myself, and you have to try to pour poison on our relationship."

"Relationship? What relationship? This sham of an engagement? You already gave him the goods. There's no reason for him to stick around now." He glared at her, as if the fire in his eyes could burn her even more than his hateful words. "I've got news for you, honey. Men are all the same, and we only care about one thing. You're just a piece of ass. And not that fine of one either. We can always find another piece that's willing and a lot less trouble."

"Get off my porch," she told him, trying to control the tremor in her voice. Her whole body was shaking with rage and terror that what he was saying might be true. "Leave. Now."

Paul took a step closer. "Who's gonna make me?"

Instead of backing down, she took a step toward him. He was a liar. She knew that. Knox had told her she could trust him. And she believed him. He hadn't left her. He'd written her a note. And this asswipe had tried to hide it from her. And make her feel like dirt about herself. Again.

Well, not this time, buddy.

She pushed back her shoulders and stared directly into Paul's beady little eyes. "Me. And Knox. I can have you arrested for trespassing. Like you said, I'm sleeping with the police. And he's *not* running away and looking for another willing piece. He's coming *home* tonight to *me*. So, I guess that means I'm a finer piece of ass than you give me credit for. Although you'll never, EVER, have the pleasure of experiencing it again. Now get the hell off my porch, off this property, and don't come back again."

For the first time, Paul's ridiculously arrogant demeanor seemed to be shaken, as he took a step away. She'd seen it, a shadow of doubt that crossed his face, his cocky mask slipping just a little before snapping back into place. But his fun-loving character was gone, replaced by the guy she remembered being married to. The one who slung hate and cruelty in every word he spat. "You think you matter, little girl? You don't. Not to me. Not to your pathetic little deputy watchdog. Not to anyone. You're not worth the shit on the bottom of my shoe."

He turned and hurried toward his vehicle, slamming the car door and spraying dirt as he peeled out and sped away.

Carley sank onto the table, not even caring that during their argument, Otis had snatched the pan of cinnamon rolls and taken off with it.

I did it. I stood up to Paul.

And he'd backed down.

She *did* matter. And she *was* worth the shit on the bottom of his shoe.

She was worthy. Of being loved and cared about by a good man. A man like Knox Garrison.

Later that afternoon, the bunkhouse was crowded and ringing with laughter as Carley finished working on her last client of the day. Phoebe had been the hit of the day, loving all the attention as she was passed around and cuddled.

Besides the woman in her chair, four of her regulars, Lyda, Aunt Sassy, Barb, and Nancy, had either stopped in or stuck around to chat after she'd done their hair. But they all stopped speaking when Knox showed up, a large vase of gorgeous wildflowers in his hands.

"Now that's a beautiful bouquet of flowers," Lyda

Hightower said loudly, then muttered, "Not like that measly thing that weasel brought in here last week."

Carley had been thinking the same thing. "What are these for?" she asked, taking the vase when he held it out to her and setting it on the kitchen counter.

"They're for you," Knox said.

"I didn't ask *who*, I asked *what* are they for?" Had he done something wrong that he was trying to get out of the dog-house for? "Are you trying to distract me from something bad you're about to tell me?"

He frowned. "No. Not at all. I've just been smiling all day from thinking about you, and I wanted to make you smile too. But you don't seem to be smiling." He lowered his voice. "Don't you like the flowers?"

She blinked up at him. "I love them. I'm just not used to someone doing something so lavish...and nice for me..."

He nodded. "Without there being strings attached?"

"Would you stop reading my mind," she said, but then couldn't help the smile that stole across her face as she looked down at the beautiful display of white and pink roses interspersed with greenery and a mix of purple statice, blue cornflowers, periwinkle stalks of delphiniums, delicate white daisies, and dainty petite sweet peas. "They really are perfect. I love the mix of colors and the blend of roses and wildflowers."

"That's the part that reminded me of you. That mix of styles."

"Yeah? You mean like a little bit country, a little bit rock and roll?"

He softened his tone. "Yeah, that. But I was thinking

more like stunning elegance yet still a little on the untamed wild and reckless side."

She smiled up at him, blinking back tears for the second time that day. "Well, Deputy Garrison, that's just about the nicest thing anyone's said to me in a long time."

"Then I need to be saying nice things more often," he said, pulling her into a hug and pressing a quick kiss to her lips.

"Hmm-hmm." The sound of a throat clearing had them pulling apart, and Carley could feel the heat rising to her cheeks as she turned back to the women in the salon.

"You know we can all see you," Lyda, the throat-clearer, declared.

"But we can't hear you that well," Aunt Sassy said. "So could you speak up?"

Carley and Knox laughed as they split apart. "I should probably finish my customer's hair," Carley told him.

"Mind if I stick around a few minutes? I had a couple of ideas I wanted to run by you."

"Sure," she said. "Have a seat."

Lyda patted the cushion on the sofa between her and Sassy, who was holding Phoebe on her lap, but he took a seat closer to the stylist chair while Carley returned to her client. She'd already dried her hair, and she'd been just finishing off her style with the flat iron when Knox had come in.

"This will just take me a few minutes," she told Knox. "But I can listen if you want to tell me what you're thinking about." *They were all listening,* she thought, noting how Lyda, Aunt Sassy, Barb, and Nancy were all leaning slightly forward so as not to miss a thing.

"Okay, sure," he said, also clearly aware of the women listening in. "So, you know how I'm always trying to fix stuff…"

"Who? You? The owner of sixty-four boxes of bartered Twinkies snack cakes? No, I hadn't noticed."

"Very funny. Do you want to hear this or not? Because I think I've come up with a semi-brilliant solution."

CHAPTER 22

CARLEY LOOKED OVER HER CLIENT'S HEAD AT KNOX AS she pulled the flat iron through a section of the woman's hair. "A semi-brilliant solution to what?"

"To the issue you were talking about last night." He lowered his voice. "About how you need to raise some quick cash to cover the deductible for you and Autumn and the building."

"It's okay," she told him. "They all know about it. We've been brainstorming some ideas today too. Although we haven't come up with much."

"Hey," Aunt Sassy interjected. "I thought my spiked lemonade stand at least got an honorable mention."

Knox chuckled. "I'd vote for that."

"You and Sassy would be the only ones then," Carley said. "So, what's your idea?"

"I was thinking about your problem and also thinking about our newly acquired multitude of baby goats, and I had this epiphany of how we could mash them together."

"An epiphany? About making quick cash using baby goats? I'm a little bit scared to ask what you came up with."

He frowned. "It's nothing weird. I'm not a monster. I was thinking about you offering one of those spa day things that women love to go to, but to have it out here at the ranch and incorporate the animals into it."

"You had me until you mixed in the animals. So, I'm not following—like you want to have the goats offer manicures?"

"No. You can offer manicures or blow-ups or whatever you call them and those things where you stick green goo on your faces, but the animals would be there, like the people attending the spa day could hold the baby goats and pet Nala while they're getting their hair done. And I could bring Sadie and Rodney too."

"So, it's like a spa day mixed with a petting zoo?" Aunt Sassy asked then shrugged. "I'm in for that."

"Yeah, I guess," he said. "And I'd be willing to help too, like I could offer five-minute foot rubs or shoulder massages or something."

"*I'm* in for that," Lyda piped in. "Put me down for two of those."

Carley chewed on her bottom lip. "You know, that does sound kind of fun. And it wouldn't cost that much to pull it off. Mainly more time than money."

"And it would be a really unique experience," Barb said. "So you could market it as something really upscale and charge more for it."

"If you made it smaller, like a more intimate group of ten or twelve people," Nancy said. "Then split it into two sessions, a morning and an afternoon, you could charge a hundred dollars a person and clear a few thousand dollars in one day."

"Although, you'd want to only charge ninety-nine, then

folks think they're getting a deal because it's less than a hundred dollars," Barb explained.

"But would people really pay a hundred dollars, or ninety-nine, for this?" Carley asked, feeling doubtful.

"For a few hours of pampering, a chance to get to hold a baby goat, help out our friend, *and* get a foot rub from a hot cowboy," Lyda said. "Sign me up. I'd pay a hundred dollars for that."

"I would too," Aunt Sassy agreed.

"There ya go," Knox said, slapping his knee. "Two down, eighteen to go."

"Okay," Carley said. "Then I'm in too."

"Awesome. And that's only half of my brilliant idea."

"I thought you said it was only semi-brilliant."

"In light of the favorable response to the first half of my plan, I'm upgrading the second-half to pure genius."

Carley chuckled and finished the client's hair by spritzing it with sheen, then giving it a quick misting of hair spray. "Okay, lay it on me."

"I think we should get Autumn to come out here and teach one of those goat-yoga classes that are all the rage right now."

Carley set down the hair spray and turned to him. "Ya know, Knox, that is pure genius. I love that idea. I just hope Autumn will go for it."

"She'll love it. It's all natural."

"What the heck is goat-yoga?" Aunt Sassy asked. "That's not some new-fangled slang for sexy times, is it?"

"No," Carley told her with a laugh. "It's just a regular yoga class, but they let baby goats climb all over the class partici-pants while they do yoga."

"That sounds kind of fun," Lyda said. "Sign me up for that too. Will Knox be leading a class?" She batted her eyes at the deputy.

"Not a chance," was all Knox had to say.

"I think I'll sit that one out," Aunt Sassy said. "That just sounds dumb to me. What if the goat poops on you while it's walking all over you?"

"Eww," Carley said, wrinkling her nose. "But that's Autumn's problem, not mine." She turned back to Knox. "And speaking of problems, these are both great ideas, but they need planning and time to get people signed up and figure out schedules and food, and we need money fast."

"That's not a problem," Lyda said. "Just make your event one of those pop-up deals. My granddaughter does that all the time. And so does my husband's social media manager. You just put the event up on Facebook or Twitter or what-ever and advertise it as a pop-up event with limited avail-ability. People jump at that kind of stuff because they love feeling spontaneous and like they're getting in on a deal that beats out other people."

"Okay," Carley said. "What the heck. Let's do it."

─────────

"I called Autumn, and she loved your ideas," Carley told Knox that night as they finished eating supper. They were sitting in their favorite spot next to each other in the glider on the porch. Phoebe had escaped the barn again and was nestled in the seat next to Carley's outside leg.

"Which ones?" Knox asked.

"All of them. She even wants to help out with the barn spa / petting zoo day. Although we've really got to come up with a better name for it than that."

"Nice. And I'm pumped that everyone likes my ideas."

"You should be," Carley said, collecting their plates and carrying them into the kitchen. "Because Aunt Sassy's backup plan to her spiked lemonade stand was to hold a ladies' night down at the Creed and have you show off your skills from when you used to be a stripper."

He choked on the sip of iced tea he'd been taking as he, the small goat, and the cat followed her in. "My what?"

Carley put the dishes in the sink, then turned back to him and pressed her lips together to keep from laughing. "I can neither confirm nor deny that there may or may not be a rumor going around that you used to be a stripper."

"You're kidding?"

"Nope."

"Oh, geez. I hope the guys down at the station don't hear that one. I'll never hear the end of it."

"I don't know," she said, offering him a coy grin. "I think you'd make a great stripper. At least you did in the dream I had about you the night of the wedding when that barrel-racer mistook you for one."

"You had a dream about me?" His lips curved into a cocky grin as he leaned a hip against the counter next to her. "Were you a stripper too?"

She nudged him in the rib. "No. Just you."

"Would you like to practice being a stripper now? You don't even need the pole, or the music, or have to dance."

"So, basically you just want me to get naked?"

"That's the general idea, yes." He raised one eyebrow. "You up for the challenge?"

She lifted one shoulder in what she hoped looked like a casual shrug, when her inner minx was jumping around as much as those goats had and already screaming "yes, yes, yes."

"I'm in if you are," she said.

"Oh, I'm in," he said, dropping his cowboy hat on the counter, then pulling his T-shirt off and tossing it across the room. "I'll race you to the bedroom and to see who can get their clothes off first."

"No fair," she said, dropping the dish towel she'd been drying her hands on and pulling her shirt over her head. "You got a head start."

He'd already toed off his boots and was halfway down the hall and shucking his jeans. He turned back to her, a vision of hard muscle in black boxer briefs, his cute grin and tousled hair sending her heart into a tailspin. "You're right. I may have had a few seconds lead, so I'll give you five seconds to catch up. But you'd better get those jeans off quick."

She shrieked with laughter as she sped to tug her jeans down and kick off her sandals at the same time.

"Two one thousand, three one thousand..." he counted slowly, still grinning as he leaned his shoulder against the wall in the hallway. "All I've got is my underwear left," he taunted, tugging the waistband of his briefs down an inch and giving her a view of his lean waist that had her wanting to jump him right there. "You'd better go faster if you want to—" his next words were interrupted as he caught the lacy black bra she'd just tossed at him.

She was laughing, unable to believe she was practically naked in the hallway racing him to see who could strip first and having so much fun as she did it.

She'd just slipped her thumbs under the elastic of the matching lacy thong panties and was starting to slide them down when Knox held up his hand and called out, "Wait."

She froze, the laughter on her lips dying.

But his smile changed from one of amusement to a wolfish grin. "I'll concede right now if you stop racing and take those off *real slow*."

Oh my.

Every nerve cell in her body tingled with anticipation as she slowly walked toward him wearing only her panties and a seductive smile. She could practically feel the heat of his gaze as it roamed over her nearly naked body. Taking a few steps past him, she stopped and wiggled her hips, then bent forward and slowly drew the panties down her legs and let them drop to the floor.

She heard him let out a groan and smiled as she looked over her shoulder at him. "You know, Cowboy, I think we're both about to be winners in this race."

"I think you're right," he said, following her into the bedroom and closing the door.

Yee-haw.

Carley had the next day off, and she spent the morning work-ing on the details and plans for the Beauty in the Barn event. They'd thrown around some other name ideas like Goats & Glamour, Paw Spa, Charm on the Farm, and Down-Home Western Spa Day, but decided to settle on something simple. She could use all the cute stuff in the description.

There were a lot of details to think through, but she loved planning things like this and within a few hours, she had a solid strategy for the day. All her ideas revolved around the theme of the barn, animals, and being in the country, like honeysuckle deep conditioning hair treatments, oat scrubs with watermelon facial masks, and *paws*itively pleasing par-affin hand remedies.

Everything had to be planned with an eye for offering value and a unique experience while still making the highest amount of profit. There were plenty of things she could do herself, like make some of the treatments, and she planned to keep the food to small snacks and lemon water versus offering an entire meal spread. She was getting really excited about it and hoped it worked as well as they thought it would.

Knox had left Sadie and Rodney at home, and he had an early report this morning, so he'd gone back to his ranch to sleep the night before. He said he'd be by late morning today, though, to take care of the chores at the rescue ranch.

She heard the sound of an engine and went out to the porch, assuming it was him, but was surprised to see Autumn instead. The yoga instructor waved, then opened the hatch-back of her Subaru and started pulling out boxes. "Come help me," she called. "We've only got two hours to set up before everyone starts arriving."

Everyone?

"Arriving for what?" she said as Autumn placed a box of yoga mats in her arms.

"The goat yoga class," Autumn said, turning to survey the farmyard. "Where should we set up? Do you think we should do it outside in the grass or is there enough room in the barn? I've had fifteen RSVPs already, but I imagine we'll have a few more that just drop in this afternoon."

"This afternoon? How do you expect to teach a class this afternoon? We don't even know how this works yet. We need to organize and come up with a proposal and a plan."

Autumn shook her head. "No, we don't. I spent half the night researching this, and I called a guy I know who does a class like this in Denver and asked him for some pointers. I used your idea of a pop-up class and posted one this morning. In the post, I told people to wear clothes they didn't mind getting dirty, to secure their hair, and that I'd bring extra yoga mats if they didn't want to use theirs. I made it sound super back-to-nature, so they'll expect it to be a little rough. I posted it around eight-thirty this morning and said we're offering two sessions with only fifteen spots available in each, and I had ten people sign up in the first half hour. And another five in the half hour after that."

"That's amazing. But still, don't you think we need to think this through or do a practice run or something?"

"No. That's half the fun of the class—it's spontaneous. And with live animals, every class will be different and none of us can plan what a bunch of baby goats will do anyway." She rested her hand on Carley's arm. "Listen, the truth is, I can't really afford to wait and make a plan. My studio's been shut down for a week already, and every day I'm losing income. You've been able to keep working by moving the salon out here, but I've just had to cancel most of my classes. I need these sessions today to help pay my rent."

Carley nodded. She knew full well what it felt like to have one day's work make or break her month, and Autumn had lost an entire week. "Okay, I get it. What can I do to help?"

"I'll need you during the class to wrangle the goats and keep them around the participants."

"How in the heck am I supposed to that? I mean, these little guys are super affectionate and love people, but I'm not sure I can get them to cooperate on a whim."

"Don't worry. I have a secret weapon." She pulled out a plastic bag and shook it. "Goat treats. I picked them up at the feed store this morning. The guy I talked to said he sprinkles these little goat treats around the participants and on their backs and then the goats just climb all over them. I guess it's just hysterical."

"It won't be hysterical if one of them poops or pees on someone."

Autumn grinned. "On the contrary, that *would* be hysterical. But apparently, they don't really pee on people and on the rare occasion that they do poop, I guess it's just like little pellets and you just scoop them up and whisk them away."

"And I suppose that's my job? I'm the pooper-scooper?"

Autumn planted a hand on her hip. "Do you know how to teach yoga?"

"No, I don't even know how to *do* yoga."

"Then I guess you're the pooper-scooper. And you really need to learn to do some yoga. It will help with your stress."

"Who said I was stressed?"

Autumn raised an eyebrow but didn't say anything.

"Oh, whatever," Carley said. "Let's go set up in the barn."

"Yes, I can't wait to meet these cuties."

"You're going to die. They're adorable."

———

Two hours later, they had everything in place and had done a couple of dry runs with Autumn and Carley doing poses on the mats while the baby goats scrambled up and over the top of them. They'd saved the treats for when they had actual class participants, but even without the food incentives, the goats just loved climbing over and around them.

Carley had called Knox and filled him in, and he'd shown up a few minutes earlier with an offer to help park cars and help wrangle the goats during the sessions. It didn't take long for the ranch's driveway to fill with cars, and then several women and a few men filed into the barn amidst excited and nervous chatter.

Carley recognized some of her friends, Nora Fisher, and Chloe, Tessa, and Quinn, but she was surprised to see Lyda, Evelyn, and Aunt Sassy carrying yoga mats into the barn.

"I can't believe you three are going to do this class," she told them as she showed them where to set up their mats.

"Are you kidding?" Aunt Sassy. "We wouldn't miss it. This is going to be a hoot."

An expensive hoot. Autumn had set the price of the class at forty-five dollars and had also put a tip jar by the door.

Everyone had followed Autumn's instructions and come wearing long sleeves and most of the women had their hair pulled up. They kept the goats in the horse stall until Autumn had time to prepare the participants and explain how the class would work. She would call out and demonstrate the poses while the goats clamored over and around them. She gave them all the choice if they wanted the treats sprinkled beside them or on their backs, and everyone chose the latter.

Chuckling with laughter, Knox and Carley walked through the yoga mats, sprinkling goat treats along their mats and in the dips of their backs and shoulders. Then with a flourish, they opened the stall door and the goats raced out, bleating and ma-a-ahing, as they scrambled over the class participants in a frenzy for affection and food.

The class shrieked and hooted with laughter as Autumn tried to yell the poses over the sounds of the excited goats. Everyone was having a great time and loving the baby goats, and Carley started to think the class was a total success.

Then, without warning, her worst fear came true.

CHAPTER 23

CARLEY SAW IT START AND THERE WASN'T A DANG THING she could do about it. But why did the mayor's wife have to be the first one that a goat decided to poop on?

The tiny round turds hit Lyda's back then rolled off onto her mat.

"Oh shit," she yelled, breaking her low cobra pose and shaking her fanny.

"Exactly," Evelyn said, cracking up as she pointed to the rolling poops.

"Help," Aunt Sassy called. "We've got a *crap*-tastrophe happening over here. Where's the poo-patrol?" She started giggling and laughed so hard, she fell sideways and almost rolled off her mat.

"It's not that funny," Lyda exclaimed, reaching behind her to brush off her back. "Is it still on me? Would somebody get them off me?"

"That is a lot of poop for one tiny goat," Evelyn remarked, scooching her mat further from the rolling pellets.

"Over here," one of the other women yelled. "This one just pooped too."

The woman next to her shrieked louder than Lyda had, startling the goat and causing more poops to pop out.

"Okay, ladies, let's all settle down," Autumn said. "Take a few deep cleansing breaths. This is a natural part of life and nothing to get worked up about. Let's get back into our poses and remember...poop happens."

"And so does pee," Aunt Sassy said, crossing her legs. "And I think I just wet my pants from laughing so hard."

"Help," a woman with a medium-length bob called. "This goat is eating my hair." She swatted at her back where one of the baby goats, it looked like Chandler, was trying to get to the treats on her neck and had gobbled at some of her hair.

Carley looked over at Knox.

"I can fix this," he said, pointing to the woman whose hair was being eaten. "I've got the hair, you take the poop."

"Got it," she said, hurrying first toward Lyda, then to the other woman, with a dustpan and brush. Thankfully, the little poop pellets were easy to sweep up and whisk away and most of the class were taking the incidents in stride, laughing and joking about whether getting pooped on would warrant a discount or cost extra because they got more of the goat experience.

Knox was able to untangle and lift Chandler off the woman's back and placate her with a few soothing words. Carley was sure it helped to have the handsome cowboy be the one to "save" her from the scary baby goat. He offered her one of his most charming grins before tucking the kid under his arm and carrying him to a different spot across the barn. The poor goat was probably just as traumatized as the woman—it was just trying to eat a snack. It wasn't his fault her hair was in the way.

The rest of the class went by without incident, and Carley was relieved to hear the laughter and great comments the class participants were discussing as they rolled up their mats and exited the barn. She was even more excited to see the amount of cash that was dropped into the tip jar on their way out.

"That went pretty well," she told Knox and Autumn after the last participant had driven away.

"Minus a few manure mishaps," Knox said. "I'd have to agree."

"I thought it went great," Autumn said, scooping up Gunther and cuddling the baby goat to her chest. "These guys did awesome and were a huge hit."

"Everyone seemed to love them," Carley agreed as Phoebe bleated and rubbed against her ankles, then put her front hooves up on her legs like a toddler raising their arms to be held. Carley couldn't resist the cutie and picked her up as well. "How could they not?"

"It looks like you all cleaned up," Knox said, shaking the tip jar.

"And with really no overhead, this whole class was pure profit," Autumn said. "With both classes today, I'll bet we'll make close to fifteen hundred dollars. And that's just in one day." They'd already agreed on a reasonable split of the profits with a percentage being donated back to the horse rescue ranch to help with the upkeep of the goats. "Another few classes and we'll be able to cover the deductible *and* my rent. I think we've got a hit on our hands."

Later that night, Knox and Carley sat on the porch together after sharing the leftover baked ziti. He'd gone back to the ranch before supper and taken care of the last of his chores, then brought Sadie and Rodney back with him to spend the night at the bunkhouse. The two animals were curled at their feet, and Phoebe, the baby goat, was stretched out in the glider on one side of Carley's leg.

Her other leg was pressed against Knox's thigh, and she was surprised at how easy and right it felt there. His arm was stretched out across the back of the glider, and she leaned back against him, nestling into his side as he dropped his arm around her shoulders and pulled her close.

"This is nice," he said.

"Yeah, it is," she agreed. "Just you, me, and our dog, cow, and goat hangin' out on the porch."

He chuckled. "I think that sounds like just about a perfect late summer night." His phone buzzed, and he checked the screen, then sat forward with a frown. "Dang. I forgot I've got a meeting in the morning. And I left the folder with all the information I need sitting on my desk at the ranch. I've got to run back out to my house to get it."

"Okay," she said, brushing off the niggling feeling that he was trying to get out of spending time with her. Or that the message he'd just gotten wasn't a notification but was from someone else wanting to see him. *Ugh.* Where did that thought come from? *Stupid Paul.* Even when she'd vowed to put him out of her life, he still had a way of sneaking in and making her feel insecure about anything good that might happen to her.

Knox pushed to his feet. "It shouldn't take but about twenty minutes to run out there and back. You want to keep me company and ride out there with me?"

Her face flushed with warmth. How had she even doubted him? Knox was nothing like Paul. And she was nothing like the woman she'd been when she'd been his wife. She was stronger now, she told herself. And Knox was a good man. "Sure, I'll ride along."

They'd been in the truck less than five minutes when Knox's phone rang. "It's the station," he said, picking up the call. "Deputy Garrison." He listened for a minute or two then said, "No problem. I'll head out there and check it out now."

"What's going on?" Carley asked.

"We got a call about an abandoned farmhouse. Apparently, the renters skipped out last week, and the landlord is out of state. Neighbors said they've heard a dog over there barkin' up a storm the past few nights and called it in. I may need to call the humane society for the dog, but first I just need to go take a look—see what's going on. Are you okay running out there with me? Shouldn't take that long and the farm is only about fifteen minutes from here."

"Yeah, of course. This is kind of exciting. I get to see you at work."

"I wouldn't get your hopes up for anything too exciting."

Fifteen minutes later, they pulled into the driveway of a rundown farm. The house was a small one-story that had seen better days. What looked to be once yellow paint was now faded to a dull beige, and the sagging porch seemed about ready to fall off. An old barn sat next to the house, the wood weathered gray and the barn door hanging askew. The rotted wood fence posts of the adjoining corral were leaning almost sideways and didn't look like they'd held an animal in a while.

As Knox and Carley got out of the truck, a small, mangy mutt squeezed out through the crevice of the barn door and raced toward them. The dog had scruffy brown and black fur and looked like some kind of terrier mix. It came racing full speed toward Knox, but in more of an "I'm so glad to see you" manner than anything aggressive.

Knox bent down to one knee, and the dog practically hurled itself into his arms. "Hey, girl," he said, ruffling her neck. She immediately rolled over for a belly rub, and Knox obliged. "Dang, but she's a cute little thing."

The dog popped up as Knox stood. "I guess we should check out the house." They started to walk that direction, but the dog raced in front of them and started barking. She hadn't even let out a yip until then. But her barking now bordered on frantic as she ran in front of them, then raced toward the barn, then came back and barked at them again.

"At the risk of sounding crazy," Carley said. "I think that dog wants us to follow her into the barn."

"I think you're right," Knox said, changing course and heading toward the barn. He pushed at the old wooden door, sliding it along the rails just enough to get through. "Watch your step," he told Carley. "It's kinda dark in here." There were enough holes in the barn roof for the evening light to shine in, but it didn't cut through to the shadowy depths.

"Oh, my gosh, it smells terrible." The scent of manure and

rotten food hit them as soon as they stepped in a few feet. The buzz of numerous flies was the only sound coming from inside. "And it's seriously creepy. What if that smell is a dead body?"

"It could be," Knox said, peering around the barn. "But I'd expect it's more likely to be a dead animal than a dead human." He turned back to her, a look of genuine concern on his face. "Do you want to wait in the truck?"

"Heck no," she said, pulling her T-shirt up over her nose. "I'm not waiting out there by myself, prime bait to be the next murder victim of the serial killer who dumped a body in here."

"That makes sense." He shook his head as he pulled out his phone and tapped on the flashlight, then shone it around the barn. "I think the smell is due more to slobs than a serial killer. It looks like the previous tenants just dumped all their trash in here." He held the light on a pile of trash bags that had been torn open and food and garbage had been strewn all over the floor. The rotten food was the main source of the flies. "It sounds like the tenants have been gone for a week or so. I'd wager that the strewn-about trash is how the dog has been surviving."

"Poor thing," Carley said, looking toward the dog, who was now standing in the center of the barn.

"Let's get out of here." He started to turn around, but the dog barked again, and ran toward them, then raced back farther into the barn. "Okay, okay," Knox said, pushing farther into the barn. "What do you want to show me?"

The dog ran toward the back where several stalls were and

stopped outside the gate of the last one. Knox approached it cautiously, his stance alert and on the defensive.

Who knows what could be in there?

Carley held her breath, praying it wasn't a body. Or an axe murderer waiting to attack them.

Knox took another step closer, then let out a whispered string of curse words that Carley had never heard him use.

CHAPTER 24

"What's going on?" Carley asked, her stomach jumping to her throat.

Knox wrenched at the gate, cursing again as he struggled with the worn-out latch, then was finally able to enter the stall. "Hey, girl, it's okay. I'm not going to hurt you," she heard him say.

A weak and frightened whinny was the reply.

Carley cautiously stepped forward, then warily peered into the stall. Bile rose in her throat, and she let out a strangled cry. A thin, black horse was standing at the back of the stall, ankle deep in soiled hay and straw. Her head hung low, and she seemed to sway on her feet.

An aching pain tore through Carley's chest as she took in the scene. The tenants had just left their animals behind—locked this horse in the stable with no way to even get food or water. At least the dog had mobility to try to forage for survival. Her heart broke as she watched the dog run in and brush her body against the horse's legs. She couldn't tell if the gesture was affectionate or protective, or maybe a little of both.

"I see her," Knox said, reaching down to give the dog's ears a scratch. "You're a good dog for bringing us to her. A real good dog."

"Who would do this?" Carley cried, brushing at the tears on her cheeks. "Who would just abandon their animals and leave them here to die of starvation?"

"Some real assholes," Knox said. She could hear the strained emotion in the tremble of his voice. "You're okay now, girl. We're here to help." He slowly approached the horse, holding out his hand to let the mare smell it. She didn't seem to have the energy to do anything more than take a cursory sniff, barely lifting her head.

"What can I do to help?" Carley, her own voice trembling as well. She swallowed back the sobs that wanted to break free, instead focusing all her energy on being strong for the horse.

"Find me a rope or some twine or something to lead her out of here. She needs fresh water and some food. She's so thin, she looks like she's starving."

Carley spotted an old lead rope hanging off the fence of one of the other stalls. She passed it to Knox, who formed a makeshift halter and carefully slid it over the mare's head, then gave a gentle tug. The horse took a tentative step forward but didn't seem to be too steady on her feet.

"Maybe we need to get her some water first," he said. "I saw a spigot outside. Can you hold her while I go try to find something to fill with water?"

"Yes. I've got her," she stated, not even hesitating as she stepped into the rancid stall and took the rope.

"I'll be right back," Knox said.

Carley slowly raised a hand, then gently brushed it down the horse's neck. The mare lifted her head with effort and nuzzled her nose into Carley's chest. "You are a sweet girl," she said, bending forward to touch her forehead to the horse's. "We're gonna get you outta here and find you some food."

The dog let out a whine and planted herself on Carley's feet. She reached down to pet her neck, not sure if the dog was whining at missing out on affection or the mention of food. "You did an amazing job of bringing us to your friend. You saved her."

"I think that crazy little dog really did save that horse," Knox said, coming back into the barn holding a rusted bucket. Water sloshed over the sides as he hurried toward the stall. "I think that's why there's trash in her stall. I think the dog has been trying to bring her food."

Her chest squeezed again as the resiliency of the scruffy mutt and for the way it had tried to take care of the horse. "Aww. You're a hero."

"I can't believe they've survived as long as they have. Thank goodness we've gotten a little rain this past week. And that this roof leaks. I imagine that's the only way they've gotten water." He held the bucket up first to the horse who took a greedy drink, then held it lower for the dog to take a turn lapping at the fresh water. "There's a few patches of grass out in the yard. Let's take her outside and see if she'll eat a little something."

Carley passed the lead rope to Knox, who gave another gentle tug and this time the horse took a few tentative steps toward him. "That's it," he told her. "Come on. Just a little ways now, and we're gonna get you out of this filthy barn."

He led her outside and to a small grassy area. The mare bent her head and nibbled hesitantly at the grass, then munched more heartily. "We need to go get my trailer so we can bring her back to the horse rescue. That's the best place to take care of her."

"You go," Carley told him. "I'm not going anywhere. These animals have already been abandoned once. I'm not leaving them again."

"Okay. Maybe that's best. It'll probably take me about a half hour to get my trailer and make it back. Are you sure you're okay here by yourself?"

"I'm fine," she said, running a hand along the horse's neck. "And I'm *not* by myself."

"You sure you're not worried about that axe murderer?" He nudged her arm, teasing her with a small quiet joke.

She peered up at him. "I'd almost welcome one to try and come at me. As angry and enraged as I am right now, I feel like *I* could kill someone. And I'd start with the jerks who abandoned these sweet animals."

"I'd help you," he said, all traces of humor gone. He leaned down and pressed a hard kiss to the side of her forehead. "I'll be back as quick as I can. Call me if you need anything."

"I will."

———

True to his word, Knox was back in thirty minutes. Carley had moved to a different spot of grass, and it looked like she had hooked one end of the rope around a fence post and was sitting in the grass next to it, holding the dog on her lap. She got up and waved as he pulled in front of the barn, and he swallowed at the emotion he felt at seeing her.

She looked fierce as she stood, a determination and a protectiveness about her as she carefully set the dog down at her feet. Her hair was wild as loose curls had come free from her ponytail, and he could see a black smudge of dirt on her arm and across the front of her shirt, but she'd never looked more beautiful.

He got out of the truck and hurried toward her and the animals. He'd been thinking about her, and them, the whole time he was gone, and the first thing he had to do was pull her into his arms and hold her tightly.

"I just needed to feel you," he said, pressing his face into her neck and inhaling her scent.

She held on just as tight, and he could feel the hitch in her breath. "Me too," she whispered. "I'm glad you're back. You made good time."

He pulled back and cupped her face in his palm. His chest tightened at the sight of her swollen eyes and red nose. "You okay?"

She nodded. "Yeah. I had a good cry while you were gone. I couldn't hold it in any longer."

He pressed a tender kiss to each of her tear-streaked cheeks. "I don't blame you for crying. I'm not ashamed to say this kind of thing makes me want to cry too. Then it makes me want to find the assholes who did this and lock them in a putrid stall to starve."

"I'll help."

He gave her another hug then pulled away. "I brought some food for both of them, but I'm anxious to get them back to Bryn's." Along with his trailer, he'd grabbed a half a bale of hay and some of Sadie's dog food.

"Me too. I called her while I was waiting, and she told me to set up a stall away from the other horses, and to call the vet to come out and check them both over. I tried to call Brody Tate, but his number just went to voicemail."

"That's probably because I was on the phone with him. Great minds must think alike," he said. "He's going to meet us at Bryn's in about half an hour."

"Oh great. What can I do to help get them loaded up and get us all out of here?" Carley gave a small shiver. "This place gives me the creeps."

"Me too," he said, peering around the ramshackle farm. "But I do need to take a few minutes and look around. Just to make sure there aren't any other animals around here."

"Oh my gosh," Carley said, bringing her hand to her mouth. "I didn't even think about that."

"I didn't either. I was so focused on getting my trailer so I could get these two out of here that I just took off. I kicked myself as I realized it halfway back to my house."

"Don't beat yourself up."

He grimaced. "It's my job to think of this stuff."

"Well, I'm sure if there was anyone around, they would have come out when I was yelling swear words at the house while you were gone."

He raised an eyebrow.

"I sort of went from really sad to really mad and couldn't

think of what else to do. But if someone's in that house, I either scared the crud out of them and they're still hiding in there, or they ran out the other side to get away from the crazy lady threatening horrible things to their ball sack."

Knox grinned. "I do like you, Carley Chapman."

She offered him a sheepish grin. "I like you too. Now go case the joint or search it or whatever cop thing you do and let's get out of here."

"Yes, ma'am."

He did a thorough search of the property while Carley gave the animals a bit of food. She didn't want to feed them too much to start to keep them from getting sick to their stomachs.

"There's no one here," he told her coming back to help load the horse into the trailer. "No sign of people or animals in the house or anywhere else in the barn. But the place has been picked clean of anything valuable. Whoever was here pretty much took everything that wasn't nailed down."

"Everything except their animals, the ones who depend on them to love them and take care of them," Carley said, her voice rising with emotion. She lifted the dog gingerly into the cab of the truck, then crawled in after him and slammed the door.

Knox started the engine and pulled out of the driveway, thankful to put the place in his rearview mirror. He reached his hand over and set it gently on top of Carley's.

He didn't say anything and neither did she. But she turned her hand over and entwined her fingers with his, then squeezed his palm tightly. She held onto him like that the whole way back to the ranch, and both of them ignored the new tears on her cheeks.

She was breaking his heart, and all he wanted to do was pull over and tug her into his lap and kiss away her pain. Finding the animals who were left behind was obviously triggering a lot of emotions for her, and he wished he could tell her that she was safe with him, that he would never leave behind what was his.

But the problem was that she wasn't his. The lines of their relationship had definitely blurred the last few weeks, especially when they'd been naked and tangled up in the sheets, but just because they'd spent time together in the bedroom, and eating together on the porch, and watching television, didn't mean they were really together. No matter how much he wished they were.

For now, he had to be satisfied holding her hand and praying the pressure of his grip holding tightly to her was enough to let her know his feelings for her were real and that he wasn't going anywhere.

It took a few hours to get the horse situated in the stall. They'd given her more hay, lined the stall with fresh straw, and cleaned her up the best they could. Brody had come over and given her some fluids and a dewormer. She was dehydrated and malnourished, but he said with some time and consistent nutrients, she should be okay.

He gave the dog a round of shots and a flea bath, then

pronounced her okay, as well. "They'll come out of this, thanks to you all," Brody had told them. "Another few days with no food and water and we'd have been looking at a very different outcome."

They'd spent another hour in the barn with the horse after the vet had left, neither of them able to leave her alone quite yet. They sat in the stall with her, the dog squished between them, taking turns passing her occasional apple slices and stroking her neck.

"I was thinking we should name this dog Angel," Carley told him as they were walking back to the house, the scruffy mutt close on their heels. "Because she was like the horse's guardian angel, watching out for her and taking care of her and trying to keep her alive. I was trying to think of a name that seemed heroic or loyal, so I also had Wonder (short for Wonder Woman), Marvel (short for Captain Marvel), and Hermione."

He nodded. "All solid choices. And I like the theme."

"So, which one?"

He shrugged. "I'm okay with whatever you choose."

"No way. We have to make this decision together since she's now our dog."

Our dog?

A weight of memories and hurt landed solidly in his chest. Kimber was the last, and only other person he'd ever shared a dog with and that had ended in his heart being trampled and had almost destroyed him. He cleared his throat, trying to clear away the memories as well. Carley *wasn't* Kimber. "I think Angel is good. She's a sweetheart too, so the name fits her."

Carley nodded. "I think so too. Any ideas for names for our horse?"

Damn. Now they were not only sharing a dog, but a horse too. In for a penny, in for a pound.

"Umm, well, she's shown quite the fighting spirit, so what about calling her Spirit? Unless you had some other ideas."

She shook her head. "No, I hadn't come up with anything yet. I think that's perfect."

"I think you're perfect."

She stopped, one foot on the porch steps and turned back to him. She didn't say anything, just looked at him, studying his face as if trying to figure him out.

His chest ached at the confusion and suspicion he saw in her eyes.

"Do you need me to tell you again?" he asked, his voice soft. Her eyes grew round, the suspicion replaced with tenderness, and he pulled her against him. Looking into her eyes, he tried to convey the depth of his feelings and the conviction behind his words. "I hate that little shit you were married to for ever making you doubt that you are now or have ever been anything less than perfect. You are beautiful, smart, funny, and one of the most thoughtful and caring people I know. You are beyond perfect for me." He froze then stumbled over his words as he said, "I mean beyond perfect *to* me."

A grin tugged at the corners of her lips then she leaned toward him and pressed her lips to his. The kiss started out soft then deepened as she kissed him with a passion and hunger that conveyed more than her words could ever say.

They stood on the porch, her one step up from him, just kissing for what seemed like days. And he could have continued to kiss her for weeks more. She felt so good, so right.

When she finally pulled back, the small smile she'd had broadened into one that promised something more, a whole lot more. "What would you say to that idea of a sleepover?"

His lips curved into a grin. "I'd say let me get my toothbrush."

She laughed. "You'd better bring your dog and your calf too."

"I'm on it," he said, already heading for the door of his bunkhouse.

"Hey, Knox," she said, causing him to stop and turn back around. "You can get your toothbrush, but I wouldn't bother bringing any pajamas."

————————

The next morning, Carley drifted awake to find herself in a cuddle puddle of several animals on top of the covers and spooned against one hot naked cowboy under the covers.

Not a bad way to start the morning, she thought, sliding her hand along Knox's thigh. She felt him wake up behind her, or at least felt part of him wake up. A naughty grin curved her lips as she wiggled against him.

"Good morning, beautiful." His deep voice drawled against her ear.

"Mornin' cowboy," she said, then froze as she heard her

front door open, and footsteps walk quickly across the floor and down the hallway toward her room.

"Carley, we're back."

CHAPTER 25

CARLEY HEARD HER SISTER'S VOICE SECONDS BEFORE Jillian's head popped around the edge of her bedroom door. Certainly not enough time for either her or Knox to even find their clothes, let alone have a chance to put them on. Instead, she clutched the sheet under her chin and hoped all of Knox's naughty bits were concealed under the covers as well.

"Hey, Sis," she said, trying to hush Sadie and Angel, who were barking at the intruder.

Phoebe woke up and started bouncing around the bed, which didn't help with the keeping the naughty bits covered situation. Nala was stretched out at the end of the bed and let out a yawn to show she was completely unfazed by the barking dogs or bouncing goat. At least Rodney was on the floor and didn't seem to care about the visitor.

Jillian stood in the doorway, her eyes wide as her mouth opened, then closed again. She raised her hand to point at Carley, then at Knox. "You guys are...I mean...you're... um...is that a baby goat?"

Before she had a chance to reply, she heard her nephew's excited voice and the sound of his sneakers racing toward them. "Hey, Aunt Carley, we're back, and we brought you something."

His mom grabbed him just as he rounded the doorway, covering his eyes and jumping in front of him. "Aunt Carley has company," she said.

"Then why are there clothes all over the floor out here? Didn't she used to always make us clean up for company?" He tried to twist around his mom. "Is there a calf in Aunt Carley's bedroom?"

She rubbed at her forehead, nudging Knox in the ribs as she heard him laughing next to her.

"Nothing like getting caught naked and with a calf and a baby goat in your bedroom," he said quietly next to her ear. She could hear the amusement in his voice.

"This isn't funny," she whispered back. Although, it was. Actually, it was really funny. She peered up at her sister who was barely holding it together, her lips pressed tightly to each other to keep from busting out laughing.

"What are you doing here?" she asked, not knowing what else to say.

"We couldn't miss your engagement party," Jillian said. "Although it looks like the party may have already started. When did you get a dog? And a goat?"

"You're one to talk. You brought a mini-horse on vacation with you. In a camper." Not much of a retort, but it was all she could think of considering her brain was a little preoccupied with the fact that she and the man she was supposed to be having a *fake* relationship with had both been caught in a very real, and very naked, situation.

Before Jillian could come back with something far more witty, because her sister could always come up with something more witty than she could, the screen door slammed again.

Oh joy, please let it be my new brother-in-law, the sheriff, Carley thought. Because not enough people were in her bedroom already.

Her new brother-in-law would have been preferable to the clop-clopping sound of hooves on the hardwood as the mini-horse she'd just referred to came trotting into the bedroom and the whole room erupted in mayhem as the dogs started barking again, the frightened goat tried to wiggle under the covers, and the cat fell off the bed. Luckily, the cat landed on her feet.

She looked at Knox, who was trying to keep Phoebe from crawling into his lap. "Can you fix this?"

He grinned as if accepting the challenge, then put his thumb and his ring finger into his mouth and let out a loud whistle. "Everybody out," he said in a commanding tone. "As excited as we *all* are to see you, we need a few minutes to collect ourselves. Then we'll meet you all out front on the porch."

Jillian shooed her son and Applejack, the mini-horse back down the hallway. "Let's give your aunt and her *fiancé* a few minutes."

"Oh, and Jillian," Knox called to her retreating back.

"Yeah?" she said, poking her head back around the door.

"If you wouldn't mind tossing me my pants from the floor out there somewhere, I'd be much obliged."

"Sure thing, Deputy," Jillian answered with a smirk at her sister. "One pair of floor pants, coming right up."

Ten minutes later, Carley and Knox emerged from the house, fully clothed and with a menagerie of animals clamoring to be let outside at their feet. As the dogs, calf, and goat raced out into the yard, Carley was finally able to give her sister and nephew a hug.

"I'm so happy to see you both," she said. "Where's Ethan?"

Jillian pointed over her shoulder to where a motor home was parked in front of the house. Ethan came out of the barn and waved as he sauntered up and gave Carley a hug. "Mornin', Deputy," he said, extending a hand toward Knox.

"Mornin', Sheriff." Knox shook his new boss's hand, then jerked a thumb toward the barn. "I'd best see to the chores. And I want to check on our newest rescue."

"I want to come too," Carley said, dragging her sister by the hand. "We rescued the sweetest horse last night. We named her Spirit." She pointed to Angel, who was racing along at her ankles. "This scruffy little cutie led us to her."

"What is going on?" Jillian asked. "When I left, you were still in your apartment and happily vacuuming away all the dog hair left behind by Milo's puppy. Now you've got a dog of your own."

"Well, he's *our* dog," Carley said, gesturing between herself and Knox. "All I have is a cat. Her name is Nala. She's the one who fell off the bed this morning. Although I really think I'm more *her* pet than she's mine. And this funny little thing has claimed me as hers as well." She scooped up Phoebe and cuddled the baby goat to her chest.

Jillian's eyes went wide. "Seriously, who are you? You have pet hair on your clothes, you're cuddling a goat, and you're not even wearing makeup."

"Yeah," Knox said, looking back and locking eyes with Carley as he pushed open the barn door. "And she's still the most gorgeous thing I've ever seen." He disappeared inside the barn, leaving Carley and Jillian standing outside, their mouths hanging open in matching gawks.

Jillian tugged at her hand. "I think there's a lot more we need to catch up on."

"Save it for later," Ethan said. "We're real happy to see you, Carley, but we just pulled into town. Your sister made us stop here first, but now I'm ready to get home."

"Me too," Jillian said, giving her sister another hard squeeze. "But I'll see you at the party tonight, and we will have time to catch up."

"How did you even know about the party?" she asked as her sister headed toward the motor home.

"Miss Evelyn called and invited us. She said she thought you might need our support."

"You didn't cut your trip short for this party, did you? It's no big deal."

"No, Carley," Ethan assured her. "We didn't cut anything short. We're home now after *extending* our vacation by a few weeks. It was just time for us to be back." He waved. "We'll see you *and* Knox at the party later."

The motor home pulled out onto the highway as a familiar truck hauling a Heaven Can Wait Horse Rescue Ranch trailer pulled in. The engine had barely stopped when Bryn already had the door open and was hurrying toward Carley, concern etched on her face. "How's the new horse?"

"I'm not sure. I was just going to check on her," Carley said. "I didn't know you were coming back today." She tried to keep the disappointment out of her voice. Not at seeing her friend, but at the fact that with Bryn home, Knox would no longer be staying in the bunkhouse next door.

"We came home a few days early," Bryn said, squeezing her arm. "We didn't want to miss your engagement party tonight."

"Oh, geez," Carley said, smacking her palm to her forehead. "Is there anyone Miss Evelyn didn't invite?"

Zane called a greeting as he got out of the truck and headed directly toward the barn, no doubt to check on the new arrival. Carley was anxious to go see her too but was more curious about the cowboy climbing out of the backseat of Zane's pickup. He had sandy-blond hair, several days scruff of a beard, and a jaw that could have been chiseled from marble. His faded blue T-shirt was wrinkled but couldn't hide his broad shoulders and muscular chest and arms. He wore jeans, a shiny rodeo buckle, square-toed cowboy boots, a gray Stetson, and aviator sunglasses—he looked like a cross between a bull-rider and a fighter pilot.

Carley nudged Bryn's shoulder. "Did you pick up a hitchhiker?"

"Sort of," she said, waving the cowboy toward her. "Carley, this is my cousin, Holt Callahan. He's Cade's brother, and he's gonna be staying here awhile."

"Pleased to meet you," Holt said, taking off his glasses

with one hand and reaching out to shake with the other. His palms were calloused, a rancher's hand.

"You too," she said. "I know your brother. And Nora's a good friend of mine." Without the glasses, she could easily see the resemblance of the two men. "Welcome home."

He raised an eyebrow as he peered around the ranch. "We'll see."

Hmm. Kind of an odd nonanswer, but with his hat pushed low and his pensive expression, he looked a bit like a broody nonanswering kind of guy.

"Come on," Bryn said, tugging at her arm. "I want to see the new horse."

That night, Carley tried on six dresses before she chose the light pink flowy chiffon one with cap sleeves that clung to her shoulders. The midi dress fell to just below her knees, but had a slight slit up one leg, and she chose a rose-gold pair of strappy sandals that had just a hint of glitter to them.

She wore her hair down but had curled it into big soft waves that had taken hours to create the effortless look. Shimmering rose-gold earrings dangled at her ears, but she couldn't decide on a necklace, so she'd gone without.

She didn't know why she was going to such effort to look nice for an engagement party that was celebrating a pretend relationship. Although, to be fair, it was the first, and no doubt, the last engagement party anyone would ever throw for her. And she *was* one of the guests of honor, so she might as well make the best of it. And for her, that meant looking her best.

It had nothing to do with the handsome cowboy she'd now looked for out the window four times to see if his truck was coming down the driveway yet. She paced the floor, checking her watch *again*. He should have been here by now. He was always early.

The sound of an engine drew her to the window again, her pulse taking flight at the excitement of seeing him and the annoyance at him making her wait. But it wasn't Knox's truck outside. It was Jillian, here to drop off the kids.

Knox had left early that morning, right after Bryn got back. He had that early meeting and had to drop off the animals and get the folder of paperwork they never managed to pick up the night before. The new horse had looked in better spirits this morning and was steadier on her feet. Carley had spent some time brushing her and hanging out in the stall with her and Angel before coming in to shower for the day.

Knowing the engagement party was that night, she'd only booked two clients. One a man's haircut, which was quick and easy, and the other was a highlight and cut, which took more time. But her client was in her early twenties and kept her headphones in the whole time, claiming she was listening to a great podcast, which left Carley to her own thoughts most of the time, and they bounced from Knox to Angel to Spirit to nervousness about the night's festivities.

Maybe it was just being with the animals who had so callously been left behind that had Carley's abandonment issues going berserk today, but she couldn't imagine leaving

Angel home alone tonight and didn't think she could bring her to the party. Thankfully, Jillian had offered for Milo and his best friend, Mandy, to come over and hang out with the animals while they were gone.

The kids didn't need much convincing, especially since a baby goat was involved, but Carley still threw in the offer of a pizza and some animal-sitting cash. She heard them excitedly exiting the car as she stepped out onto the front porch.

"Wow, you look amazing," Jillian said, standing up behind the car door. "That dress is gorgeous, and your hair. Wow."

"Thank you," Carley said, unable to help wishing that those were the comments she would have hopefully been hearing from Knox right now.

"I love your dress," Mandy said, coming up the steps.

"Yeah, you look really pretty, Aunt Carley," Milo said, coming up behind Mandy. "Are you okay if we go on in? I can't wait to show Mandy the baby goat."

"Knock yourself out. Phoebe and Angel are inside, but there's seven more babies to play with out in the barn."

"Cool," he said, pushing through the front door so he and Mandy could start the cuddle-fest.

Carley tilted her head at her sister's outfit of sweats, sneakers, old T-shirt, and messy bun piled on top of her head. "No offense, but you *don't* look so amazing. What's going on? Aren't you coming to our party?" She tried to keep the panic out of her voice. "First Knox is a no-show, now my own sister. Maybe I should stay home too."

"What do you mean Knox is a no-show?"

Carley shrugged. "He was supposed to be here half an

hour ago, but I haven't heard a word from him. No text. No phone call."

"That's weird."

"Is it? You know I don't have the best track record when it comes to men sticking around. Maybe this whole engagement party idea finally shook some sense into him, and he's backing out while he still can."

"No way. I've seen the way he looks at you. Maybe it had something to do with the station. Ethan got called out to an emergency. Maybe Knox had to respond too."

A glimmer of hope bloomed in Carley's chest. That explanation made sense. She prayed that was the reason and that her first instinct of him dumping her was wrong.

"Also, I am, of course, planning to come to the party," Jillian said. "My day just got away from me with all the cleaning and reorganizing of moving from the camper back into the house. I'll be a little late, but I'll be there. If I rush it, I can hopefully make it within the next hour."

"Get out of here then. And hurry. I have a feeling I'm going to need you tonight."

She went back inside and checked her phone. No texts. No missed calls.

The party was starting in fifteen minutes.

She spent the next thirty minutes talking to the kids about the animals, paying the pizza delivery guy, and anxiously checking her watch. At quarter after the hour, she made the decision that she just had to go without him.

Evelyn had put too much time and effort into throwing a party for them, she couldn't be a no-show as well. She knew what it felt like to be waiting and not having someone show up. She hadn't expected to have that feeling with Knox though. A stark reminder that she wasn't worth showing up for.

She was surprised at the number of cars lining the streets around Evelyn's house. This was supposed to be a small party, but it looked like half the town had shown up. Evelyn lived in a giant Victorian in the oldest part of town. The street was wide with a canopy of trees overhanging the center, and Evelyn's home was at the end of the block, a grand house with a long sweeping veranda running the length of the front and wrapping around the side. Wicker furniture with chintz cushions decorated the porch, now lit with carriage lights and twinkling lanterns hanging from the railings.

The sounds of laughter and a string quartet came from the house as Carley hesitantly walked up the stone steps. Surely that was a recording, and Evelyn hadn't really hired a small symphony to play for the evening.

Her stomach roiled and pitched with nerves. What was she doing? And where the hell was Knox? This was crazy. She was walking into this house to celebrate a lie with people she actually cared about. She couldn't do this.

She turned to go but was stopped by Lyda Hightower and her husband sweeping up the steps behind her. "Hello Carley," Lyda called out, marching up and hooking her arm around Carley's elbow. "You look gorgeous, as always. I simply love this dress."

"Hi, Lyda. Mayor," she said, nodding a greeting to the well-dressed distinguished silver-haired man on Lyda's other side. "And thank you. You look beautiful too. Is this dress new?"

Lyda waved a hand over the floral-print designer gown that skimmed her ankles at the just the right length to show off a pair of nude Louboutin kitten heels on her perfectly manicured feet. "This old thing," she said, with just the slightest hint of a Southern accent. "I've had it in my closet forever."

Somehow Carley doubted that, and from the bemused smile on the mayor's face, it appeared he did too.

"Now, where's your handsome fiancé?"

"Oh, he had a work thing," she said, hoping her tone sounded casual as she went with Jillian's assumed explanation for his absence. "You know Knox, always the dedicated public servant. Deputy duties first, fiancé duties second."

"Yes, I know all about having your man in public service," Lyda said, but her tone was one of pride rather than annoyance as she smiled at her husband. "Well, it seems like we arrived just in time to walk you in then."

"Yes, thank you," Carley said, the ease in her tensed shoulders indicating her relief. Although coming in with the mayor and Lyda would be much more of a grand entrance than the way she'd planned to sneak in unnoticed.

"Look who I found outside," Lyda said, announcing their arrival to the whole room as they stepped into the large marble foyer filled with beautifully dressed people holding small plates of hors d'oeuvres. "The guest of honor. Or one of them at least. Deputy Garrison is protecting our fair city of Creedence, but he'll be along shortly." Lyda squeezed her arm before letting go and heading into the fray to mingle.

As much as she hated being the center of attention, Carley was thankful Lyda had announced to the whole room why Knox was missing and had given a reasonable explanation. She only prayed that it was the truthful one.

It seemed like her assumption was correct that half the town had shown up. She saw Chloe Bishop, now Chloe James, on the arm of her new husband and chatting with what looked like the rest of the entire James family. Amber and Brandi were there, both dressed up and chatting together like the fight at the salon over Buster Jenkins had never happened. Even Erica, her stylist, was there with her husband, who was proudly walking around with baby Lily strapped to his chest. It felt strange, and dishonest, to have so many people who cared about her and Knox show up to offer them good wishes, when all of this was a sham. And they weren't even a couple. Heck, he hadn't even bothered to show up tonight.

Although now a part of her was starting to worry. The side of her who had always been sure he'd leave was warring with the side of her who felt like she really knew Knox. And knew this wasn't like him. Her head hurt thinking about all the possible places he could be, but her heart only knew one thing—he wasn't here. With her.

She waded through the guests, waving and smiling hellos as she tried to find a glass of something to drink and a corner to hide in. Or maybe she could find Cletus and hang out with the bulldog all night. But apparently luck was *really* not on her side tonight.

The side parlor looked empty from her vantage point,

and she made a beeline in that direction, but as she turned the corner into the room, she came face-to-face with the one person she never expected to have at her engagement party.

"Paul." She said his name as more of an accusation than a greeting. She felt like a broken record, asking him the same question time and time again, but it was still the most befitting for the situation. "What the hell are you doing here? At *my* engagement party?"

He wore an expensive suit with new alligator skin boots, both of which she was sure had been at the expense of his grandmother. Both the boots and the rattlesnake rattle encased inside his bolo tie seemed fitting to his personality. The grin he wore reminded her of the crocodile who ate the canary as he said, "I think the more important question *isn't* why *I'm* here, but why isn't your supposed fiancé here?"

CHAPTER 26

Why wasn't Knox here?

Paul had a valid point.

"No," Carley said, struggling to hold her ground and not let him get to her. "I know the answer to that question. But I don't understand why you would *want* to be here. Other than to torment me."

Paul pressed a hand against his chest. "Dang. You really know how to hurt a guy. Especially since the reason I'm here is all for you."

"For me? How do you figure?"

"I figure I'm the one who's going to be here to pick up the pieces when this guy decides to dump you too."

She sucked in her breath. How did he always know what words to say to hurt her the most? It was like he knew right where her gaping wound was and enjoyed pouring salt directly into it. She blinked back the sting of tears in her eyes, not wanting to give him the satisfaction of knowing his comment had hit its mark.

"Carley, there you are. I've been looking all over for you," Jillian said, walking briskly into the room and throwing her arms around her sister in a hug. "Don't you dare let that little maggot get to you," she whispered fiercely into her sister's ear. "You hold your head up."

She squeezed her sister, drawing strength from Jillian's whispered command. Taking a deep breath, she lifted her chin and pushed back her shoulders. "Thanks, Sis."

Jillian hooked her arm around Carley's. "Let's get out of here."

Paul's self-righteous smile felt like he knew he'd gotten to her. He aimed a sleezy nod at her sister. "Hello, Jillian, always good to see you."

Jillian huffed and nodded back as they pushed past him. "Hello Dickface. *Never* good to see you."

Carley tried to hold in her laugh as she saw Paul's smile slip the slightest, but she couldn't hold it in. She and Jillian busted out laughing together as they hurried down the hall and back into the living room. "Thanks for saving me, Jil. I don't know how I got cornered in there with him."

"Anytime."

"You look great, by the way."

"Thanks," Jillian said, fluffing the side bun she'd twisted her hair into. She wore a periwinkle midi dress with a square neck and thin shoulder straps and a pair of low-heeled silver sandals. Silver earrings with glittering blue stones in the same shade of periwinkle dangled from her ears. "Not bad for getting ready in thirty minutes."

"Yoo-hoo, Carley," a voice called from across the room.

Carley looked over to see Aunt Sassy bustling toward her, weaving her way through the partygoers. Sassy had on a belted jumpsuit with wide palazzo black pants and a sequined hot pink bodice, so it was easy to spot her in the crowd.

"Congratulations," she said with a flourish as she threw

her arms around Carley, then whispered in her ear, "Meet me in the kitchen right away, but don't tell anyone besides Jillian." Raising her voice to a normal level she added more dramatically. "So good to see you. But I've got to go now." She drifted off one direction while discreetly pointing Carley in the other.

"She's not much of an actress," Carley said in a low voice to her sister. "But I'm just curious enough to see what she's up to. Follow me to the kitchen."

They wound their way through two rooms, exchanging pleasantries as they went, then finally pushed through the door into the large kitchen. On the far side of the kitchen, she could see Evelyn, wearing a gorgeous peach gown, standing next to a breakfast nook and using a wad of bloodstained gauze to dab at the forehead of a man seated at the table who was holding a bag of frozen peas to his cheek.

The man's back was to her, but Carley recognized the broad shoulders, tousled dark hair, and deputy uniform. "Knox," she said, rushing to him, as dread and fear roiled through her stomach.

He turned at her voice and pushed up from the chair as he tossed the bag of vegetables on the table. "I'm sorry I'm late, darlin.'" The side of his eye was swollen and bruised, and his cheek was scraped and bleeding. He had a cut on his lip, and his shirt was covered in dust and dirt.

She threw herself into his arms, heedless to the mess of his clothes, hugged him close then pulled back to look at his face. Wincing, she gingerly touched a spot on his cheek that didn't look hurt. "What happened? Are you okay?"

He nodded but pulled away from her. "I'm fine, but I don't want to mess up your dress." Even though his one eye was swollen, she could still see the tenderness shining there. "You look stunning."

She waved away his compliment, the words she'd been craving to hear earlier that night. Now she only wanted to know what happened. "Forget about me. Are you really all right? Should we take you to the hospital?"

He shook his head. "No, I'm really fine. It looks worse than it is. And I'm not going anywhere. This is our engagement party, and I'm not about to miss it."

"Who cares about the dumb party. I care about you," she told him.

"I care about what in the dickens happened to you," Aunt Sassy said from behind her. "Am I the only one who's curious?"

"Heck, no," Jillian said. "I'd also like to know what was so dang important that you stood my sister up and then got yourself beat up for."

"I'm sure you'll hear about it," Knox told Jillian. "Since your husband was involved too." He held up his hand. "Don't worry. He's fine. Like really fine, not like my kind of fine," he said, indicating his face. "He's just still down at the station filling out paperwork."

"That's good to know," Jillian said. "Thanks for telling me."

He nodded. "You're welcome. Now as for what happened, I'm sure it's not as interesting or as exciting as any of you are imagining. We responded to a domestic dispute earlier this evening—Ethan had asked me to come along because we'd dealt with this particular guy before, and he was usually trouble. And tonight was no exception. We got the family away, but the husband did not take kindly to our asking him to leave the home. Then we explained that we were not asking but telling, and he thought it would be a good idea to take a swing at me. And now he is in jail and hopefully rethinking that decision and the ones where he decided to harm his wife and child."

Evelyn picked up a new piece of gauze and reached toward his head, but he shook his head. "I appreciate it, Miss Evelyn, but really, I'm fine. I don't need anyone to make a fuss over me. I feel bad enough that I wasn't here for Carley, I don't want to ruin your party too." He reached for Carley's hand. "I'm sorry you had to greet all those guests by yourself. I'm ready to go out there with you now."

"Not dressed like that you aren't," Aunt Sassy. "Your clothes are filthy, and you've got blood in your hair."

"I can fix that," Lyda said, rushing into the kitchen in a swirl of perfume and carrying a hanger holding a dress shirt wrapped in plastic. "I happened to still have my husband's dry cleaning in the car after picking it up this afternoon. This shirt might not be an exact fit, but it's starched and pressed, and it should come close enough. I can't do anything about the pants, but I found a freshly cleaned tie in the stack as well." She handed him the shirt and tie, then pointed to the kitchen sink. "You can wash up right there and then change your shirt, and you'll be good as new."

"Or, you can use the washroom in the hallway," Evelyn

told him, tossing a look at Lyda, who stuck out her tongue at her old friend.

"You okay with this?" he asked Carley, gesturing to the shirt and tie, then pointed to his face. "And with being seen with me like this?"

She nodded, so relieved that he hadn't intentionally stood her up or abandoned her. "Yes. I'm okay. And Lyda already told everyone you were going to be late due to official business."

"Then I'd better get changed."

Ten minutes later, he came back into the kitchen, his hair was wet but free of blood. The dress shirt was a little snug, the muscles of his broad chest and arms stretching against the fabric when he moved, but not one woman in the kitchen minded. Especially Carley.

He stuck out his elbow for her to take. "You ready to go join the festivities?"

She smiled up at him and took his arm. They walked back into the party together amidst cheers and shouts of greeting and congratulations. As they worked their way through the room, they eventually ran into her least favorite person.

"Paul, I'm surprised to see you here," Knox said. "But we appreciate you coming out to tell us congratulations."

Carley pulled her shoulders back and held firm to Knox's arm, determined to show Paul that he no longer had any power over her.

"I'm just here to support my wife," Paul said, his face twisting into an ugly sneer.

"*Ex*-wife," Knox said before Carley could. "And you don't

have to concern yourself with anything Carley does anymore. She can take care of herself. And I'll be here when and if she needs me."

Take that, Dickface.

She loved that Knox didn't claim to be the one to take care of her now, that he gave her all the credit for standing up for herself. She knew she could lean on him if she needed to, but he saw her as someone capable of taking care of herself. And she just might have fallen a little harder for him in that moment.

―――――――

Even though they'd had a late night, Carley was up early the next morning. She hated to admit how much she loved waking up curled against Knox's side, and how much she was getting used to it. Especially after how heartbroken she'd felt the night before when she'd thought he'd stood her up. Everything about their relationship was like a crazy rollercoaster of ups and downs. But she had no problem admitting how amazing those *up* moments were during their time together before they'd fallen asleep.

She and Knox both had the day off, and she would have loved to have slept in, but she had too many things to do today. Earlier that week, with Autumn's help, she'd posted the pop-up event for Beauty in the Barn to be held this afternoon, and she'd quickly filled the twelve available spots and collected the ninety-nine-dollar fee from all of them online.

Now she just had to make sure they got their money's

worth. Angel and Phoebe followed her out to the barn where they'd planned to hold the event. She set up six stations and had timed the spots so the women would rotate through, the first one finishing just in time for the next round to start their cycle through. She gave each spot a fifteen-minute time limit and set up each one to be a pampering experience.

Within a few minutes of starting to set up, Jillian arrived, and then a freshly showered Knox came out to the barn with travel cups of fresh coffee for each of them. Autumn arrived midmorning followed by Evelyn, Lyda, and Aunt Sassy, and suddenly it felt like not just setting up for an event, but another party. Many hands made light work, and they had everything set up just in time for Bryn to make it home from her shift at the diner with sandwiches and chips in hand to feed the hungry helpers.

Aunt Sassy, Lyda, and Evelyn had signed up for the spa day, figuring they'd earned some pampering after helping set everything up, and the other nine women all showed up by two. There was an excitement and giddiness in the air that Carley figured had more to do with Knox's presence in the barn than the cuddly animals or spa treatments. The swelling around his eye had gone down some, but the scrapes and bruising gave him an even more rugged look. Carley thought even with the black eye, he was still so damn handsome he took her breath away.

As each woman entered the barn, Carley gave them a pink-and-white gift bag that Bryn had made containing beauty supply samples, bottles of water, and small tubes of hand lotion and lip balm.

Bringing in the color scheme of the salon, she'd chosen all the decorations and the supplies in either pink or white, giving the barn a quaint feel. The air carried the fresh spa-like smell of eucalyptus, thanks to the scented oil diffusers Autumn had brought. Add in a sprinkling of adorable baby goats running up to greet the guests and their Beauty in the Barn spa day couldn't be more charming.

Carley handed out directions and assigned each woman a place, then set the timer for fifteen minutes. She was in charge of the station for facial masks and cleansing, she'd asked Jillian to do paraffin hand treatments complete with a five-minute hand massage, Erica had agreed to come in and offer mini manicures, Autumn was doing a meditation corner with some easy stretching, one station had a comfy chaise to take a ten-minute power nap, then wake up to lemon water or hot tea and a selection of tiny bakery desserts, and the pièce de résistance, the station she figured brought in the quick sign-ups and the willingness to shell out almost a hundred bucks, was the head and neck massage given by a handsome cowboy.

And of course, at each station, there was the opportunity to cuddle or pet or visit with one of the farmyard animals. The goats were making themselves available for pets as they bounced from one person to the next, each bounce sending up giggles and coos of adorableness. Angel was curled in Aunt Sassy's lap as Carley spread a facial mask across her cheeks. Knox had brought over Sadie and Rodney, and the golden retriever was lapping up every affectionate head pat and neck scratch while the calf wandered along in her wake.

Tiny the pig and Shamus the mini-horse had come in to see what all the ruckus was about, and Carley laughed as she saw Lyda trying to sneak Tiny a miniature chocolate mousse. Nala, the cat, had even agreed to show up. She was parked firmly in the napping station, curled against Evelyn's side, who had fallen fast asleep the second she'd lain down on the chaise. She might have even been snoring, but they were going to blame that on one of the horses.

The participants were free to wander around and visit the horses in their stalls, and Knox was showing a woman how to feed Sienna a sugar cube off her palm.

There was one animal missing, but Carley was fine if Otis decided to stay away. He'd probably just try to find a way to run off with the snacks. Although his absence did make her a little nervous, and she wondered if he had somehow found a way into the bunkhouse and was eating everything in her pantry while she was distracted in the barn.

All in all, the day was a huge success. Even if Aunt Sassy had complained that she thought there was going to be a stripper and had shot a meaningful look at Knox. All the women left with happy smiles, and most had even contributed to the tip jar Autumn had insisted they leave by the barn door.

Evelyn was the last to leave and she pulled Carley aside as Knox was putting back the stack of hay bales they'd used to create the meditation corner. "I wanted to talk to you a minute, now that everyone's gone and your event is finished."

"Good," Carley said. "Because I wanted to talk to you too. I needed to say thank you again for throwing us such a wonderful party last night. I know it didn't go exactly how we'd planned, but it was such a thoughtful gesture and I know it took a lot of work."

"Oh, don't worry about that. It was fun. And Lyda and her staff of minions helped so it wasn't even that much work." She picked up Carley's hand and gave it a squeeze. "But the most important part of the night was that it worked."

"What worked?"

"The party worked to finally convince Paul that you and Knox were really engaged and that he wasn't going to waltz into town and just woo you back. That and the fact that I had a meeting with that developer yesterday morning and shared with him that Paul had no claim to that building and that under no circumstances were you and I planning to sell it."

"Good for you. Did you tell Paul about the meeting?"

"I certainly did. And I told him I loved him, but I also love you and that he needed to stop whatever game he was playing because all the business nonsense with that fool developer was over. And there was no way he was getting his hands on our building."

"Wow. How did he take it?"

"About as you'd expect. A bunch of bluster and some wheedling and attempts to charm me back to his way of thinking, but I stood my ground, and he got the message. In fact, he packed up his stuff this morning and hugged me goodbye, telling me he'd talked to a rodeo buddy of his and he was headed to Wyoming to look into some new exciting business opportunity."

"Wait. You're telling me Paul left town this morning? Like he's really gone?"

Evelyn nodded, and Carley let out a thankful sigh of relief as she hugged the older woman to her.

"Oh, my gosh. I feel like I can breathe now."

"That's not all you can do now," Evelyn told her, squeezing her hand again. "Now that all this business with my grandson is over, you can finally concentrate on your relationship with that handsome deputy and decide if you're ready to admit that for all your waffling around about if your feelings are true or not, what I saw last night in the kitchen when you thought Knox was hurt was most definitely real. I know you all care about each other, but now it's up to the two of you to decide what you're going to do about it."

"Thank you," Carley said, giving her another hug instead of an answer. "I'm so thankful I have you in my life."

"Right back at you, kiddo," Evelyn said, squeezing her back, then patting a hand gently against her cheek. "And you're not getting rid of me any time soon. We're stuck with each other. And with our building. I also heard from the insurance company this afternoon, and they are covering the whole claim."

Carley pressed a hand to her chest. "Wow, you are just full of great news. You have eased every one of my burdens. Anything else?"

"Nope. That's all I've got. But now I'm pooped, and I'm going home to spoil that beautiful bulldog of mine."

"Give him a cuddle for me. I heard you took him to visit Dottie."

"I did. I found out which care center she was in, and we surprised her. She was so happy to see her baby. But she told me she didn't know when she was going to be discharged, that it might still be months now, and I told her Cletus could stay with me as long as she needed him to."

"You are one special lady, Evelyn Chapman."

Evelyn took Carley's shoulders and peered into her eyes, her gaze steady and direct. "So are you, Carley Chapman. And don't you dare let anyone make you think otherwise."

Knox came out of the barn then, Angel racing along at his heels. "I think we've got everything put back to rights in the barn. And Otis finally showed up, and he and I split the last few desserts."

"Perfect," Carley said, laughing as she gave a nod to Evelyn.

"I'll see you later, Deputy," Evelyn called out with a wave as she headed toward her car. "You did great today."

"Take care, Miss Evelyn. Thanks again for the party last night. And for the frozen peas."

"Any time, honey," Evelyn chuckled.

They watched her drive away, then Carley turned toward Knox. "She's right, you know. You did so great today." She wrapped her arms around his waist and hugged him. "You were amazing the way you charmed those women. They all loved you. And I love you for all the help you've given me."

He squeezed her to him and whispered against her hair, "I love you, too."

CHAPTER 27

CARLEY STOOD STILL, STUNNED BY HIS WHISPERED words. Had he just told her he loved her? Like loved-loved her? No. Surely not. He must have said he loved *helping* her too.

But if he did say he loved her, then that meant that this whole fake relationship thing was as real as she hoped it was. It meant that he wanted to be more than friends, or in their case, friends with benefits, and he had genuine feelings for her. Like she did for him.

As soon as he'd said…whatever he'd said…Knox's muscles stiffened, then he quickly let her go and turned away as if looking for the dog. "Here, girl," he said.

"Wait, Knox," she said, putting her hand on his arm. "What did you say?"

He shook his head and looked at something in the distance over her shoulder as if trying to remember. "Um, what, I don't know."

Her shoulders fell, and a solid rock of pain thumped in her stomach. Surely if he'd just declared his love for her, that would be something he'd remember. She must not have heard him correctly.

Maybe she'd just heard what she wanted to hear, what she

wished he would say. Because as scared as she was, there was no denying that she'd been falling in love with him too.

But apparently, she'd been reading his signals wrong. And honestly, they'd both said this engagement was just a cover story from the very beginning. And now that Paul was gone, there was no reason for them to keep up the charade. So, if Knox wanted out, now was his chance.

"I got some good news from Evelyn," she said, crossing her arms over her chest.

"Oh, yeah?"

"Yep. Not only is the insurance company going to cover our claim, but she told Paul the deal with the developers is over and there's no way she's signing over our building to him. And I guess he packed up his stuff this morning and left town."

Knox's eyes widened. "So, Paul is gone? Just like that?"

"Yep." She took a step away from him, as if already working to rebuild the walls she surrounded herself with. "So, we don't have to pretend anymore." She tried to keep the hopeful tone out of her voice, but inside she was praying he would take her in his arms and declare his love for her and tell her he wasn't pretending anymore.

"Oh," he said, as he scrubbed a hand through his hair. "Well, that's good. I guess." He looked toward the bunkhouse with…what? Sadness? Regret? "And now that Bryn's back, I guess I won't be needing to stay here anymore." He pushed his hands into the front pockets of his jeans. "I mean, I'll still be around if you want to talk, or you can text me or we can meet for coffee or whatever."

He'll be around to talk? What the heck did that mean? Now that he knows Paul is gone, was he dumping her? Just like that? She didn't know what to say.

And apparently neither did he.

"Well, I'd better get my stuff together and get these guys home," he said, nodding to Sadie and Rodney who were sacked out on the front porch with Angel.

"Yeah, sure."

He looked at her for a few seconds more. Did he want her to stop him? To invite him to stay?

Forget that. He seemed to be making his position clear. If he wanted to stay, he would.

"Yeah, so I'll go do that now, I guess." He turned and headed for the bunkhouse.

The next morning, Carley headed toward the barn, wanting to check on Spirit—and if she were honest, maybe hoping Knox might show up.

It hadn't taken him long to pack up his truck, and she'd purposely stayed inside the bunkhouse when he'd driven away. She'd checked her phone for the hundredth time before she went to bed, but he hadn't sent her his usual "goodnight" text. She let Phoebe, Nala, and Angel all sleep with her, surrounding herself with animal cuddles, but nothing could make up for the absence of the warm cowboy on the other side of the bed.

After a cruddy night's sleep of tossing and turning and

second-guessing just about every decision she'd ever made, she finally got out of bed when she saw the sun coming up and made herself a strong cup of coffee. She'd taken an extra-long, extra-hot shower, letting the water run over her back as she leaned against the tile wall and sobbed. Then she lifted her face to the spray, letting the water wash away her tears and tried to imagine all her sorrow swirling away down the drain.

She'd spent the next few hours trying to keep herself occupied, to keep her thoughts off him and all the time they'd spent together the past few months, but nothing worked. Hopefully spending time with and brushing Spirit would at least occupy her hands.

Angel ran along at her heels. The little dog had been both a comfort and a source of distress as her very presence reminded her of Knox.

A deep baritone voice could be heard singing softly as she stepped into the barn, and her heart leapt in hopes it was Knox. It was coming from the direction of Spirit's stall, and as Carley got closer, she recognized the old Bob Seger tune. But it wasn't Knox who was singing.

It was Bryn's cousin, Holt Callahan. His hat was hanging on the outside of Spirit's stall, and he crooned softly to the horse, singing as if the song were written about her, as he gently ran a round brush over her coat.

Carley stood still, not wanting to intrude on the moment, but also entranced by the scene. She remembered the rough feel of the cowboy's calloused palms, but those same hands seemed so soft as he gently brushed them over the neck and back of the horse.

As transfixed as Carley was, Angel was more interested in seeing her friend, or maybe she wanted in on some of the cowboy's sweet affection, because she slipped under the gate and went trotting into the stall to circle through Spirit's legs. The horse bent her head to nuzzle her nose against the dog, and Carley wanted to cry at the tenderness of their friendship.

"Well, hello, there," Holt said, reaching down to scoop up the scruffy dog. "Where'd you come from?" He turned around and spotted Carley standing a few feet away. "Hey. Sorry, I didn't hear you come in."

"I didn't want to interrupt," she said, taking a few steps closer to fold her arm over the stall door. "You've got a nice voice. Spirit seemed to be loving the song."

He shrugged. "Bryn told me she'd been abandoned, and I just figured she could use a little extra attention. Hope that's okay."

"By all means," she answered. "I feel terrible for what happened to her, and the dog. It was some pretty awful conditions we found them in. That mutt has been getting tons of attention, so I'm happy to have as much love poured onto the horse as we can."

"She seems like a real sweet mare. Gentle as all get out. She's just been standing here letting me brush her for the past twenty minutes."

"Well of course, what girl wouldn't love having all the attention of a cowboy petting and serenading her?"

He raised an eyebrow and offered her a roguish grin that had her rethinking the way she'd phrased that. But her cheeks still warmed at the lingering glance he gave her.

"You seem to know your way around the barn," she said, changing the subject. "Do you have horses too?"

His casual smile fell, and a shadow of grief and pain crossed his features for just a moment as he reached for his hat and pushed it on his head. "Nope. Not anymore." He answered with a finality that didn't welcome any more discussion about it. Opening the stall door, he stepped out and closed it behind him.

"How long are you in town for?" she asked, walking out of the barn with him.

He shrugged. "Not sure. I'll be stickin' around for a bit. Gettin' my head on straight and trying to help out Bryn around here." He glanced toward the farmhouse. "Some of my best memories growing up were spent here—with my grandparents, and my brother and cousins. We all spent most of our summers here."

"What a great place to grow up around."

"Yeah, it was." He reached down, picked up a stick, and tossed it for Angel. The dog went racing across the driveway to retrieve it and bring it back. "It *still* seems like a pretty great place."

"I agree," she said, just as the hoard of baby goats who had been bleating in the barn for attention finally made their escape—they were going to have to figure out how to goat-proof that latch—and all seven of them came running out, tangling around Carley's legs and jumping up on her for pets.

Trying not to step on them, she lost her balance and stumbled forward. Holt reached out to grab her, wrapping

EVERY BIT A COWBOY   325

his arm around her to keep her from falling, then hauling her back up to her feet before letting her go.

Laughing, she tried to pet all the goats at once while keeping her balance this time. "Oh, my gosh, thank you," she told Holt, who just tipped his hat and took the stick being offered by the frantically tail-wagging dog to throw again.

———

Knox pulled his truck into the driveway of the rescue ranch, and the small gift bag in the seat bumped against his leg. He'd totally blown it with Carley the afternoon before, and he hoped the gift and his apology would be enough to get him back into her good graces. Because he had things to talk to her about.

He was such an idiot. He couldn't believe he'd blurted out that he loved her. Then she'd thrown him even more when she'd told him Paul had left town and so their pretend engagement was over.

He hadn't known what to do, or say, so getting out of there seemed the best manner of choice. But as soon as he drove away, he knew it had been the wrong decision. And he'd fussed and festered about it ever since. He'd taken his horse out that morning after he'd finished his chores, and as he galloped him hard across the pastures, he'd come to what he hoped was the right decision this time.

The pieces of the wooden box Carley's grandmother had given her had been sitting on his workbench since he'd brought them home that day it had been broken in the salon.

It didn't take him long to repair the damage and restore the box to its original state. He'd polished the wood, then lovingly wrapped it after putting a small gift inside.

His plan was to present the box to Carley and tell her how he felt. That he was in love with her and wanted their relationship to be real. But driving up to the barn, he saw Carley standing outside, laughing with Bryn's cousin, who had his arm around her and was playing fetch with *their* dog.

A nauseous feeling rolled through his gut, up his throat, and suddenly he felt dizzy and in danger of losing his breakfast.

Their dog.

Memories of his relationship with Kimber pounded through his head. He'd thought they were on the same page, thought they'd had the real thing. But as soon as he'd told her he loved her and they'd gotten a pet together, she'd freaked out and taken off, *with* their dog.

Was the same thing about to happen with Carley? What if he told her he loved her, and she told him none of it had been real and the whole thing had been a charade? Yeah, they'd had great sex, but sometimes sex was more about the feeling and not the *feelings*.

He parked the truck and grabbed the bag, his gut still ready to heave, as he walked toward her. She watched him, one hip jutted out, her hand in her front pocket, her chin tipped up as attitude rolled off her in waves.

Her hair was pulled up in a messy ponytail, and she had on a frayed pair of cutoff jean shorts, a pink T-shirt that read "Beauty School Dropout," and a pink pair of Converse sneakers, but she looked just as gorgeous to him now as she had the other night when she'd been all fixed up for the party. If she only knew how beautiful she truly was.

"Hey," he said. *Great opener, dude.*

"Hey," she said back.

Angel came racing toward him, circling his legs and whining for his attention. He bent to pet her and scratch her belly.

Bryn's cousin—what was his name? Hal? No, Holt—touched Carley's arm. "I'll talk to you later."

"Yeah, see you. And thanks for your help with Spirit this morning," she said.

"Anytime." He nodded to Knox, then sauntered off toward the house.

"How did he help with Spirit? Is she okay?" he couldn't stop himself from asking. What had that guy done to help *their* horse?

"She's doing well. He was just brushing her. Giving her some attention."

Her words felt like an accusation—like maybe she thought *he* was ignoring the horse. Or was he just reading something into her tone that wasn't there?

"That's good," he managed to say.

"What are you doing here?"

No, there was definitely something in her tone. She sounded different. More distant. And no wonder—he'd been a royal jackass the day before.

He held out the gift bag. "Here. I brought you this."

She took the bag but didn't open it. Letting it swing by her leg, she studied him. "Anything else?"

He shrugged, the queasy feeling getting worse. Nothing about this felt right. "I just thought, you know, with Paul gone, maybe we should talk. About, you know, us, and..." He didn't know what to say. He wanted to tell her he cared about her. No—screw that, he wanted to tell her he was in love with her. That instead of a fake relationship, he wanted to have a real one with her. He wanted all of this to be true.

His gaze cut to the ring on her finger—his grandmother's ring—and all he could think was how much he wished he'd had a chance to have given it to her for real.

She must have seen his gaze drop to her hand because she followed it with hers, then he heard her sharp intake of breath as she must have realized he was looking at the ring. "Oh, my gosh. Of course, you're here for the ring. I'm so sorry. I should have given this back to you yesterday."

"No, that's not what I..." But his muttered words were too late. She'd already taken off the ring and pushed it into his hand. Was she really ready to give up on them so easily? Or was there never an "us" to begin with?

The dog whined, then trotted over and sat on Carley's feet.

And that simple act completely did him in.

"I'm sorry. I can't do this," he said. All the old feelings of betrayal and rejection came rushing back from the last time he'd given his heart to a woman, and she'd shattered it into a million pieces, then doubly crushed it by taking their dog.

He couldn't open himself up to that kind of heartbreak again. He wouldn't. It was better for him to walk away first than to get in any deeper and risk her walking away from him.

"I gotta go. Paul's gone, so you don't need me anymore." He couldn't look at her. "Take care of yourself, Carley. You should keep the dog." He turned and walked to his truck, his fears coming true as his heart—the broken one he'd thought being with Carley could repair—shattered once again.

CHAPTER 28

CARLEY WALKED BACK TO THE BUNKHOUSE, HER BODY numb. Sinking onto the porch steps, she let Angel crawl into her lap and cuddled her against her chest.

She was so stupid. How had she let herself believe a man like Knox Garrison—a good man—would ever be interested in sticking around for a woman like her?

She'd known he was going to leave her. They always did. But she thought she'd protected herself—kept enough of her guard up—she didn't think it would hurt this damn bad.

Emotion burned her throat, but she fought the tears stinging her eyes. She looked down at her hand, empty and bare without the ring she'd worn so proudly.

Don't you cry, dammit.

Was that the only reason he'd come? *No.* She looked down at the gift bag she'd almost forgotten she'd had in her other hand. Peeling through the layers of tissue, she reached in and pulled out the wooden box her grandmother had given her.

She couldn't stop the tears that fell now as she saw that Knox had repaired it. There was no sign it had ever been broken.

Why had he brought her this beautiful gift—this loving gesture—if his intention was to come here to break up with her?

She took in a shuddering breath. Had she been reading this

all wrong? A spot of color caught her eye, something peeking out the edge of the box. She carefully opened the lid, and a sob escaped her as she saw the blue sage wildflower sitting inside.

His words came back to her from the night they'd practiced kissing on her porch.

"You sure have pretty eyes," he'd told her. *"They remind me of a mountain lake the way they change from green to blue depending on the light and what you're wearing...makes me think of the blue sage wildflowers growing up the side of the mountain behind my ranch."*

Those words, and this sweet wildflower he'd handpicked and put into this box to give to her, were not the words and actions of a man who was just pretending.

She peered down at the box and could feel the love radiating off it. Angel licked at her chin and let out a whine.

You should keep the dog. The last thing he said to her.

This wasn't all about protecting her from Paul. It was about him protecting himself from her. She was not the only one who'd had their heart broken, not the only one who'd been rejected and left behind. Had Knox left her before she had a chance to leave him?

She thought back to the things she'd said the day before, when she'd told him that Paul had left town so they didn't have to pretend to be together anymore. She'd been testing the waters, hoping he'd say he still wanted to be with her. But maybe he'd heard that she didn't want to be with him.

She lifted her chin and drew in a deep breath. It was true she'd been left behind before, but in the past she'd accepted her fate, and taken on the fault and guilt of it, blaming herself for not being good enough or worth sticking around for.

But she wasn't that same little girl her father had left behind. And she wasn't that same young bride that Paul had so easily discarded.

She'd learned to stand on her own two feet, to run a successful business, to offer friendship and be part of a community. She had changed and grown in the last five years. Hell, she'd grown in the last five *days*. She'd stood up to Paul, something she'd never thought she could do before. She'd taken an unlucky circumstance that had happened to her when her shop flooded and instead of giving up, she'd brainstormed fun and innovative ways to make money and do something for others. She'd helped to rescue an abandoned dog and horse, rehomed a despondent bulldog, and found a clever use for eight adorable baby goats, who Autumn had already been talking about adopting.

And she'd fallen in love. With a man who had made her feel like she mattered, like she was important, like she was worthy.

Angel licked her chin again. So why the heck was she still sitting here? For the first time in her life, she wasn't going to just sit back and accept her fate. She was going after what she wanted. She was going to stand up and fight for the man she loved.

She *did* love him. Now she just had to tell him. And if Knox didn't want her, then so be it. At least she would have tried instead of giving up.

It took her less than five minutes to put the box and gift bag inside, grab her purse and Angel, and peel out of the ranch. Another ten minutes, and she was turning off the highway and pulling up in front of Knox's house.

She stopped the car, grabbed the dog, and marched up the steps to knock on his door. She could hear Sadie barking inside and Knox's firm command for her to settle down. Pushing her shoulders back, she stood up tall, ready for battle, ready to fight for the man she loved.

He opened the door, and his eyes widened at the sight of her. "Carley. What are you doing here?"

"First of all, I'm here to give you this." She pressed Angel into his arms.

He held the dog to him as she wiggled and squirmed, trying to crawl up his chest to lick his face. "I don't understand."

"She's *our* dog. And the first thing I need you to know is that I have no intention of leaving you and taking her with me."

His brow furrowed in confusion. "Oh-kay."

"And the second thing I came to tell you was..." She faltered. "Damn, I really should have thought more about what I was going to say. I was just in a such a hurry to get here," she said out loud, but it was more to herself than him.

She tilted her head up and looked at the ceiling of the porch, then back at him as she suddenly knew *exactly* what to say. "You know, this house has always been special to me. It's the one I've seen in my dreams when I imagined *home*. But now I realize that it wasn't the house but the man who lives inside the house who should have been in my dreams. Because when I was in the arms of that man, I finally found my true home."

"Carley."

She shook her head. "Let me finish. In the past, when a man walked out on me, I let him go. But not this time. This time, I'm standing up and I'm fighting for what I want. But I need to know if I'm in this fight alone or if you're in it with me. I want to know where I stand with you. I *need* to know how you really feel. Please, Knox. Tell me."

He set Angel down on the porch, and she lay down next to his feet. He lifted his eyes to look into hers. "This is hard."

"I know. It is for me too."

"I have never met anyone like you. From the first time I saw you, I knew you were something special. You're smart and thoughtful and funny. You always make me laugh. You're one of the most generous and kindhearted people I know. You light up a room just by walking into it. And when you smile at me, *just at me*, I feel like the luckiest man alive. You are so beautiful, inside and out. I was lost from the moment I met you. I guess what I'm trying to say is that even though I started this whole fake engagement thing, none of the last several weeks has been pretend for me. My feelings for you have always been real. And they scare me to death." He picked up her hand and held it to his heart. His voice was soft, but she heard him loud and clear this time. "I love you."

She intertwined their fingers then pulled their hands from his chest to place them on hers. "You told me once that I could trust you with my heart. That you wouldn't break it. Now, I need you to trust me with yours, because I love you, Knox Garrison, and I promise I won't break your heart."

He pulled her to him and kissed her hard. Wrapping her arms around him, she held on tight, kissing him back with all the love and passion she'd been holding back the past few weeks.

When he finally pulled away, he gazed down at her, and she felt the love he held for her. "I'm sorry if I hurt you."

"I'm sorry if I hurt you." She touched his cheek. "So, what now? I know I love you, but I'm not sure where we go from here."

He smiled tenderly down at her. "Don't worry, I can fix this." He pulled something from his pocket, his grandmother's ring she'd given back to him earlier that day. "When I looked at this ring on your hand today, I *wasn't* thinking that I wanted it back, I was wishing that I'd had a chance to give it to you for real." He took a deep breath, then his smile widened as he let it out. "I want to give it to you now, as a promise, for our future together." He held the ring out to her. "Carley Chapman, I am truly, madly, deeply in love with you. Will you marry me?"

She shook her head. "No, Knox."

His eyes widened. "*No*?"

"Wait, I mean yes, of course I'll marry you." She plucked the ring from his hand and slid it back on to her finger. "Because I am truly, madly, deeply in love with you too. But what I meant was, no, *you* don't get to fix this one." She smiled up at him. "Because from now on, *we're* gonna fix it. *Together*."

THE END…

…AND JUST THE BEGINNING…

Can't get enough of Creedence Cowboys?
Read on for an excerpt from Book 1 in
the Creedence Horse Rescue series.

a Cowboy STATE OF MIND

THE STILL-NAMELESS DOG JUMPED INTO THE CAB AS ZANE Taylor opened the door of his pickup, and he absently patted its head and rubbed behind its ears. The dog leaned into him and got that blissed-out look on its face, and Zane's tension eased a little as it always did when he interacted with an animal. The late spring sun warmed Zane's back, and as soon as he turned his attention away from the dog, he felt the weight of the decision he bore on his shoulders. His former boss, Maggie, had been nagging him to come back to his old job on her Montana ranch. She'd taken in a herd of wild stallions, and she needed him. He'd gotten by so far with vague replies, but it was time to give her an answer. Time to get back on the road and out of Creedence. Except the reason he was so fired up to leave was also the reason he wasn't ready to walk away.

He shrugged the soreness from his shoulders. He'd had a good morning with Rebel, the headstrong black stallion he'd been working with for weeks now. Maybe the horse could feel the warmth in the air as well. Although it *was* Colorado, so they could still get a snowstorm or two before spring reluctantly slid into summer.

"Nice job today, horse whisperer," Logan Rivers, his current boss, and friend, hollered from the corral where he was putting another horse through the paces.

Zane waved a hand in his direction, ignoring the comment, as he turned the engine over and pulled the door shut. He wasn't fond of the nickname, even though Logan had been using it since they were in high school and working summers at Logan's family's ranch.

Zane could admit grudgingly that he did have a gift with horses, especially the dangerous or wild ones, somehow connecting with the animals better than he ever did with people.

The black-and-white border collie mix rested her head on Zane's leg, and he stroked her neck as he drove toward Creedence, where no one was a stranger and everyone knew not just *your* business, but your cousin's as well.

He lowered the windows and turned on the radio, contemplating the errands he needed to run after he grabbed a plate of biscuits and gravy at the diner. The thought made his mouth water. So did the thought of hopefully seeing a certain blond waitress who had been taking up way too many of his thoughts these last few months.

He slowed, his brow furrowing, as he recognized that same waitress's car sitting empty on the side of the road. The car was an old nondescript blue sedan, but there was no mistaking the colorful bumper stickers stuck to the trunk. A bright blue one read "What if the hokey-pokey really is what it's all about?" and the hot-pink one above the back taillight read "It was me. I let the dogs out."

His heart rate quickened as his gaze went from the empty vehicle to a hundred yards up the road, where a woman walked along the side of the highway, her ponytail bouncing with each step and a light-colored dog keeping pace at her heels. Which was pretty impressive, in and of itself, since the dog had only three legs.

But then, everything about Bryn Callahan was kind of bouncy, and she was just as impressive as her dog. The woman was always upbeat and positive. Even now, with her car sitting busted on the side of the road, her steps still seemed to spring, and the bright sunlight glinted off her blond hair.

He drove past the abandoned car and onto the dirt shoulder as he slowed to a stop beside her. "Need a ride?"

She turned, her expression wary, then her face broke into a grin, and it was like the sun shining through the clouds after a rainstorm.

"Hey, Zane," she said, the smile reaching all the way into her voice as she grasped the door handle. She looked steadily into his eyes, her gaze never wavering, never sliding sideways to stare at the three-inch, jagged scar starting at the corner of his eye and slicing down his cheek. Most people couldn't keep their eyes off it, but Bryn acted as if it wasn't there at all. "I sure do. I was supposed to start my shift at the diner ten minutes ago."

She opened the door, and the dog bounded in, hitting the floorboards, then springing onto the seat to wiggle and sniff noses with the border collie. They could have powered a wind farm, the way their tails were wagging and their little butts were shaking.

"Hey, Lucky." He leaned in as the dog leapt over the collie's back and into Zane's lap, where it proceeded to drench his face in fevered licks and puppy kisses. Lucky was like a hyper three-legged Tigger as he bounced from Zane's lap back to the collie, over to Bryn, and back to Zane.

"Lucky, get off him," Bryn scolded. She tried to push her way into the truck as she got her own slobbery reception from the collie.

Zane chuckled and grabbed her hand to help her into the cab. But his laugh stuck in his throat as heat shot down his spine and his mouth went dry. He swallowed and tried to focus on assisting her, instead of staring at the area of bare skin he glimpsed as the top of her dress buckled and gaped from her movement. It was just the side of her neck, but it was the exact spot he'd spent too much time thinking about kissing.

"Silly mutts." She laughed as she tossed her backpack on the floor and plopped into the seat. Her hand was soft, but her grip was solid, and for a moment, he wondered what would happen if he didn't let go. "Wow, what a greeting," she said, as she released his hand to buckle herself in.

Zane's eyes were drawn to her legs like bees to honey. The woman had great legs, already tan, and muscular and shapely from her work at the diner. Her white cross-trainers were scuffed with the red dirt from the road, and she had a smudge of dust across one ankle that Zane was severely tempted to reach down and brush away so he could let his fingers linger on her skin.

Bryn wore a pink waitress dress, the kind that zips up the front, with a white collar and a little breast pocket, and the fabric hugged her curvy figure in all the right spots. For just a moment, Zane imagined pulling down that zipper—with his teeth. His back started to sweat just thinking about it.

Simmer down, man. He took a deep breath, utilizing the stress-reducing exercise he'd learned in the military, and tried to think of something witty to say. He didn't usually let himself get carried away with those kinds of fantasies. But he didn't usually have Bryn in his truck, filling his cab with the sound of her easy laughter and the scent of her skin—traces of honeysuckle and vanilla and the smell of fresh sheets off the line on a warm summer day.

"That dog is serious about kissing. I haven't had that much action in months." He winked, then laughed with her, pulling his hand back to ruffle Lucky's ears as the dog settled into the seat next to the collie. He tried to play it off like a joke, to settle his pounding heart, when what he really wanted to do was pull her into his lap and kiss her face and throat the way Lucky had done to him. Well, not *exactly* the same way.

Bryn snorted and scratched the ears of the collie, who was softly whining as she pressed into Bryn's shoulder. "He's just happy to see you. It's been a while, ya know?"

"Yeah, I know." It had, in fact, been months since he'd seen her.

"Well, Lucky has noticed you haven't been around much." She dropped her gaze and her voice as she focused on petting the dog. "We both have."

Both?

"Are you saying you missed me?"

"I didn't say *missed*. I said noticed."

His shoulders slumped. Of course she hadn't missed him.

She playfully nudged his elbow, and he felt the heat of her skin against his arm.

"Of course I missed you. You all but disappeared after the great Christmas pie bake-off in December."

He chuckled as he shook his head. "I still can't believe we made fifteen pies in four hours."

"I still can't believe you wore a frilly apron with a glittery cupcake on the front."

He raised an eyebrow. "What other kind of cupcake is there? And I liked that glittery color. I'm thinking of having it added to the paint job on my truck."

A laugh burst from her. "I dare you to."

He let his voice drop and offered her what he hoped was a flirtatious grin. "I do enjoy a good dare."

She chuckled, then lowered her gaze to the dog's shoulder, where she scratched its fur. "So, why *didn't* I hear from you? Was it something I said or did?"

Yeah, it was everything you did—everything that made me want and hope and wish for something more. "Nah. I was going to call you, but we got real busy at the ranch. Then I heard you started dating some rough-stock cowboy, and I didn't want to overstep."

"Is it overstepping to be my friend?"

He cocked his head, eyeing her. "Is that what you want me to be? Your friend?"

"Of course. I didn't give you my number for you to *not* call me."

Wrong question, dumbass. Should have asked her if *all* she wanted was to be his friend. He offered her a shrug. "I'm not much of a talker."

"That's perfect. Because I can talk up a blue streak, and I'm always on the lookout for a good listener."

He chuckled. "I can do that. I can probably even throw in an occasional grunt of agreement just so you know I'm paying attention."

She giggled softly, and the sound swirled in his chest, melting into him like molasses on a warm pancake. "That sounds great."

"I'm happy to lend an ear, but shouldn't your new boyfriend be the one listening?"

She huffed, then muttered, "Not hardly."

"Uh-oh. Trouble in paradise?" He hoped.

She shook her head. "No trouble. Not anymore. It's safe to say we broke up."

"Sorry to hear that." *Not really.*

"Don't be." Her expression hardened, but she didn't say anything more.

No problem. He didn't want to continue *any* conversation that had her shoulders slumping and pulled her lips into a tight frown. "What happened to your car?" Zane asked, drawing his gaze back to the road as he eased the truck onto the highway. Not that her broken-down car was a great topic, but at least it took the focus off her broken-down relationship.

"Who knows? This is the third time it's conked out since Christmas."

"Have you called someone about it?" *Like me.* Yeah right. Why would she call *him*? Hadn't they just established that he'd been avoiding her for the past several months?

"No. What good would it do to call someone when I don't have any money to pay them anyway? Last I checked, my bank account was holding steady at six dollars and eighty cents."

"I could take a look at it for you. And I wouldn't charge you more than a smile." Ugh. Did that really just come out of his mouth? It hadn't sounded half as dopey in his head.

"That would be very neighborly of you," she said, ignoring his dorky comment and flashing him a brilliant grin. "That's a price I can afford. But you don't have to. I know Logan's keeping you pretty busy out at Rivers Gulch."

Neighborly? He didn't want to seem neighborly. He'd been trying for flirty, but his efforts had apparently fallen flat. *Wait.* How did *she* know Logan had been keeping him busy at the ranch? Had she asked about him? "I've got time," he assured her. "I'll take a look at it when I'm done in town. See if I can spot the problem at least."

"That would be so great." She ruffled the neck of the black-and-white dog, who had settled down next to her. She seemed to draw stray animals like a magnet. "You picked a name for your dog yet?"

"She's not my dog."

Bryn rolled her eyes and let out a small chuckle. "*You*

might not think so, but *she* does. Every time I see your truck, she's ridin' shotgun. Why do you think she does that if she doesn't consider herself yours?"

He shrugged, his tone even and dry. "She must like my winning personality."

A laugh escaped Bryn's lips—a sound that filled the cab of the truck, and his heart, as if the door of a dark room had been cracked open to let in a shaft of light. "I'm sure that's it," Bryn said, still chuckling.

A grin tugged at the corners of his lips. This woman made him smile, even when she was giving him a hard time.

"How's your dad doing?" she asked.

The smile fell from his lips. "Stubborn as ever."

His dad's heart attack had brought him back to town earlier that winter, only long enough to get the old bastard back on his feet. But then Logan lost his hired hand and had offered Zane a job helping at the ranch and with the horses, and a couple of weeks had turned into a couple of months.

He and his dad had reached an uneasy truce. As long as Birch took his meds and stayed off the sauce, Zane agreed to remain in town. They mostly stayed out of each other's way, but occasionally found themselves watching a hockey game together, especially if the Colorado Summit were playing, and Creedence's hometown hero, Rockford James, was on the ice.

But lately Zane had felt the familiar itch—the need to move on when he'd stayed in one place too long and gotten too comfortable with having people around him. An itch that was made worse by the desire to see the blond waitress who was taking up space in his mind and under his skin. And that was an itch he had no business trying to scratch.

"He seems to be doing better lately," he told Bryn. "So I'll probably take off pretty soon. My old boss is harping on me to come back to Montana. She took in a new herd of wild stallions and needs someone to break them."

"Oh," Bryn said, the word a soft breath on her lips. "I didn't realize you were leaving. When are you going?"

He murmured something noncommittal about it not being today, then lifted his shoulders in a dismissive shrug as he pulled into the parking lot of the diner and parked in the shade of a giant elm tree.

"Then how about coming in and having some breakfast? On the house." She laid her hand on his arm and gave it a gentle squeeze. "It's the least I can do for giving me a ride into town."

He shook his head, only slightly, not wanting to move too much for fear of dislodging her hand. The weight of it settled something inside him. "You don't owe me a thing for the ride. I was happy to do it. But I will come in for a bite. I've been thinking about Gil's biscuits and gravy, and there's a pretty cute waitress I wouldn't mind getting a cup of coffee from."

ACKNOWLEDGMENTS

As always, my love and thanks goes out to my family! Todd, thanks for always believing in me and for being the real-life role model of a romantic hero. You make me laugh every day and the words it would take to truly thank you would fill a book on their own. I love you. *Always*.

Special thanks goes out to my youngest son, Nick. Throughout the writing of this book, we were going through a massive home renovation that involved a thirteen-foot addition, demoed walls, open rafters, freezing temperatures, and a kitchen gut and complete makeover. We had workers in our house, constant interruptions, no kitchen, and a million decisions to make—none of which helped with my writing creativity. Thank you, Nick, for all your help during this time—for your encouragement to write all the words and for your help with the subcontractors, the construction, and the building and installing of twenty-six IKEA cabinets. You offered a hug when I cried and a listening ear when I needed to vent, but most of all, you could always make me laugh. I love you to the moon and back, two hundred and forty thousand times.

Such a huge bucketful of thanks and acknowledgment goes out to one of my writer besties, Anne Eliot, for your constant and consistent encouragement and support in both my writing journey and in making this book happen. I will never forget our virtual/Marriott writing retreat— staying up late, Facetime sprints, eating chocolate, both in our perfect snuggled-in writing spots, and of course, the all-important hot tub break. You are always willing to listen and talk (or argue—lol) through plotting struggles and character crisis, and we always have the most fun doing it. Thank you for your steadfast belief in me and for alternately holding my hand and lovingly pushing me to the finish line of this book.

This writing gig is tough, and I wouldn't be able to do it without the support and encouragement of my writing besties who walk this journey with me. Thank you to Michelle Major and Lana Williams for all the encouragement and the hours and hours of sprints and laughter. Thanks, Michelle, for your unending support and for always listening. XO. Thanks to Sharon Wray for always being in my corner and for being with me for that final sprint-a-thon push to the deadline of this book. You all are just the best.

I can't thank my editor, Deb Werksman, enough for believing in me and this book, for loving Carley and Knox, and for making this story so much better with your amazing editing skills. I appreciate everything you do to help make the town of Creedence and my motley crew of farmyard animals come to life. Huge thanks to Susie Benton for the grace and support you offered me when I was having the roughest time with life getting in the way of turning this book in. And holy hot cowboy, thank you to Dawn Adams for the most gorgeous cover that perfectly captures Knox and the horse rescue farm nestled against the mountains of Colorado. I love being part of the Sourcebooks Sisterhood, and offer so many thanks to the whole Sourcebooks Casablanca team for all your efforts and hard work in making this book happen.

A big thank you to my family. I appreciate everything you do and am so thankful for your support of this crazy writing career. Special thanks goes out to Dr. Rebecca Hodges, my sister, and Dr. Bill Bryant, my dad, for always being willing to listen and offer sound veterinarian counsel when I call with frenzied questions about my farmyard crew of animals and rescues. And a big thanks goes out to my sister, Kate Erickson, for all your help and ideas for the fun goat yoga scene.

I have to do a shoutout to my wonderful hair stylist and friend, Melissa Chapman, to whom this book is dedicated. Thanks for all the hours of listening and talking through plot ideas and for all your advice, ideas, and guidance in making sure I got all the beautician details right in this book, from setting up Carley's temporary shop to how to rinse out a permanent.

Huge thank you to my agent, Nicole Resciniti at the Seymour Agency, for your advice and your guidance. You are the best, and I'm so thankful you are part of my life.

Big thanks goes out to my street team, Jennie's Page Turners, and for all my readers: the people who have been with me from the start, my loyal readers, my dedicated fans, the ones who have read my stories, who have laughed and cried with me, who have fallen in love with my heroes and have clamored for more! Whether you have been with me since the first book or just discovered me with this book, know that I write these stories for you, and I can't thank you enough for reading them. Sending love, laughter, and big Colorado hugs to you all!

ABOUT THE AUTHOR

Jennie Marts is the *USA Today* bestselling author of award-winning books filled with love, laughter, and always a happily ever after. Readers call her books "laugh out loud" funny and the "perfect mix of romance, humor, and steam." Fic Central claimed one of her books was "the most fun I've had reading in years."

She is living her own happily ever after in the mountains of Colorado with her husband, two dogs, and a parakeet who loves to tweet to the oldies. She's addicted to Diet Coke, adores Cheetos, and believes you can't have too many books, shoes, or friends.

Her books range from Western romance to cozy mysteries, but they all have the charm and appeal of quirky small-town life. She loves genre mashups, like adding romance to her Page Turners cozy mysteries and creating the hockey-playing cowboys in the Cowboys of Creedence. The same small-town community comes to life with more animal antics in her new Creedence Horse Rescue series. And her sassy heroines and hunky heroes carry over in her heartwarming, feel-good romances from Hallmark Publishing.

Jennie loves to hear from readers. Follow her on

Facebook at facebook.com/jenniemartsbooks, or Twitter at @JennieMarts. Visit her at jenniemarts.com and sign up for her newsletter to keep up with the latest news and releases.

HOW TO HANDLE A COWBOY

One of *Booklist*'s "Best Romances of the Decade"
from bestselling author Joanne Kennedy

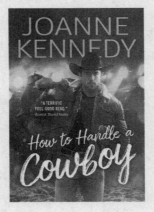

Sidelined by a career-ending injury, rodeo cowboy Ridge Cooper has nothing to do at his family's remote Wyoming ranch but sulk. Desperate to find an outlet for the energy he's always devoted to his sport, he offers to teach rodeo skills to the kids at Phoenix House, a last-chance group home for foster children.

Inner-city social worker Sierra Dunn has been exiled to Phoenix House for blowing the whistle on her boss. She intends to prove herself and move on, until Ridge's grit and determination to create a foster family of his own have her re-thinking everything she thought she knew about love.

**"Realistic and romantic... Kennedy's forte
is making relationships genuine."**
—*Booklist* Starred Review

For more info about Sourcebooks's books and authors, visit:
sourcebooks.com

ONE HOT COWBOY WEDDING

New York Times bestselling author Carolyn Brown's inimitable sass and Texas twang at its best

His grandfather's will requires Ace Riley to get a wife and stay married for a year if he wants to inherit the ranch. He turns to his friend Jasmine King for what was supposed to be a secret wedding followed, after a year, by a quiet divorce. That was the plan... But when they win a contest in the little wedding chapel in Vegas, the secret marriage is exposed to the national media and all hell breaks loose. And media attention isn't the only thing that's heating up, as Ace and Jasmine find it increasingly hard to stay just friends...

"Fresh, funny, and sexy."
—*Booklist* for *Love Drunk Cowboy*